D1678236

Works by S.M. Perlow

Vampires and the Life of Erin Rose

Novels
Choosing a Master
Alone
Lion
Hope
War

Short Stories
Alice Stood Up

—

The Grand Crucible

Novels
Golden Dragons, Gilded Age

—

Other Works

Novels
Stealing the Holy Grail

Short Stories
The Girl Who Was Always Single

STEALING THE HOLY GRAIL

S.M. Perlow

Bealion Publishing

A Bealion Publishing Book

Copyright 2021 S.M. Perlow

All rights reserved. No part of this book may be used or
reproduced in any manner whatsoever without written permission,
except in the case of brief quotations embodied in critical articles
and reviews. For information, contact S.M. Perlow.

This book is a work of fiction. Any references to historical events, real
people, or real places are used fictitiously. Other names, characters,
places, and events are fictitious, and any resemblance to actual events,
places, or persons, living or dead, is entirely coincidental.

Editor: Sarah Carleton, Red Adept Editing Services
Cover design: Streetlight Graphics
Formatting: Polgarus Studio

smperlow.com—updates, social media links, and more
information about the story

ISBN: 978-0-9992858-5-5

1.0.0-p1

For the inspiration, thank you,
Geoffrey, Chrétien, Wolfram,
both Dr. Joneses, and everyone in between

1

Arthur said it would be just like this. In the darkness, Perceval smiled, catching his breath as he rested against the rough wet trunk of a tall pine tree. Lightning filled the sky. Steady drops of rain penetrated the forest canopy, hitting his short brown hair hard. He closed his eyes and could hardly hear the dogs barking behind him or their masters behind them anymore. Thunder rolled softly.

Loudly and clearly came Perceval's memory of his king's warnings. "It will not be easy," Arthur had said at the Round Table in Britain three years before. "If it were easy, we would already have it here, to be celebrated as it should be. This gift of God's, this proof of His great sacrifice, would be revered in this room. Or at least, we would know where it is kept or hidden and revere it better from afar with that true knowledge." Arthur glanced over his shoulder at Merlin, who leaned on his staff, then his eyes returned to the table to meet Sir Gawain's. "No, this quest is to be fraught with peril." Arthur looked at his greatest knight, Lancelot. "You will be confronted by enemies and obstacles of all kinds." He turned to Lancelot's son, Galahad. "You will be tested." Then he spoke to twenty-year-old Perceval, the youngest in that noble group and a month in King Arthur's service. "You will face evils beyond comprehension, Perceval. Are you ready?"

Woof! Woof! The dogs had caught Perceval's scent. He steeled his gaze and wiped rain off his face. Lightning flashed, and Perceval searched for an opening among the trees. Three years and countless struggles had brought him across the narrow sea to Francia and to the Ardennes Forest in the northeast. He *was* ready, he assured himself. He'd been ready the day that Arthur asked him and every day since.

Perceval drew his straight sword from its scabbard on his hip. He wore a coat of chain mail over his tunic, and a long knife hung, sheathed, off his belt. If he could find a place in the open to make a stand, he vowed to again prove his worth, but trees towered everywhere.

Woof! Woof! WOOF!

Perceval pushed himself off the pine trunk and ran, leather boots sliding and whooshing with his high steps through the wet underbrush, which he could hardly see.

Woof! Woof!

He held his free left hand in front of him, lest he suddenly slam into an unseen tree.

Woof!

Thunder boomed. Lightning flashed. Perceval glanced behind while he ran.

WOOF!

A rustling sound near ground level had to be the beasts. At the height of a man—a giant man—two red eyes burned through the woods.

"Agh." Perceval stumbled on a log. To his left, another pair of menacing eyes stared.

WOOF!

Perceval hurried right, legs and arms pumping. Those eyes belonged to demons, not men, he reasoned. Their sickly slanted shape, their blazing bloodred color—not human at all. And those dogs surely had been loosed from the gates of hell.

"Evils beyond comprehension," Arthur had warned.

Red eyes ahead—Perceval skidded to a stop.

Boom! Thunder. The sky glowed white.

Behind him, closing in, came an unblinking stare.

Boom!

For three years, Perceval had fought thieves and wicked men. He'd rescued lords, ladies, and their kin from evildoers and depraved criminals. He'd won every knightly tournament he fought in, even against valiant brothers of the Round Table.

Woof! Woof!

But always, it had been men or women, not demons—not Satan's dogs.

Boom! Thunder cracked and rolled in a low drumbeat.

Fiery eyes glowed to the left. Raindrops pelted Perceval's head and slid down his face, blurring his sight, blurring everything. King Arthur had been prescient.

BOOM!

Into darkness, Perceval ran right up a rocky slope. *Give me a clearing!* he cried in his mind. Daytime was not near—the sun's rays did not lurk over the horizon, poised to banish

3

the foul creatures or aid Perceval in fighting them. He glanced skyward. *God, give me but a small space to see my enemy in its true form and force. Let me know what I face, and, Lord, I will not fail you!*

The hillside blocked Perceval to the left. Behind him, the hounds barked. Demon eyes shone to his right.

He raced forward, up the hill. *Torchlight!* Running harder, Perceval slipped but caught himself and pressed on. The light, ablaze on the hillside, illuminated a gap in the trees. He *would* see his enemies plainly. Up the hill he went, but no one was near the fire.

He would wield the torch as a second weapon—he could distinguish its orange-and-yellow flames at the mouth of a cave in the hillside. Perceval gripped his sword. He would make his stand for God. To free His people on His good earth of the evil raised that night, Perceval resolved to send those foul beasts back to where they came from.

Into the clearing he burst.

"Perceval."

He halted, watching the cave mouth, sword ready.

A gray-bearded knight stepped out into the light, sword sheathed on his hip. "Welcome." A red cross boldly shone in the center of his bright-white tunic. His silver mail sleeves gleamed. The thunder rolled low.

Perceval's breathing stayed heavy. "Who are you?"

"I am Sir Berthold," the knight said in the Celtic language of Perceval's homeland. "I am to show you in from the rain and to take you to what you have long sought."

Perceval lowered his sword.

4

"You've been a good knight, Perceval," Berthold continued. "You've been honorable and have done great deed after great deed. You've been always victorious in battle, and above all, you've been a model example of chivalry."

Perceval shook his head. "I've tried."

Berthold smiled. "And you have been humble." He took the torch off the hillside.

Behind Perceval, lightning faded. Three pairs of fiery eyes shone in the trees.

"Others in my order," Sir Berthold said, "have been playing their part with tricks of red light—and very real dogs—to ensure that you found your way here." He motioned toward the cave. "Please."

Perceval sheathed his sword and headed into the darkness. Berthold followed. His torch lit the brown walls and low ceiling more than anything ahead of them.

Wiping rainwater from his face as best he could with his wet tunic sleeve, Perceval considered the wisdom of taking the unknown knight at his word, but Berthold felt true. If he or those with him meant to harm Perceval, they could have done that outside the cave.

Perceval wondered if he would see the Holy Grail straight away. For Berthold had to be taking him to the grail. *Will I hold it tonight?* His concern about trusting Berthold sank beneath the mountain of questions he wanted to ask the knight. *How old is he? The grail gives everlasting life, according to the stories. Has Berthold been around since the beginning— since the days the son of God walked the earth?*

It grew cooler as they went. The sounds of their boots, especially Perceval's wet ones, hitting the hard ground accompanied the torch's burning. Perceval couldn't blurt those questions to the holy knight.

What does the grail look like? Perceval had imagined it, and when he was asleep, his mind free to wander, for years he had dreamed of that sacred vessel. *Did I picture it true?*

Surely not. It had to be more beautiful and splendid. More radiant.

At a fork in the tunnel, they veered right.

"Not far now," Sir Berthold said.

Perceval wouldn't ask those questions. He would not be so rude.

He wondered which of his brother knights he would see at the tunnel's end. If he'd proven worthy, of course Galahad had also.

The glowing from a chamber ahead of them steadily grew. Surely Lancelot would be there to greet him, or those who were there would regale Perceval with the story of Lancelot reaching the grail. Back at Camelot, one day soon, they would all rejoice and share their stories.

"You are the first in some time," Berthold said as they entered a small room wider than it was long. Torches high at each corner illuminated the minimal space and the bold blue-and-red embroidery on the single wooden chair against the rear wall, but they did not penetrate the openings to other tunnels to the chair's left and right.

Holding his torch steady, Berthold stepped to Perceval's side. "Sir Perceval of Wales!"

From the tunnel on their right, a taller, broader-chested knight appeared, adorned in the same red-cross-decorated tunic over gleaming chain mail. His sword sheathed, he moved aside from the entranceway and clasped his hands before him.

From that same tunnel, a middle-aged, clean-shaven man limped out, his face pained, holding hands with a tall woman with long blond hair who helped him walk. He wore the same tunic as the knights, with a red cloak wrapped around him and a golden crown askew on his head. A red cloak hung on the woman's shoulders, too, boldly contrasting with her long white gown.

The man grimaced. The woman—stern faced, statuesque, and beautiful—guided him into the chair. The grimacing man—perhaps the king—rested his head in his palm and stared down, keeping still, like the still air in the room, which smelled... empty. The woman looked at the passageway they'd come from.

An angel emerged. Perceval, his mouth agape, let himself blink. The woman stepped out, holding before her a long wooden spear as high as the room would allow. *Spear of Destiny*, Perceval thought. She appeared younger than the woman beside the chair, and her lustrous brown hair ran down the back of her pure-white long-sleeved gown.

She was so pretty she *could* have been an angel. She smiled confidently, walking toward the king, her gaze fixed on the long iron head of the spear that had pierced the side of Jesus Christ, crucified outside the walls of Jerusalem.

The seated king silently mouthed words to the ground.

The torches crackled. Leather sandals on her feet, the angel moved across the room without a sound.

A second brunette angel followed the first, carrying a ring of twisted wooden strands on a pillow of white satin. Perceval gasped. *The Crown of Thorns!*

Trumpets sounded but only in Perceval's mind. He hadn't known the crown had survived. The music of heaven soared.

His heart pounded. Toward the tunnel on the left, the first girl had passed the king, holding the spear. The second woman approached him, her face full of joy, focused on her precious thorn-spiked relic. The stoic woman standing beside the king kept watch on the entranceway to the right. The knight there hadn't moved an inch.

Perceval dropped to a knee.

A third angel—a blonde, the prettiest young woman in God's kingdom—carried in her outstretched hands a silver goblet. Such magnificence was beyond anything he'd imagined. She bore the Holy Grail, the goblet that had held the blood of their slain savior. *The blood of God.*

Perceval crossed himself. *Thank you! Praise you, Lord!*

Perceval's smile waned. Unlike the others in the procession, the girl with the grail did not smile. She was taller, her hair only reached her shoulders, and at a second glance, he noticed dark streaks mixed with the blond. Her eyes seemed heavy.

The grail neared the oblivious king.

Oh, sweet grail.

The king moaned, but the woman beside him had her

8

attention on the goblet. Shifting her eyes to its bearer, she raised a brow.

The younger beauty, keeping the grail steady before her, raised an eyebrow in response. The woman with the king grew stern. The grail bearer rolled her eyes. Then, passing the woman, she finally formed a smile to match the brunettes'.

The holder of the spear neared the tunnel entranceway to Perceval's left. What power it had he did not know, but he felt lucky to have seen it. He thanked the Lord and decided to ask the holy knights about it later. The young woman lowered the spear and entered the dark tunnel, and Perceval's heart sank.

Then the confident, warm girl carried the Crown of Thorns into the tunnel, and when she disappeared, Perceval's heart sank further.

But it soared again at the sight of the grail. *How long will I be in its presence? How soon will I sip its water?* He choked up and thanked God for deeming him worthy.

The bearer of the grail looked at him. Perceval couldn't breathe, beholding her blue eyes, her fair skin, and those soft pink lips. Then she, too, disappeared into the tunnel with the grail.

Without another sound, the king rose with the help of the woman. She walked him to the tunnel where the others had exited. The knight at the entranceway followed them.

Perceval let himself take a breath.

Sir Berthold turned with his torch toward the tunnel Perceval had entered by. "Come."

Perceval stood. "I…"

"Please." Berthold rested his hand on Perceval's shoulder.

Perceval started into the tunnel. *Was that it? All those years to see it but not to hold it?*

He turned to Berthold. "Wha—"

"You're a good knight, Perceval," Berthold said. "You honor the Lord with your ways. Thank you."

With each step, Perceval's heart darkened more. *What comes next?* He clung to the hope that something did. They reached the fork in the tunnel and continued out. *I won't be allowed to drink from the grail?*

"I cannot hold it?" Perceval asked, the forest looming before them.

Wind and rain howled. Lightning flashed.

"No."

Thunder boomed louder and louder. *How did I fail?*

At the cave mouth, Berthold stopped, so Perceval did too. Berthold said, "You did not prove worthy."

"I—" Perceval shook his head. "I—"

Berthold walked back into the cave, and Perceval watched until he disappeared.

Boom! Thunder struck.

What happened? What did I do wrong? Perceval recalled the procession. The spear, the crown… he fell to his knees. He saw the grail in his mind.

Tears welled up. *That most holy cup. That life-giving goblet.*

And the girl who carried it. Tears rolled down Perceval's face. Wet wind hit the exposed back of his neck. He pictured all three who carried the relics and could see them in their white gowns, but the details of the first two faded. Perceval remembered the grail bearer's big feline eyes—those sad eyes—dark-rooted blond hair, and thin wrists that stretched out beyond the ends of her sleeves.

What will Arthur think of me? The grail had been within Perceval's reach, but he, Arthur's knight, was not worthy to drink from it. Or even to hold it. And his thoughts lingered as much on the girl who carried it as on the grail itself.

Perceval watched the rain outside. Bright flashes filled the sky. In the tunnel, there was only darkness.

He got to his feet. Shoulders sunk, nose running, Perceval stepped out into the storm. *What did I do wrong?*

2

"Perceval the Brave," Cera said quietly.

She was alone in her little candlelit chamber in the cave in the middle of the Ardennes Forest before dawn, the morning after King Arthur's renowned knight had failed before her king. Wearing her long white gown, she ran a comb through her shoulder-length dirty-blond hair.

"More like Perceval the *Mute*."

She raised an eyebrow. Her mother, Diana, had made the same gesture at her when Cera neared with the grail, nervous for Perceval. But Cera didn't smile like she had forced herself to the night before.

"Mother…" She scowled. "I'm no child."

Cera was *her* child, her mother reminded her often. But no fifty-six-year-old woman should be commanded by the facial twitches of her parent. Cera had given her mother what she wanted, except it hadn't been for her mother. She'd smiled for Perceval.

And not because he was so handsome…

Not only because of that, anyway.

"Princess Cerise," Sir Deverel said on the other side of

the heavy curtain covering the chamber entrance. "Are you ready to go?"

Cera put her comb in her leather satchel then walked to the curtain and pulled it open. "Mm-hmm."

"Let me carry that," he said.

Cera threw the bag's strap over her shoulder across her body. "I can carry my own bag, Sir Deverel." She walked past him into the tunnel.

———————————

The trees out the small square window of the carriage grew thinner as they headed southwest to the city of Reims. Mireille, who had carried the Crown of Thorns in the procession, sat beside Cera on the cushioned seat that hardly provided greater comfort than a good leather saddle. Sir Deverel rode on horseback behind them, Sir Alan rode ahead, and Sir Berthold drove the carriage. The three knights were correct that a pretty young woman riding outside the carriage would draw people's notice. As was always the case with their order, they did not want that, and while Cera would have happily dealt with the attention, she didn't feel like arguing with them about it at the outset.

And she only appeared young, of course. She looked just like the twenty-four-year-old Frankish girl she'd been when she started drinking regularly from the Holy Grail back in 491. The year was now 523. Jesus had died almost five hundred years before, her order had guarded the grail ever since, and Cera had been drinking from it most days for more than thirty years. Her eyes looked... deeper, she thought, but otherwise she hadn't aged a bit. None of them had.

Members of the order had died, though—like her father—when their efforts for secrecy failed and powerful forces came for the holy relics they kept. Even the grail could not bring people back from the dead, and while her father had fallen along with too many others over the centuries, never had the grail, the spear, or the crown been taken from them.

They had, however, buried or hidden the relics on rare but well-chronicled days when they'd split up to travel, as always, and were overrun. The prudent course then was to hide the relics and flee. Later, they would return to retrieve them, sometimes in greater numbers, sometimes with just a few knights in secret.

And most often, attackers were common thieves, oblivious of the sacred objects the order carried. The order easily repelled such aggressors, so skillful were the knights and so fresh and strengthened by the holy waters of the grail. Cera welcomed any chance to join in with her knives, like the short silver-handled ones strapped to each thigh below her gown.

That day, they carried the Crown of Thorns—the irresistible weapon—in a locked chest beneath the floorboards of the carriage. Diana, Josephus—the order's king—and a few others transported the grail, taking a different route to Reims. Others rode a third way with the Spear of Destiny. Among them was Mabyn, who had carried the spear in the procession.

Despite her mother's constant condescension, Cera

didn't hate her. She didn't hate Josephus, either. But she did hate how they used the grail.

Cera rested her head against the side of the carriage. *Dammit, Perceval.*

They spent the night camped off the road. Cera could have slept under the stars, like the knights, but if she had suggested it, they would have insisted the grail princess have a tent, albeit a simple one, to avoid drawing attention. She had the energy to renew the decades-old argument but decided to save it.

They reached Reims the next day, in the middle of its pale-gray afternoon. Sir Berthold, Sir Alan, and Mireille went straight to Lord Voclain's palatial stone home by the river, where much of the order would gather by evening. With a nun's hood pulled over her head, Cera walked the dirt streets to the old city's church, with Sir Deverel escorting.

And silently, Cera cried. A mother with two children huddled in her arms sat against a low stone wall, looking colder than they should have on that autumn day. A filthy man leaned against a mud building, coughing repeatedly and roughly. Past him, a body lying prostrate might have been a corpse. King Theodoric cared little for those people, Cera had long before realized. He cared even less than his father had.

"Please, sir." A gaunt young boy approached Sir Deverel, hand outstretched, palm up.

The knight shook his head.

"I'm hungry." The boy held his stomach. "I'm so hungry."

Tears streamed down Cera's cheeks, hidden by her hood.

"I'm sorry." Deverel put out his arm, and the boy stopped short of it.

Perceval wouldn't have done that, Cera told herself. He would have given the boy a bit of bread from his satchel or dried meat if he had any. But not Sir Deverel. And Cera couldn't give the boy any food or drink or money either. The reasons had been made very clear to Cera so many times over the years. "It would draw unwanted attention" and "We have loftier goals," she was told. If she'd disobeyed and sold her fine things to raise funds to feed the poor, it wouldn't have lasted. She couldn't feed a whole city for long, let alone the many towns and cities across Europe.

Perceval cared too. Tales of his exploits, like those of many knights, had come to Cera and her order—the maidens he saved from evil men, the thieves he brought to justice at the behest of lords and ladies, his prowess in battle, his commitment to God. But stories also reached their ears of Perceval teaching a lesson to the brute who bullied the townspeople in Bedford and convincing Lord Urban to share his bounty with the hungry in Gloucester.

But to Cera's immense frustration, Perceval the Caring didn't matter to anyone in her order. Those deeds amounted to footnotes in the ledger. The council deemed Perceval the Gallant Warrior Knight worthy of appearing before the grail. Cera clenched her fist. Perceval the Too Quiet had shown up. Or Perceval the Too Humble—or the Too Overwhelmed. It didn't matter. He'd failed his test before Josephus.

With tear-filled eyes, Cera glanced behind them at the boy. All she wanted was to give him—and all of them—a drink. The grail could nourish that boy. It couldn't resurrect the corpse lying on the street, but it could cure the coughing man and warm the freezing family. With the grail, Cera could help the whole city.

But the grail hadn't reached Reims yet, and when it arrived, it wouldn't be for those people. Lord Voclain would get a sip, as would Cera and her companions. But otherwise, the grail would stay secret, the exalted aim of chivalrous knights, the prize to be won through acts of valor and great deeds on behalf of the most prominent, those who already had so much. Perceval would understand why that was all wrong.

Her tears had dried by the time they reached the church, one of the few other stone buildings in the city. Sir Deverel pushed open the big door. Inside, Cera pulled down her hood and wiped her face with her sleeve. Pale light seeped through open windows into the cool rectangular room. Flames flickered atop thin golden candlesticks upon the white-cloth-draped altar. A huge wooden cross hung above it on the wall. A sculpture of Mary near the altar stared at Cera. It was plain white marble and wasn't large, but as she stared back at it, Cera felt tiny.

"Sister," the old approaching priest said. "Good sir. I am Father Fremont."

"Father," Cera said, Mary's gaze fixed on her over his shoulder. "May... may I make a confession?"

Sir Deverel shifted beside her. She and the order had their own priests who said Mass and heard their sins, but Cera didn't want to talk to any of them.

"Of course." Father Fremont motioned to the pair of chairs facing each other on the left wall, one cushioned—for him—and one bare wood.

Cera followed him there while Deverel headed to the pews, genuflected, then sat, hands clasped, head bowed.

At the chairs, Cera glanced at the knight. "Is there anywhere private?"

Father Fremont nodded. He led them to the far corner of the church, through a wooden door into a small room used to prepare things for Mass. Both seats there, on adjacent walls a few feet from each other, were cushioned.

He closed the door. They sat, and with kind eyes, the priest asked, "My dear, how long has it been since your last confession?"

"Not long." Cera turned away from him. "And far too long."

Father Fremont frowned. "Tell me what you mean."

"My sin"—she picked at a chip in the stone wall with her fingernail—"which I ought to have confessed sooner, is of inaction."

"What should you have done?"

Cera looked at him. "So many are hungry. So many are ill and suffering."

"And you could feed them? You could see them healed and well?"

"I believe I could."

"I know not how you could manage that." Father Fremont pointed at Cera. "But I know full well that despite your appearance, you are not a nun."

"How can you tell?"

He moved his hand up, down, left, and right, in the sign of the cross. "Not once from you since you've been here."

"Oh!" Cera sat straight. "I'm sorry."

He smiled and returned his hand to his lap. "It's quite all right."

Cera grasped the side of her hood. "It's to blend in. My friends and I are just passing through."

Fremont nodded.

"I am not a nun, Father, but I am a woman of faith in our Lord. Tremendous faith. I had a plan to do more." She shook her head. "It didn't work out."

"Why not?" he asked.

"It's... hard to explain."

He didn't flinch.

"Things didn't go how they were supposed to," Cera added.

"So that's it, then?"

"For me, with the company I keep... there was a chance, and it failed. I'm afraid that *is* it."

"Maybe it isn't." He shrugged. "I don't know your plan, but if you possess the faith you say you do, if it is tremendous and if you are telling me your sin is inaction, then the only penance I can prescribe is to try again or to try something else."

Cera opened her mouth to respond but got no further.

"You want me to tell you to pray?" Father Fremont turned up his palms. "Fine. Say a Hail Mary on the way out. Say an Our Father. But then act. You're young, but you don't seem like a naive girl. Whatever it is you think needs doing, if it is truly righteous, *do it*." He stood, opened the door, and walked out of the little room.

Cera watched him head to the opposite side of the church and join Sir Deverel, who was examining a small painting. She crossed her arms, allowed her head to fall all the way back, stared at the ceiling, and let out a huff. "Perceval… you weren't supposed to fail."

After a few deep, exasperated breaths, she got up and went out to a pew near the altar. Cera knelt and did make the sign of the cross this time before sliding onto the bench. She clasped her hands and began the prayer in her mind. *Hail Mary, full of grace, the Lord is with thee…*

———————

Josephus, Diana, and the knights with them met Cera and the others at Lord Voclain's that evening. The Holy Grail they'd brought safely with them would have nourished them all, but Lord Voclain insisted on treating everyone to a feast of freshly hunted game and his best red wine. Cera headed from her private room to the main hall for dinner.

While knights made their way in, Lord and Lady Voclain, gray-haired and refined, chatted at the entranceway with golden-crowned Josephus and Diana. The order's king and queen were the significantly older pair but appeared markedly younger. Father Niels and Mireille headed past them into the hall. Cera's mother, in a light-blue gown, spotted her daughter, who wore her usual white.

"Cera," her mother called down the hallway. She touched Josephus's arm. "Dear, I'll be just a moment."

He nodded without interrupting his conversation.

Diana came over to Cera. "How are you? Sir Deverel said you were crying on the way to church earlier."

Cera crossed her arms. "He's spying on me now?"

Her mother frowned. "He's concerned about you." She smiled. "He likes you."

"I know he does."

"And? He's a valiant knight. He's kind and, I can't help but notice, quite easy on the eyes."

"Mother…"

"You've been alone for a long time, and like Deverel and Josephus, I worry about you. Alone is no way to go through life, especially not a life such as ours."

"I hate being alone." Cera uncrossed her arms. "Deverel is a fine knight, and as you say, he *is* easy on the eyes. But he's not the man for me."

"Diana," Josephus called from the main hall.

Cera's mother flashed him a smile.

"I was crying because of the suffering people," Cera said. "Nothing new."

"Diana," Josephus called. "Please, it's time."

"Will you talk to Josephus again?" Cera asked while she and her mother headed to the main hall. "Try to convince him."

21

"He's convinced you are wrong. In his bones."

Cera stopped. "What do you think?"

"That we've had this conversation for too many decades." Her mother kept going. "I'm as tired of it as he is."

Entering the room, Cera shook her head at the silver plates and fine wine pitchers set on the table before them. She called to her mother, "And why do we bother with all this?" Cera wished the dinner was going to those in Reims who actually needed it.

Her mother glared at her while taking the chair beside Josephus, who sat at the head of the long table. A small iron chest at his feet contained the Holy Grail, for after the meal. On his other side sat Lord and Lady Voclain. Cera sat down next to her mother. Down the table, Father Niels, Mireille, Mabyn, and two dozen knights had filled in the rest of the seats. A crackling fire heated the hall.

Lord Voclain offered a short prayer of thanks for the food.

"Amen," all said, and then, around the table, two-tined forks skewered quail, sharp knives cut in, and chewing and swallowing intermixed with rising conversation.

"Lord Voclain," Josephus said. "Thank you for your most generous hospitality."

"Anytime, old friend." He motioned down the table. "You are all welcome anytime."

Josephus and most of the others nodded graciously.

"How goes your work?" Lord Voclain asked.

He knew all about the order. Select members of his family had for centuries. The order relied on allies like them to move across countries and keep their secret.

Cera shook her head at her silverware on the table and took a sip of wine. "Tremendous faith," she'd told Father Fremont. *Tremendous uselessness*, was the thought she kept coming back to. She examined the decorated goblet in her hand—it was ornate compared to the clean sides of the Holy Grail. Cera peered inside. No gold lining.

Cera sighed. She was the fifty-six-year-old princess of a silver-walled, gold-lined cup. She let her other hand rest on her gown on her thigh, feeling the knife strapped beneath it. But she couldn't do anything with it. With dozens of knights at the table, Lord Voclain, Mireille, Mabyn, Diana, Father Niels... she wouldn't stand a chance. And Cera didn't *actually* want to fight them. They weren't the enemy. They were just wrong.

Cera caught Sir Deverel watching her from across the table a few seats down. He smiled. She quickly looked away.

Cera put down her wine and loudly pushed her chair back. With all eyes on her, she went around to the head of the table, crouched beside Josephus, and opened the chest. On a concave pillow of white satin, surrounded by cushioned walls, lay her cup.

Cera grabbed it, filled it halfway with water from a pitcher on the table, and gulped it fast. The familiar coolness rushed within her while she returned the grail to the chest, closed it, and nodded to everyone. "Good night."

Cera went to her room and shut the door, but she hadn't retired there to sleep. Not yet. She didn't have a better plan than the one that had failed, but unless she'd badly misjudged Perceval, he was still the key to everything with the grail, and though it mattered less, he was also the answer to her prayers for the company of a man who understood the world as she did.

Cera sat at the old wooden desk, where a thick candle burned. The boy on the street asking for food that afternoon came to mind, and she swallowed hard. To make things right, to help that boy and all the rest, Cera would wait a little longer.

And do more. She had to convince her order to invite Perceval before them again, and most importantly, she needed to ensure that Perceval didn't give up on the grail.

She took the quill from beside the jar of ink, dipped it in, and, on parchment, wrote in the language of Perceval's people in Britain:

Sir Perceval of Wales,

I pray this letter finds you well.

Cera paused and considered. Then, careful to avoid revealing certain details, in case the letter fell into the wrong hands, she continued.

But if it does not, and you are unwell because of what happened—or rather, what did not happen—in the cave in the Ardennes, do not lose heart.

Of course, he would have lost heart. They all did when they failed. Cera and everyone in her order had heard countless stories of once-great knights crushed and broken. She thought about what Perceval might need to hear.

You are a good knight.

Cera shrugged. *Direct but true.* She tapped the quill on the edge of the ink jar then wrote,

You should be proud. King Arthur would be proud of you.

They all longed to do well for their luminous king.

I am proud of you.

Cera held her quill point over the ink, pondering the bit about her. She could start over—burn the parchment and redo the letter without it. Except she *was* proud—proud and thankful that at least one knight was out there who cared.

Keep going. Fight well. Fight for God, and by God, fight for his people. Be the valiant knight. Be the generous knight. We will not forget you. Next time, be the caring knight whom I've heard tales of and saw in your eyes that you were.

The candlelight flickered. *That should do it,* Cera

thought, *if the letter finds him.* She pulled a gold coin from her purse and placed it on her desk. She'd visit the priest in the morning and, in private, ask him to find a rider who would take on the task of locating Perceval out in the world and delivering the letter. *Which could take a while.* She stacked a second gold coin atop the first.

At the bottom of the page, she signed in an abbreviated way, which seemed safest.

C

She pursed her lips then returned the quill to the page and finished her name so that when he finally succeeded before the king, Perceval would know what to call her.

Cera

3

Roan woke with the weight of Lorette's petite head on his broad chest and the scent of her brown hair in his nose. He lay on her soft bed, half covered by thick blankets, with a pitcher of wine tipped over on the table beside him. The sun rose beyond the small windows in the stone walls. In the southeast of Britain, Roan held Lady Tadman of Sussex, yet his mind lingered on a raven-haired beauty from his homeland across the North Sea.

Lorette lifted her head. "Last night was fun." The young woman couldn't have been much older than twenty, which made her twenty years his junior. She kissed his short black beard and his neck, over thin wisps of his long hair, then laid her head back on his chest near his two black chain necklaces. Lorette had been married to Lord Tadman for a month. Word of her beauty had spread, so Roan had come.

"It was, actually." Roan closed his eyes, and vivid images of the woman he did not hold in his arms—of *her* head on his chest and his head pressed against her chest—filled his world.

Lorette lifted her head again. "'Actually'?"

Roan moved her off him and slid out of bed. From the floor, he grabbed his worn coal-gray trousers and, while pulling them on, heard a low thumping outside. The sound of horse hooves drew nearer and louder.

"Lorette!" came a cry from a distance.

"He's returned?" Lorette sat up, holding her blanket to her. "It should not have been for days."

Roan sat on the bed and slipped his feet into his black boots. "I sent word that your husband should come today. This morning."

Lorette squinted. "Why?"

"Pain," Roan said.

"What? Pain?"

Roan pulled his black tunic over his head, in the process stretching out his shoulder, which had been tight ever since the battle of Badon. "I suffer worse, but his pain will be of a similar sort. He should feel it, and I wish to witness it."

Lorette leaned away. "You're sick."

The approaching horse slowed.

Roan flared his eyes, tapping a finger to his temple. "Aye."

"What will you do?"

The horse stopped, and its rider's feet hit the ground.

"I never really know until I do it." Roan buckled his belt, securing his big sword and knife on his side, then drew close to Lorette. "But if he insists on fighting me, I'm liable to kill him." Roan left her room, the door half open behind him, as he heard a door past the main hall, around the corner, opening.

"Lorette!" an anxious male voice called. "Lorette, are you all right?"

Silence in the bedroom.

Roan headed down the hall, past the long table, toward the voice.

Lord Tadman rounded the corner. "Who are you?" The lean young man halted with his hand on his sheathed sword's shiny handle. "What are you doing in my home?"

Roan remained beyond his reach. "I'm Roan."

"What have you done?"

Roan put out his hands. "She invited me in for dinner." He smirked. "Then she invited me to bed."

"Never. Lorette!" Lord Tadman yelled past Roan. "Are you all right?"

"I am!" she called from her bedroom.

"See," Roan said. "We had a fun night together."

Lord Tadman drew his sword. His eyes narrowed and lips tightened, but Roan needed more from him. *More pain.*

"She showed me a good time," Roan said. "Showed me things in that bed of yours that I've never seen before. Never even heard of!"

"Liar!" Lord Tadman stepped to Roan, chopping his blade down.

Roan shifted back and shoved the off-balance man to the floor. "There it is! That's what I wanted."

Tadman got himself up, chest heaving. Lorette, wrapped in her blanket, appeared at the opposite end of the room.

"I'll go in peace," Roan said.

"Peace?" Lord Tadman swung high, and Roan ducked it.

29

Lorette covered her mouth with her hand.

"I didn't come here to kill you." Roan drew his longer, heavier sword. "But maybe I should have."

Tadman swung his blade, and Roan parried it as if knocking aside a twig. Roan attacked, and Tadman blocked weakly. Roan slashed across his knee, which buckled, sending him again to the floor.

"My lord!" Lorette called.

Tadman grimaced, holding the wound. "They will hunt you if you kill me."

"They could try," Roan said.

"They'll kill you."

"They could not." Roan bent down to him. "But if they did, I would not care."

Lord Tadman's blade slowly angled toward Roan. "Then you won't care if—" He lunged.

Roan shifted aside, the blade missed, and when Tadman spun to strike again, Roan's sword tip was waiting. He drove it through Tadman's gut and out his back.

Lorette gasped, her face filled with anguish, then Roan's pain grew as well. It wasn't supposed to be her.

"Wh… why?" Lord Tadman managed as Roan withdrew his blade. Tadman slumped, and his blood pooled around them.

He, not Lady Tadman, was supposed to feel it, Roan thought. *Nothing goes right! Not even that.*

"Grr…" Roan turned his back to the lady. "Grah!" Roan roared and heard her retreating behind him. With her dying husband's blood dripping off his blade and the soles of his boots, Roan left.

An hour later, famished, Roan rode his horse into Cruchester. The small town had been established by his Saxon countrymen when they came to the island of Britain in the fourth century, first as raiders then as soldiers hired by the failing Roman state to help fight against the Picts in the north. Roan tied his horse outside the town's lone tavern. No heat from the pitiful fire in the middle reached him when he pulled open the door.

The fat bartender and single barstool occupant looked at Roan. An older man at a small table, slurping a spoonful of soup more loudly than anything in the place, did not. Roan marched to the side of the bar opposite the other haggard customer, whose long hair appeared even more tangled than his own. *Maybe—mine might actually be worse,* Roan realized.

The bartender approached.

"Ale," Roan said.

The bartender reached for a mug.

Roan pointed his thumb at the man at the table. "Got more soup?"

"It's last night's," the bartender said.

"Don't care."

The man at the end of the bar squinted at Roan, who glared back. The barkeep set a tall mug of brown ale before Roan then headed to the pot by the fire. With his eyes fixed on the other patron, Roan set a gold coin on the bar—from the sack he'd taken off Lord Tadman's horse—then took the mug and chugged it. The patron gave a toothy grin, yellow and foul except for blank spaces where teeth should have been.

The bartender placed a steaming bowl before Roan.

Roan pushed his mug forward. "Another."

The barkeep took the gold coin and the mug while Roan ate a spoonful of hot and exceptionally bland soup. Roan moved bits of it around in a futile effort to identify them, then decided he didn't care what they were. He grabbed the mug from the returning bartender's hand and washed the soup down with a long drink of warm ale.

"Roan," the man at the end of the bar called out. "Roan the Relentless."

Roan burped. "So what?"

"That's you."

"What of it?"

The patron pointed his mug at Roan. "It's not yet midday, and Roan the Relentless is downing mugs of ale in Cruchester's dingy old tavern."

The bartender frowned at the man.

Roan finished his second mug and slid it for a refill. "So are you."

"But I'm no one," the man said.

"Neither am I!"

"But you are." He leaned toward Roan. "Son of Osred, who is King Aelle's most senior chief."

"Second son." Roan began ale number three and growled, "Let me eat in peace!"

"All right!" The man sat back. "All you had to do was ask."

Roan spooned out some soup, listened to the fire's faint crackle… and, washing the lingering insipid flavor from his mouth with ale, found himself unable to think of a reason to stop gulping until none remained. "More!" He slid his mug to the bartender's open hand.

"Fearsome warrior," the other patron said to the bartender, who refilled the mug. "Never lost in single combat."

Never lost a fight, true, except that doesn't matter. Everything that did matter, Roan *had* lost.

The bartender set his mug down. Roan grabbed it and sipped. *I never would have brought them to this dreary bar.* He drank faster. He might never have been to a bar like it again. That part of his life would have been over.

He took a quick breath then drank on, staring at the wall but seeing them in their home, at the table. Roan saw them making hearty stew together over the fire. Who could have imagined he would be cooking? But he remembered it. He remembered them in their yard, in the sun, and then in bed. Not as fine a bed as Lady Tadman's, but so much finer too.

Ale seeped from the corners of Roan's mouth onto his beard as he tilted the mug farther. Lorette had wept as she fled back to her bedroom. He'd heard it but wouldn't look. Despite his cruel intentions, there'd been something good between them.

Roan slammed his empty mug on the bar. *But it paled.* The others stopped chatting to look at him. His relationship with Lady Tadman paled compared to what Roan had before, and a paled good was worse than nothing at all.

And now Lady Tadman's husband was dead, leaving her alone. Alone like Roan.

"Are you okay?" The other patron appeared concerned.

"No!" Roan slid his mug to the bartender.

"What are you doing here?" the other man asked.

Roan assumed he meant the tavern, not *here* in the larger philosophical sense. "I've gotta be *somewhere*. Where's my ale?"

"Then you're not joining in the tournament after this?" the patron asked. "I suppose that would be a lot to drink beforehand, even for a man of your repute."

Roan burped. "Tournament?"

The bartender brought Roan's full mug, which he began drinking immediately.

"Lord Wheatley's. Out over the big hill. That's why no one's here."

Roan pointed his mug at the patron. "Why are *you* here?"

"I prefer the peace and quiet."

Roan shook his head. He considered the bowl of mysteriously bland soup but opted instead to polish off ale number five.

From behind a knight's tent and table, Roan watched a young squire cup his hands over his eyes to block the shining sun. Sword drawn, Roan snuck up on his prey, who peered down the hill to the plain where a dozen warriors battled on foot in the tournament melee. Onlookers watched from a loose ring around the action, some standing and others seated in the grass or on blankets. Roan knocked the top of the squire's head with the pommel of his sword, and the young man crumpled to the ground.

From the table, Roan grabbed a dirty white tunic that hardly fit his big frame and yanked it over his clothes. He scoffed at the cross etched in a nicked and dented helmet—at the notion of the Christian God protecting its owner from *him*. The helmet went down past his cheeks when he slid it on. Through the eye-level slit, past the loose strands of hair smushed against his forehead, Roan could see well enough.

He mounted his horse and charged for the melee, his throat parched. Roan could have used some water. The earth bobbed more than it ought to have as he bobbed in his saddle. He could also have used a couple fewer mugs of ale. But it wouldn't matter.

Spectators pointed, and the combatants might have noticed his approach had their focus not been on their foes, the sword thrusts and swings between them, and the resulting clanging and smashing of metal on metal and wooden shields. But Roan wouldn't sneak up on them and attack from his horse. He didn't seek those or any advantages. He wanted to fight. He wanted a challenge—a distraction.

Roan burst his horse into the middle of the action, and attention shot to him, as combat ceased, heavy breathing taking its place.

"Who goes there?" a knight in a spotless silver helmet called.

Roan swung his leg over his saddle, dropped beside the knight, and stumbled. "Grr." Roan collected himself, shouted, "Grah!" and shoved the man.

The knight staggered. "You cannot join now. We've already begun!"

Roan drew his blade. "Then don't fight back." Roan wrapped his second hand around his sword's long handle and chopped hard into the knight's round shield. He chopped again at the solid wood and kicked the knight, who shuffled farther back while ale sloshed in Roan's stomach and he fought for his own balance.

The other knight from the pair Roan had interrupted thrust his sword at the Saxon, who leaned away to avoid it. Roan punched the knight's cheek hard. The knight swayed lazily over Roan, whose fist drove him to the ground.

With loud clangs and smashes, other fighters resumed their battles. They had let Roan into their game, but it was no game to him. The first knight charged. Roan set his feet and shook his head quickly to focus.

He swung fast to meet the attacker's sword stroke, knocking the knight's blade aside. Roan drove his shoulder into the man, who fell backward to the ground.

Roan slashed downward, and the knight parried it. Roan kicked his ribs. He kicked aside the knight's shield, drove his knee down into the man's chest, and grabbed the knight's sword arm when he tried to swing. Roan ripped the handle from the knight and held that sword and his own crossed over the knight's neck.

"I yield!" the knight cried from behind his polished helmet. "Stop! I yield."

Roan's chest heaved. The clattering of other battles slowed. Roan held both swords firm.

"He yields!" the second warrior called. "Come, man, you've won. Let him be."

Roan observed the watching, frozen combatants. *I could slaughter them all, but then what?*

Roan's gaze turned skyward, into the sun-drenched blue. He knew what came after that field—who and what his mind would dwell on and churn over mercilessly. Even the melee offered no real respite.

Schvt. Roan sliced both blades through the knight's neck and watched blood run from it onto the grass.

"Ugh," Roan let out as the second warrior tackled him to the ground. Roan dropped the dead knight's sword and threw his attacker away.

Another charged Roan, who parried his sword strike. Roan spun and knocked aside a sword then slashed its wielder's shoulder. From behind, hands grabbed Roan's right arm, then two had his left, and both his arms were stretched out wide.

A knight in an orange tunic approached. "Who are you?"

Roan pulled inward. "Grr." His mouth wide, he pulled harder. "Grraa!" Roan dragged his two captors forward. He stomped one's foot, and its owner's grip loosened. Roan elbowed into his chin, and he let Roan go. Roan smashed the face of the young man holding his left arm then grabbed him and thrust the tip of his sword to the man's jugular.

"I yield!" the bloody-nosed man cried.

"He yields!" The knight in orange halted. "What do you want?"

"Pain!" Roan huffed and pressed his blade against the

skin of the young one's neck. "Death! I had to see it and live it. So do you!" Spectators rose to their feet. Squires ran closer from their tents. No one nearby moved a muscle. "They're dead."

"Who?" the knight in orange asked.

"Both!" Roan lowered his sword and shoved the young man away. "They're *all* gone!" Roan stomped to his horse and mounted it then pulled off his borrowed helmet and dropped it to the ground.

"Roan," a pointing knight said.

"Son of Osred," said another.

Roan spun his horse away from the melee.

"Relentless," someone said.

"All gone," Roan said softly before taking a deep breath. "Yet I go on." He kicked his horse's sides and shouted, "Ya!" Through a widening gap in the crowd, they sped off.

4

And now Arthur is dead. In Wales, Perceval sat on the ground alone in the small house in the woods where he'd lived before becoming a knight. The fire in the central hearth smoldered. His hair a mess, his face unshaven, he shivered in the crisp morning air. Perceval tilted back the jug he'd bought in town—half a day's ride away—sipped from the thin layer of wine at the bottom, then leaned his head against the wall of mud reinforced with straw. He didn't know exactly how long it had taken him to drag himself there from Francia after that awful night in the forest. He had returned to the cave the following morning to find it empty, and his journey home had been a slow, lonely blur, much of it walking beside his horse, Ociel, because there was no reason to hurry.

Why rush anywhere to do anything, he'd thought, *when I have no idea in what way I failed before the grail?*

He'd replayed the events in the cave—and the whole night leading up to it—so many times, but no answers accompanied those memories. No hints about what he should have done differently. No clues. "You did not prove worthy," Sir Berthold had said in final judgment.

Perceval had been home a long time and only asked the current date when fetching the jug of wine. It had been eight months since Francia. His two brothers and father had never lived in the house. They died earlier, in battle alongside King Arthur—king of all the Britons—against the invading Angles and Saxons to the east. Arthur prevailed, halting the Germanic people's advance halfway across the island of Britain, but Perceval's brothers and father fell on the field for the cause. Heartbroken and holding tight to the one son she had left, his mother had moved with Perceval out into the woods, away from the world of knights and court and battles and quests. Perceval wished he'd listened to her when she'd warned him to avoid it all.

Sitting there with his wine, he wished that when an old knight, lost and famished, had wandered to their home when Perceval was seventeen—seven years before—he'd let the man go on his way with directions and a bite to eat, as his mother had pleaded for him to do. Perceval shouldn't have prodded him for stories that kept him around. He shouldn't have asked the knight where he'd been, what he'd seen, and what noble deeds he'd done. Perceval cringed, recalling how when the knight mentioned King Arthur, Perceval had hung on every word, absorbing the stories like a sponge, and begged for tales of the king's court at Camelot and the Round Table knights.

Perceval sipped his wine and wished, most of all, to have not ridden off with him the next morning, set on learning his knightly ways and joining that renowned group of Arthur's. *God, why did I do it?*

Perceval swallowed hard, recalling the day he'd learned that his mother's grief at her son's parting—her certainty that his fate would be as grim and short as his brothers'—proved more than she could stand. She took her own life a month after he left. Since death at one's own hand could not lead one to heaven, Perceval's rash choice to leave had driven his mother to hell.

He extended his empty hand and grasped—but for nothing. Had he achieved the grail, then at least he could have found a reason, a purpose, in it. But after all he had done and all those he had helped, he'd proven unworthy to drink from God's precious cup or to be long in its presence. He'd been hastily ejected from the presence of all of them, in fact—the knights, that troubled king, and the blond angel who carried the Holy Grail. Perceval had taken a route far around Camelot on his return to avoid the castle or its scouts beyond the walls. He couldn't bear to tell Arthur of his failure.

Perceval grimaced, and his eyes watered. There was news in town that Arthur had died. *In battle? With his peerless sword Excalibur in hand and Merlin at his side, how could he? And if not in battle, then how did he die?* That bright beacon—that bulwark against the invaders from the east—had fallen and with no heir to succeed him.

A tilt of Perceval's jug brought no liquid to his lips. He peered in, and sure enough, it was empty. Perceval looked around his barren home.

Without King Arthur in command, with General Constantine elevated to king, how long will it be before the

Angles or the Saxons from the east reach Wales in the west? Whichever of the war-hungry kingdoms came to claim his homeland, Perceval wondered, if he resisted and met his end, whether he would join his mother in that infernal doom.

Knock, knock, knock. "Sir Perceval?" a young-sounding man said. *Knock, knock, knock.* "Sir Perceval, are you there?"

Who would come here? Perceval got his aching self up and, jug in hand, answered the door.

"Sir Perceval?" the young man asked, one hand on the reins of his hard-breathing horse.

"I am." He squinted at streaks of morning sunlight through the treetops. "Just Perceval."

"I tried here once before, months ago, but found no one at home." He reached into his leather satchel, retrieved a folded paper, and held it out. "Thank God you are here now."

Perceval took the letter, which was sealed with white wax. "Who sent this?"

"I know not its author." The courier mounted his horse. "But the priest in Reims impressed upon me, in no uncertain terms, the importance of seeing it delivered and keeping it secret. And I have seen it so. Godspeed, Sir Perceval." He rode away into the woods.

The single piece of parchment had been folded neatly in thirds. The white seal was plain. Perceval put down the wine jug, broke the seal, and opened the page.

Sir Perceval of Wales,

At the bottom, the signature read *Cera*, a name he didn't know.

> *I pray this letter finds you well. But if it does not, and you are unwell because of what happened—or rather, what did not happen—in the cave in the Ardennes, do not lose heart.*

One of *them* had sent it.

> *You are a good knight. You should be proud. King Arthur would be proud of you. I am proud of you.*

Perceval checked the end again. *Cera. Could it be from her?* His heart raced.

> *Keep going. Fight well. Fight for God, and by God, fight for his people. Be the valiant knight. Be the generous knight. We will not forget you. Next time, be the caring knight whom I've heard tales of and saw in your eyes that you were.*

> *Cera*

That angel from heaven, the fair bearer of its most precious cup. Perceval had wept for her as much as for it. The letter had to be from her. None other had looked into his eyes, save Sir Berthold, whose name did not grace the page.

Cera. The angel had a name.

43

Next time, she'd written. Perceval covered his heart with his hand. Both sank. He *had* lost heart, as she commanded him not to. Not dreaming the letter, or any like it, possible, he had lost himself.

He kicked the wine jug into pieces. *Eight months.* Now, most certainly, Perceval knew he did not deserve God's grail. *How can I be worthy of Cera or her company?*

He held himself up against the doorframe and reread the letter.

… do not lose heart… I am proud of you… Next time…

He would be worthy, Perceval decided. He crossed himself and looked skyward. "Thank you, Lord." He pressed the letter to his heart.

Be the valiant knight, it said, and he vowed to be that every day forward, without interruption and without fail.

Be the generous knight. Of course he would be.

And she'd said, *be the caring knight.* He always tried to be caring. But apparently, he had not been so before the grail. He resolved to never make that mistake again, anywhere.

In the stream behind his home, Perceval washed his clothes, armor, and helmet. He gave his face a close shave and neatly trimmed his hair. Wearing his coat of mail over his beige tunic, he secured a round wooden shield to his horse's side. He filled his canteen and loaded a pack with a bit of food on the chestnut-brown mount, planning to get more on the road.

Perceval said a prayer of thanks to God and asked for

opportunities in his travels to prove himself worthy of the grail and of Cera. He *had* to be worthy when next they met. He needed to be able to look into her eyes and know he was the knight she'd described in her letter.

Shame crept over Perceval.

He drove it away. Never again would he falter. He would not crumble and retreat to his mother's house or to anywhere. He would make Cera proud. Perceval pictured himself with a hand on the grail and one of hers on it also, and then he imagined his hand touching her soft fingers holding the silver goblet.

Perceval gave a last glance at the house, for he did not plan to ever return. He would travel to the cave in the Ardennes, in Francia, the site of his shortcoming. He didn't expect to find the grail or its guardians there, but that chamber within those caves in the forest seemed the appropriate place to resume his quest in earnest after he saw to things at Camelot.

Upon his horse, Perceval started east for the castle, a couple of days away, to pay his respects to Arthur, to be sure Guenevere was doing all right without her husband, and to ask Merlin exactly how his king had died.

Perceval rode the rest of the early-summer day, and when the sun hung low in the sky and some distance remained between him and Camelot, he neared Lord Yardley's estate. They'd met at court years before, and it had been a pleasant exchange, so Perceval decided to seek the lord's hospitality for a hot meal.

Fenced-in cattle grazed beside his home. Long lines of crops began on the other side. Chickens wandered within the larger fence surrounding it all. The main stone house, with space for multiple rooms, contrasted sharply with the smaller wooden structures for his servants and those down the hill in town. Perceval tied Ociel outside the lord's main house and knocked on the thick door. A young boy strained to crack it open.

"Hello, young man," Perceval said down to him. "I am Sir Perceval of Wales."

"My father isn't home," the boy said.

"But I am." A round middle-aged woman stepped behind him and opened the door wider.

"Lady Yardley?" Perceval asked.

She nodded. "Good evening. Your name is familiar to me. My husband spoke of you and all of Arthur's knights."

"Spoke well, I hope."

"Of course." She smiled. "Won't you come in?"

"If it's not too much trouble, I would indeed."

She moved her son aside.

Perceval entered. "I've been riding all day, and—"

The lady peered past Perceval, left and right, before closing the door.

"Is someone out there?" Perceval asked.

"No," she said. "But there will be."

"Oh? Are you expecting guests? I would understand if—"

"Not guests."

"Thieves!" Her son threw up his hands.

"Three of them," Lady Yardley said. "If not more.

46

Stealing crops and cattle. Ever since King Constantine called my husband to Camelot and now off to war, most mornings when we wake, something is gone. My servants, bless them for trying, wound up bloodied and bruised the night they confronted them. Three men, they said. Big men."

"I see." Perceval rubbed his chin. "Well, it is set to be a warm night. If you would permit me, I'll wait out for the thieves and see if I don't have better luck stopping them and persuading them not to return."

"Oh, no." Lady Yardley set her hand on his arm. "I couldn't ask you to do that. Please, come in and have a plate with us. I've made plenty for dinner."

"You have not asked me to take on the task, but I insist. It is my duty as a knight of Arthur's and a man of God. You two and your servants should not be prey to criminals."

"Thank you, Sir Perceval." Her eyes shifted up. "Thank God."

"I thank him, also, for this opportunity." Perceval reached for the door then turned back. "Do you... I was away when it happened. Do you happen to know how King Arthur died?"

"I don't. It's so sad, though. Such a loss."

"Indeed it is." Perceval pulled open the door.

"Wait," Lady Yardley called. "Let me get you some bread at least."

Perceval waited, exchanging funny faces with her son, until she returned with a loaf of bread and some dried beef. Then he went out and sat behind the house, with a view of the cattle and the fields. When darkness fell, he moved to where candlelight from inside did not reach.

———————

A quarter moon was rising. Stars had been twinkling for hours, but Perceval didn't trace patterns in them, like on so many nights when he'd camped out on the road. He imagined Cera, smiling, handing him the grail. He held her hand while sipping its precious drink.

He heard rustling out in the field. Perceval scanned the dark property. An opening gate creaked near the cattle. Whispers from that direction meant at least two men were conversing. Perceval crept low toward the cattle, hoping the animals would block the view of him from those out there.

"This one," a male voice whispered.

"No, no," another said, his voice louder as Perceval neared. "Here, this one."

Two sets of legs moved among the animals within the fence, but Perceval couldn't spot the third. He curled his way around the fence, toward the gate they'd entered by, where the two of them led a single roped cow. They were both big men. Perceval couldn't see their faces but made out a sword on one man's hip and a knife on the other's.

At the open gate, Perceval stood. "Stop."

The thieves froze. "Who's there?" the one with the rope over the cow asked.

"I am Sir Perceval of Wales, and you are trespassing on Lord Yardley's land and stealing from him."

"He ain't here," the same one said, letting go of the rope.

"Lady Yardley is, and her son. And you commit crimes against them. Leave now, and do not return."

"Good idea. If we take them all now, we'll never have to return."

Perceval drew his sword. "I cannot allow that."

The other thief drew a long knife and approached. In the darkness, Perceval could make out the whites of their eyes.

The swordsman drew his blade. "There are three of us." He advanced.

"So I was told." Perceval raised his sword and said softly, "God protect me."

The swordsman swung, and Perceval parried. His companion thrust his knife, and Perceval dodged then ducked a sword stroke and chopped low across the knifeman's shin. Groaning, the knifeman dropped to his knee. Perceval cut at the swordsman, who parried weakly. Perceval swung, and the man's blade barely got there. Perceval shot his sword to the man's neck.

"Hey!" The third in their group—a woman with a knife—skidded to a halt just out of reach.

Perceval looked from her to the wounded knifeman then met the swordsman's eyes, the tip of Perceval's blade remaining steady at the man's jugular. "I asked you to leave."

"We will." He dropped his sword to the ground.

"Smart," Perceval said. "Why bother carrying the weapon when you or your friends won't have right hands to use it?"

"Hey now." The man put up his hands.

"Ah-ah." Perceval inched the blade nearer. "You are thieves, and you have been caught. That is a punishment you would *not* forget."

"We won't forget!" the swordsman said.

"We won't," the woman echoed.

Perceval turned to the man with the knife.

He stood. "We won't forget."

"And you will not come back here," Perceval said.

"We won't," they all answered.

Perceval lowered his sword. "I am also Perceval of the Round Table. King Arthur may be gone, but I am not. Lord and Lady Yardley—my friends—know how to reach me. If anything more is stolen from them—any single thing—I will know of it, and whether you are the thieves responsible or not, *you* each will pay with a hand. Do you understand?"

"Yes, yes, we do," they replied.

"Good." Perceval moved aside.

The swordsman shifted a cautious step then went to the woman. The man with the bleeding shin limped their way.

With his free hand, Perceval grabbed the dropped sword by its handle, flipped it, and caught its blade. He held it out to its owner. "Take it."

Cautiously, the man grasped the handle.

Perceval held it firm. "Don't use it for this. God is watching. Think of your soul."

The man nodded.

Perceval let the blade go. "But without King Arthur, if the Angles or the Saxons make it this far, you may need it to defend yourself and those you love."

While they walked out of sight, Perceval sheathed his sword and thanked God for the strength both to prevail and to show them mercy. He asked the Lord to lead the three of them to a better path than thieving.

———————————

Lady Yardley kindly invited Perceval in for breakfast in the morning. Over the hearty meal, he explained to her and her son what had happened with the thieves. She thanked him profusely and, of course, unnecessarily, for—as Perceval explained again—he'd done no more than perform his duty. Afterward, he rode for Camelot.

By midafternoon, the wide gray stone castle loomed on the tree-covered hill in the distance. The square towers stood at each corner, along with the one in the center, but only a lone, thin green banner flew on one side tower instead of the array of reds, blues, and yellows on every tower that Perceval had grown used to.

On he rode, as he had countless times before, past the little lake, up the hill, and through the trees until he reached the main gate. The guard above the two big doors peered down, unmoving, so Perceval announced himself.

"I am Perceval, knight of the Round Table."

"It appears you are." The guard motioned behind him.

With a *thunk* and the *stretch* of thick ropes, the doors opened inward. Only a few people were ambling about. Slowly, Perceval rode in. A scattering of guards on the walls in pairs conversed quietly. Another, alone, had his arms crossed and head bowed. A merchant's cart stood barren and unattended. No music fluttered like during Perceval's past visits. He dismounted, and not a guard or young man ran to take Ociel's reins, so Perceval walked with him toward the great hall, lamenting how everything had faded with the brilliance of Arthur.

Perceval tied up Ociel, ascended the wide staircase, and pulled open the great hall's heavy door—and found the Round Table before him. *Thank God.* The room with high ceilings was only a little longer than it was wide. At its right wall, the pristine white sculptures of Mary and Jesus topped brown marble pedestals, while a third pedestal remained vacant, without the likeness of Saint Peter that Arthur had commissioned for it. The wooden crucifix on the far wall still hung.

"Perceval." His dear friend entered through the door on that wall.

Perceval smiled. "Sir Galahad."

Their embrace beside the table and Galahad's hearty pats on his back were the first warmth Perceval had felt since arriving at Camelot.

"Young one." The auburn-haired knight, solidly built as Perceval and standing but half an inch taller, backed away.

"By one year," Perceval said.

Galahad smiled. "How are you? We had not heard anything of you for some time."

"I am well. Now. I was lost for a spell, but I am found and steeled in my purpose."

Galahad raised an eyebrow. "Which is…?"

"The grail, Galahad. Still the grail." Perceval pictured its smooth sides. "Did you… have *you* seen it?"

"No." Galahad's eyes fell. "I have not. We all failed Arthur."

Perceval knew he had failed most spectacularly. "It's out there. I... I know it's out there, waiting for someone worthy."

"Good man, Perceval. You may honor our departed king yet."

"What happened? Did he fall in battle? Where is Merlin? Where is Queen Guenevere? How is she doing?"

"Where to start?" From the table, Galahad pulled out the nearest chair. Perceval sat. Galahad took the next one around, leaned out, and spoke as if to the empty chair across the circle. "Guenevere has gone south with my father."

Perceval sat back, recalling the queen and Sir Lancelot happy together in courtly conversation.

"Arthur's death hit her hard, but she seemed to find real comfort with him," Galahad continued.

Perceval remembered them dancing together joyfully the evening they all celebrated Guenevere's sister's marriage, after a generous amount of wine had been drunk. Lancelot was older, but the difference hadn't seemed so great.

"Where is Merlin?" Perceval asked.

Galahad turned to Perceval. "Advising King Hengist now."

"King Hengist?"

"He leads a people called the Jutes," Galahad explained. "From across the North Sea, near where the Angles and Saxons come from, but farther north."

"Does Hengist seek to conquer the entire island of Britain, like the others?"

"He does."

Perceval crossed his arms. "Then he would have been Arthur's enemy, and Merlin has allied himself with him."

"The peace of Arthur's reign is ending, and I think the old sorcerer aims to ally himself with the imminent war's eventual victor. Hengist, with his brother Horsa at his side, is an iron-willed warrior leading a powerful people."

"King Hengist may be the victor *because* Merlin has chosen his side to offer counsel to. Will you fight with King Constantine against him?"

"No." Galahad shook his head. "Gawain, Bedivere, and Sagramor are, but I've no interest in that war—or in any. I will leave Britain soon. Like you, I still seek the grail."

"I've seen it. The Holy Grail." Perceval could no longer keep it from his friend—Galahad, the truest and most worthy of Arthur's knights.

Galahad nodded. "I, too, see it night and day, when I sleep and dream, when I ride and my mind wanders, and when I pray to the Lord in thanks for all he has given me, including the quest for his most holy grail."

Galahad didn't understand Perceval meant he had seen it literally. Perhaps Galahad's kindness and deep-rooted goodness didn't let him fathom that it would not have been the first thing Perceval said the instant he came through that door and they embraced. But Perceval couldn't bring himself to correct Galahad and explain his failure.

"How did Arthur die?" Perceval asked.

Galahad shrugged. "One morning, here in the castle, he did not leave his room. When his servants called, Arthur did not answer. They found him dead in his bed. Maybe poison?

Guenevere returned to the castle that afternoon and wept over his body. Excalibur was nowhere to be found." Galahad leaned closer. "Nor was Merlin, and scorches marked the sleeve of Arthur's robe."

"No..." Perceval scrunched his face. "Merlin would never. He was Arthur's most trusted advisor—his teacher for years, since before Arthur became king. They were dear friends."

"Aye. And maybe a candle made those marks on Arthur's robe weeks before, or months, and went unnoticed or uncared about."

Or the ball of fire ever burning atop Merlin's long staff made them, Perceval thought. But it just seemed unbelievable.

"Sagramor especially," Galahad continued, "rides to battle set on confronting Merlin about it. To know why he switched sides. To demand the truth."

"Good," Perceval said.

"Knowing these new details, will you join them? And King Constantine?"

Perceval pictured Cera. "No." She held the grail. "I know it's out there, Galahad. The Holy Grail. Whatever happened to Arthur, I will honor him by completing the quest he sent us on. Gawain, Bedivere, and Sagramor are plenty to confront Merlin, no matter the tricks or spells he may employ against them. I will honor them, too, and you, and all of us who once sat at this table with King Arthur. You will not be alone out there, Galahad. I will search for the Holy Grail, and I will achieve it."

Perceval rode east for three days through Saxon lands, prepared to answer any who questioned him with assurances in their language that he was not riding to battle against them. Fortunately, it proved a lonely journey, though he would have preferred it if he and Galahad could have sought the grail together. They both agreed with Arthur, however, that such a holy quest surely included personal tests, which needed to be confronted alone. Nothing Perceval had been through had changed his mind about that.

On the southeastern coast of Britain, the scent of salt in the air grew pronounced as he reached the port town of Dover, the last hour of his ride after sunset. In the morning, Perceval planned to cross the sea to Francia. In the meantime, he headed to the tavern to have a meal before setting up his small tent outside of town for the night. Smoke rose from the sturdy Roman-built tavern's chimney, and the smell of cooking meat emanated.

He pulled open the door and stepped inside. From the far corner of the wide room—dim but brightened by the fire burning in the hearth—a big, haggard man in black, with long black hair, yelled, "Are you next?"

Perceval didn't answer despite all the eyes on him.

"You can't have her!" the man screamed, clutching the pretty woman at his side.

A smaller man in a clean gray tunic walked over, while patrons resumed their drinks and conversations and the man in the corner kissed the woman with him.

"Who is he?" Perceval asked the approaching man.

"Roan."

That Saxon name Perceval knew. "What's his problem?"

"The woman is Lady Stanton. She went missing a week ago, and *Lord* Stanton is offering a bounty for her return. We tracked her here. They"—he pointed at two dazed and bloodied armed men leaning against the wall adjacent to where Roan sat—"came with me. Roan wouldn't let her go."

Perceval watched Lady Stanton laughing at whatever Roan had said. He guessed she was ten years younger than Roan. She lifted a mug for a long drink, and Roan did too.

"Doesn't seem she's eager to go," Perceval said.

"No," the man said. "But Lord Stanton is very worried, as are their two children. The older boy beseeched me to bring his mother home."

"As she is the lord's wife," Perceval said, "he is within his rights to command her to return to him."

"Yes."

Though Perceval wore his mail armor as ever, to be ready for any enemy, he didn't touch his sword on the way over to the aisle between the tables leading to Roan and Lady Stanton. Roan's big sword lay next to its sheath on the table before him. The Saxon had a reputation as a fierce warrior, which he'd earned over more than two decades of pitched battles, single combat, and tournaments. While it appeared those decades had taken their toll on him at the edges, he struck Perceval as powerful. Dangerous. Roan never stopped in a fight until he won, they said, so Perceval had no intention of starting one with him.

Lady Stanton turned to Perceval, then Roan did the same and looked at him with hollow eyes that flared and tightened. "You *are* next." Roan stood from the bench.

Perceval stopped halfway to his table and put out his hands. "I'm not here to fight. Lady Stanton, your husband is worried about you."

"Let him worry," she snapped.

"Your children are as well."

She slammed her mug down. "Let *him* deal with those brats for a change."

Perceval clasped his hands before him. "Roan, is it?"

The Saxon pointed at the knight. "Who are you?"

"Sir Perceval of Wales."

Roan formed a grin. "One of Arthur's."

Murmurs and whispers filled the quieting tavern.

"Until the day I die," Perceval said.

Roan wagged his finger. "Gonna be sooner than you think."

"M'lady," Perceval said. "Where can I tell Lord Stanton you will be tomorrow so that he can speak with you?"

"Nowhere! Tell him I hate him. You tell him to leave me be!"

"He is your husband," Perceval said. "He has the right. If things are such that you don't want him to be your husband, then speak to him and settle it. I'll be there as well to ensure that you're treated fairly."

"Huh!" She threw her head back. "You think it's that easy? Ha! You think he'd let me go? You're a fool."

Roan shook his head. "The world's not that easy, boy."

"It could be," Perceval said. "It may be. Let us try."

"The world is hard." Roan clenched his fist. "It's pain

and death, and when we find a person—when we make a time that isn't unbearable—the good's ripped away so there's nothing left but pain."

"I had heard you were married," Perceval said to Roan.

Lady Stanton shot a glance at Roan, his hollow stare returned, and Perceval began to make some sense of the man.

"She died," Roan said. Lady Stanton softened.

"I'm sorry," Perceval said.

"God took her!" Roan called out to the silent tavern then focused on Perceval. "If the god of your Bible is real."

Perceval stepped toward him. "He is."

Roan picked up his sword. Perceval stopped with his hand on his sword's handle.

"Then he's a monster!" Roan roared. "Madeline died! Our son died!"

Lady Stanton put her hand on his side.

Roan pushed it off. "And you… look at you."

She leaned away.

"A pale shadow of that woman," Roan went on. "You're nothing." Roan squinted. "What would Aedre think of *you*? Go!" He pointed at the door. "Get out of my sight!"

Hand covering her mouth, she rose.

"Go!" he shouted.

She ran past Perceval and out the front door.

Roan pointed his sword at him. "And you…"

"I've no quarrel with you," Perceval said.

"You couldn't let me have one night of peace. One night without…" Roan brought his hand to his temple and grimaced. "Without *this*."

"My only concern is for Lady Stanton and her family."

"It's too much." Roan balled his fingers into a fist. "It's too hard!" He slammed his fist down then shoved the table away.

"Please, sir," Perceval said. "I am sorry for you. I cannot imagine—"

"Does your god protect you?" Roan made his way around the askew table.

"He always has." Perceval glanced at the scattering onlookers.

Roan kept coming. "He can't protect you from *me*."

Perceval drew his sword. "Stop this."

With two hands, Roan raised his blade. "Grah!" He chopped down.

Perceval managed to parry the mighty blow and set his feet better. Roan swung. Perceval met it firm. "I don't want this."

Roan's eyes flared. "I do!" He swung his sword again.

Perceval deflected it, slid back, and slashed. Roan dodged—the big man was fast—and swept low. Stepping back, Perceval blocked his sword—but not Roan's fist across his face.

"You die tonight," Roan snarled.

Perceval spat blood from his cut lip.

"Just like all of them!" Roan advanced, swinging high.

Perceval parried. Moving back, he blocked, stepped backward again, and parried again and again.

Perceval sliced across Roan's thigh. The man didn't

flinch. Perceval dodged a sword strike, running out of space behind him. Roan smashed Perceval's face and threw Perceval into the tavern wall.

Perceval snapped his neck to the right, avoiding a punch. Twisting left, he avoided Roan's fist and punched straight into Roan's nose, sending the big man reeling.

"Stop!" Perceval yelled, catching his breath. "The lady is already gone."

Roan fumed, and red covered his leg beneath his cut pant.

"It is *done*," Perceval implored.

"Grah!" Roan rushed forward and rammed his shoulder into Perceval's chest, pinning the knight against the wall. His fist caved Perceval's stomach, and air rushed from the knight's lungs.

Roan's left hand both held his sword and kept Perceval's sword arm pinned against his body. He drove his other fist into Perceval's gut, where rattling chain mail hardly dulled the blow.

Roan ignored Perceval's lefty punch and smashed Perceval's face. Then he punched his stomach. Perceval couldn't breathe. Roan hit him again. Perceval's sword arm wouldn't move. No air.

The grail...

Roan bashed Perceval's face.

Cera...

Roan held Perceval's arm tight.

Next time, she had written.

Perceval drove his knee into Roan's groin, and the blows

upon him stopped. He did it again, and Roan lurched backward. Perceval sucked in a huge breath. Roan glared, breathing hard and fast.

With his right eye swollen half closed, Perceval spat more blood. "This is over." He stepped toward the front door.

The wild man raised his blade and charged. Perceval slid aside, and the big man spun to block a sword strike. Now Roan, not Perceval, stood against the wall. Perceval swung low, and Roan blocked. The knight's elbow slammed Roan's head into the wall, shutting the Saxon's eyes. Perceval whipped his sword at his neck.

Roan parried, as if by reflex, then opened his eyes. Perceval swung high, and Roan parried but missed the next slash across his arm. The knight sliced Roan's already cut leg, and the man dropped to a knee.

Perceval swung his sword toward Roan's neck. Roan ducked then rose fast, punching up into Perceval's chin so hard that the knight flew backward into the quiet tavern air.

Perceval hit the ground. His head smacked it, and his sword rolled from his hand. Roan, his balance lost, landed on top of him.

All around Perceval, the patrons in the firelight blurred. Roan's weight on Perceval again robbed his lungs of vital air. He pushed upward, but Roan wouldn't budge.

Roan tried to lift himself but fell back on Perceval with a huff. He dropped his sword and, with both hands, pushed himself high enough to punch at Perceval's face—lazily. Then he collapsed atop Perceval, and they both breathed hard.

Roan's neck stretched tall as a small hand lifted his head by his sweaty hair. The hood of a young brown-haired woman fell as she sliced a gold-handled knife across Roan's neck. Blood spilled onto Perceval's chest.

Roan gagged. Perceval tried to push himself backward, out from under him, but he couldn't, and the woman held the bleeding Saxon. "Go to hell, Roan," she said. "Take your broken self there and burn."

Roan's eyes closed, and she let go of his hair. Perceval rolled Roan's lifeless body off and breathed easier.

The man in the gray tunic came over and crouched. He pointed his thumb at the seething woman with the bloody knife. "Lady Tadman had her own run-in with Roan a while back, like Lady Stanton's. Lady Tadman offered us the same as Lord Stanton for an opportunity to do what she just did, so we took both jobs." The man patted Perceval's shoulder. "Thanks to you, we'll get paid for this one at least."

Grimacing, his right eye now swollen completely shut, Perceval got to his feet then retrieved his sword. "Come on," he said to the man.

"Where?"

Perceval pointed his sword at the door. "Lady Stanton is out there alone in the dark of night. We need to find her."

"We won't split the reward another way." The man motioned to his companions sitting against the wall. "It's three ways only."

Perceval cleaned his sword's sides against his pant leg then sheathed the blade. "I don't want your money. But God as my witness, I will see Lady Tadman and Lady Stanton home safely." Perceval started for the door, and when no footsteps followed, he turned around. "And you good people will assist me."

Lady Tadman moved first, then the man in gray motioned to his two dazed companions, and all three followed Perceval out of the tavern.

5

Instead of getting up and returning to the church in Guérande, the nearby town where her order guarded their holy relics, Cera stretched out again on the ocean beach at the western end of Francia. While her long-sleeved white gown covered her legs and concealed the pair of daggers strapped to them, her ankles and heels felt the late-spring evening's cool sand. The sun was setting, but Cera had seen so many sunsets, and she hadn't ridden out for that one.

She laid her head back, listening to the rolling waves, enjoying the chilly, salty air, and smiling widely. That afternoon, word had reached the order that Sir Perceval had resumed his knightly ways—no details, but after months without any news of him, he'd been spotted at Camelot in his armor with his weapons. Cera didn't know if her letter had found him or if achieving the grail had again fixed itself at the forefront of his mind.

But it must, she thought. *It's Perceval. How could that not be his chief goal?* And even if he hadn't yet explicitly set his sights on it, his nature—the deeds he would do—would surely put him on a path toward the grail.

Of course, no one else in Cera's order cared about the development. Their interest had moved on from Perceval to other knights. But she hadn't moved on. No other knights would see things Cera's way or find it in their hearts to help her do what she would ask them to do. The seed of hope that had been replanted in her in Reims, when she'd sent her letter, had finally begun to grow.

Cera almost squealed with delight before she shivered and sat up. The sun had gone entirely below the horizon. Her horse, tied up away from the water, stood in the dimming light. Cera sighed. The news that day was thrilling, for sure, but she had more waiting before her regardless. Cera put on her sandals, got up, and rubbed her arms for warmth while heading to her horse.

"Should we head back?" Cera asked the animal, turning to the waves, brushing her hair from her face to see clearer. "I'll miss this. I'm ready to move on, but I've enjoyed our time here. Haven't you?"

Her horse nodded.

"I knew it." Cera got up on the saddle, and they began the short ride back to town. She figured she would have missed dinner by then, as she'd planned from the outset. She'd simply have her drink from the grail before heading to bed.

Cera's mind wandered to handsome Perceval and to things she'd tried not to let herself dwell on for fear nothing would ever come of them. Now she recalled from their brief encounter, as vividly as she could, his sharp features and alluring eyes. She wanted to know the man behind them, to finally connect with someone who shared her point of view—or if he didn't right away, she hoped he would eventually. She imagined him without his tunic and armor, and her without her gown, in his strong arms, held tight against his fit body.

With Guérande in sight, Cera wondered if Perceval had returned to Francia or stayed in Britain. She hoped he'd left and hadn't gotten caught up in the fighting for control of the island. While just war certainly provided opportunities for knights to show their valor and commitment to God, danger reigned during the chaos of pitched battles. Perceval could handle himself in battle, or any situation—Cera did not doubt it. Yet she didn't want him around that heightened risk regardless. Francia offered a safer path back to the grail.

BOOM! Flames exploded in a red-orange sphere ahead, huge from the town's building tops, into the early night's waning blue sky.

Cera halted her startled horse. Broken timber and stone flew. The fire shrank and burned off a single roof, that of the tall church where her order had the relics.

"Ya!" Cera got her horse moving fast, her mind racing, trying to think through who might have attacked, for that explosion had been no natural fire.

How many members of the order were caught in the blast? Have the relics in the basement—has the grail—been damaged or stolen?

"Ya!" she cried. *Mother, please be all right.*

Families with children hurried away from the burning

church. Men rushed toward the river with buckets.

"More water!" one cried as Cera charged into town.

Fire raged off the rear of the church's roof, and a hole had been blown out the back of its western wall.

"What happened?" Cera called to anyone she passed as she neared the building.

"Fire!" yelled a man walking speedily with two full buckets of water. "A blast like I've never seen!"

"Whoa!" Cera stopped at the church entrance, which had so far been spared from the flames at its rear, and dismounted.

On the street at the far end of the church, past hazy heated air, two people—gray robed and hooded—mounted waiting horses, leaving a handful with no riders. The person in the lead turned to the other, and through the haze and fire, Cera could not make out a face. The person pointed right with a long thin finger, and in the palm of a half-open hand, flames churned in a small ball.

"Merlin!" Cera stepped that way.

The riders sped off.

"Diana!" Josephus screamed from the church, his voice distant but unmistakable.

Cera ran to the door, shoved it open, and entered the hot, crackling building. She recoiled when a burning piece of roof fell at the far end, near two knights' bodies. Cera rushed right to the basement door and hurried down the stone staircase.

"Brave Diana." The king's voice deepened.

Cera rounded the corner. Bloodied knights of her order stood at the far end of the lamp-lined low-walled tunnel, outside the room where the relics were being guarded. Cera stepped over the lifeless bodies of two men in gray robes like those she'd seen outside and one of the order's knights lying facedown between them.

Sir Deverel turned to Cera. "They attacked from a new tunnel. It was hidden. We did not know of it."

"We should have known," Sir Phelan growled.

"Thank God the relics are safe," Sir Alan said.

"And my mother?" Cera asked.

The knights parted, and Cera stopped at the room's entranceway. The three iron chests of their most precious relics remained. Two more fallen knights of the order lay on the floor, along with a pair of robed men and their knives.

Tears streamed down Josephus's face. "Goodbye, my love." He held Diana's burned, blistered, unbreathing body.

Cera's mother's hand still gripped her sword.

"We *know* it was Merlin who attacked us." Cera threw her hands up emphatically from a middle seat at the long table in the crypt below Würzburg Cathedral in east Francia. It was near midnight. Knights and a priest of the order filled every chair but one. "We've known for two months, and we've done nothing!"

Seated at the head of the table, King Josephus responded, "We do not know. You continue to assume."

"He wielded a ball of flame!" Cera shot back.

"Whoever did it wore a hood and a mask," Josephus said.

"And did not carry a staff," Sir Berthold, beside him, added.

"Go ask him." Cera leaned forward. "They say Merlin has the ear of King Hengist these days." She looked around the table. "Go—tonight, right now. Go to Britain and confront him. Any of you, please."

Like the corpses entombed around them in the cool subterranean chamber, the people at the table gave no answer.

"My mother is dead!" Cera motioned to the empty chair at the end of the table opposite Josephus. "Your queen is dead! Burned to death by that wizard, that fiend! Avenge her!"

"I miss her dearly," Josephus said. "For hundreds of years, your mother would have been seated in that chair of honor, and I would have looked to her for counsel and, these last years, for comfort. You know I miss her, but what you ask is not our way. She would agree. We withstood the attack. The spear, the crown, and the grail are all safe. There has been no follow-up attack. One day, be it someone else or that same group, there will be a next attack, and again, our order will survive it. Until then and after, we will not seek revenge. We will not lash out in our own attack. We will use our strength to protect the relics and remain the end goal of a quest—a way of life that demands devotion to God, chivalry, and fighting for good."

"But not 'good' for everyone," Cera said. "Knights all over Europe—knights like you all were—come to the aid of lords and rescue wealthy ladies, but there are so many others we could help."

"In Cologne…" Sir Willard raised a finger. "I—"

"That one time," Cera said. "Thank you, truly, Sir Willard. But it was one time in a whole career. At this moment, out in this very city are so many ill and hungry, yet we do nothing. The grail could heal them. The grail could feed—"

"We've had this discussion." Josephus pointed then wagged his finger. "It would not work. Men—entire kingdoms—would wage war over the grail, and it would end up in the hands of who knows who."

"But—"

"I will not argue this again, Princess."

She slumped in her chair.

"It is your privilege to carry the grail," the king said. "By birth and because of your devotion to God, and most clearly your devotion to His people. But you do not have to carry it. You could leave us and it."

Cera glared at him.

"The choice is yours," he added.

"I carry the grail to honor God's power and His love and compassion," Cera said. "I also *choose* to remain because with my mother gone, you will hear my counsel, and maybe eventually, you will listen."

Josephus's eyes widened. "Good. As long as it isn't the same argument, again and again."

Cera backed her chair out and walked away.

Josephus began, "And now—"

Cera turned around. "What of Sir Perceval?"

"What of him?" Josephus responded.

"He has returned to his knightly ways." Cera turned to Father Niels. "For a couple months, at least. I saw the notes you made in his section of the ledger."

The priest shrugged. "Being thorough. Adding an addendum to his case."

"Invite him before us again," Cera said.

"We cannot," Sir Berthold said.

"No, you *do* not."

Josephus sat back and put out a hand. "Cerise—"

"Just…" She pointed at him then at Father Niels. "He is a brave knight. Skilled in battle and truly devoted to God. With the many we lost in the attack, don't give up on Perceval. Don't close the case."

Josephus leaned forward. "Princess—"

"I don't want to hear it." Cera put out her hands. "My mother is gone. That is her daughter's counsel. Good evening to you all."

Leaving them behind her, Cera took her long gray cloak from a hook on the wall and wrapped it around herself. She connected its gold clasp at her neck while ignoring the details of their resuming discussion. At the top of the winding staircase, she emerged in the cathedral's nave and almost slammed the small door behind her. She certainly could have, she decided. The place was empty at that late hour. But it didn't seem right. Christ hung crucified behind the altar, the sculpture complete with the wound on the right side of his chest that represented the one made by the tip of the spear the order kept down in the crypt. His head bore a replica of the Crown of Thorns they protected in another chest.

And in a third chest, on a bed of white satin, lay Cera's

charge, the grail in which Josephus's father, Joseph, had caught some of Jesus's blood after Joseph had taken their crucified savior's body to wash before entombing it. Joseph never knew of the grail's power.

If he had, Cera wondered, *is this what he would have wanted? Is this what the man whose blood it was would have wanted?*

She huffed and headed for a small door beside the cathedral's larger front one.

From the shadows in that corner emerged Sir Deverel. "Princess Cerise, if you're going out, let me get an escort for you."

Cera flashed a pretty smile, walked beside him, and turned aside so he couldn't see her reach into an unclosed pocket in her gown. From the sheath on her thigh, she grabbed her dagger.

She slid behind him, pulled his head back, and his body tensed, with his fingers wrapped around his sword handle. But Cera had the edge of her blade at his neck. "Ah." Cera pressed her knife gently into his skin. "No, no, Sir Deverel."

He let go of his sword.

"No escort for me tonight." She lowered her weapon and shoved him away. "You wouldn't strike me with that sword anyway."

"M'lady—"

Cera pointed her dagger at him. "I can obviously take care of myself." Then she pointed it at the crypt entrance. "And I'll be back before they're done with their meeting. They won't know." She headed for the door.

"Princess—"

Cera pulled it open. "I'll be down by the river. If I've *not* returned before then, you can all come rescue me." She exited into the warm, clear night while the door banged shut behind her.

A big moon glowed overhead. Cera walked straight away from the cathedral and downhill between low houses, toward the River Main, spinning her knife in her hand forward, stopping it, and spinning it in reverse. *Let someone bother me. Let them get in my way and see what happens.*

She checked behind and did not see Sir Deverel following. If he were, she had no doubt she could have her knife, or the identical one on her other leg, at his throat again, for he was young—by her order's standards—and, though skilled, not skilled enough to stop her. She ceased her knife spinning. He, like all of them, didn't deem Cera's skill in combat an actual threat to be on guard for. She had no doubt about that either.

They'd seen her fight the odd would-be thief in their travels, and they'd seen her do to them what she'd just done to Sir Deverel, and more, but they considered it amusing, not the real her. And they'd told her as much. It was a series of little tricks, a game a young girl played for fun and would outgrow. They had no idea that at a dinner Josephus had insisted on to celebrate her fifty-seventh birthday that March, *not* using her knives had been the furthest thing from her mind.

To those knights, she was the ever-beautiful princess who carried the grail they revered. Her still-twenty-four-year-old face and body were symbols of the everlasting life God's grail provided. To them, she lived intertwined with the Holy Grail for her role in the spectacle of the procession and as part of the prize the knights earned through lives of bravery, chivalry, and devotion to God. They looked at her passionately because of her presence in the holy fulfillment of their lives' work. And Cera was pretty and a girl, and they were men, but for those with lust mixed into their gazes, the grail quest drove them chiefly.

Cera shook her head and flipped her knife. A few of the knights had kissed her hand with tenderness beyond a polite greeting. A few even kissed her cheek or neck in search of more, but whenever Cera asked if they had other ideas of how the grail might be used, or she began to mention her thoughts about it, the knights all answered with uncomfortable blank stares. Cera's questions and alternatives ruined the end of their quest, and since her efforts at reasoning got her nowhere, she stopped their advances.

Cera smiled at the knights and politely explained that on account of her being the "grail princess," their encounter could go no further than the soft kisses already rendered. She asked if she could rely on them to protect her as they would protect the grail. They hastily agreed, thanked her for the mission, and parted with renewed purpose.

Cera reached the riverbank and walked in the low grass along the calm moonlit water. Perceval would understand, she assured herself. It would not be a blank stare when they spoke, when she held his hand and explained why Josephus and the whole order were wrong. Cera's mother hadn't understood, Josephus never would, but Perceval would, and he would agree with her about what they had to do. And when his brown eyes told Cera he did, *she* would kiss *him*. He was the prize to be won, not her.

Slosh—Cera heard it behind her and turned to see a growing ripple.

A hand wrapped around her wrist. Cera spun back toward a tall woman who was prying Cera's fingers off her knife. The woman wore black leggings and a blue shirt cinched by a thin coal-gray corset.

She held the knife and let go of Cera's arm. Her brown hair was pulled tightly behind her pretty face, and her red lips formed a smile. "Cera—"

Cera stepped back, got the dagger off her other leg, and pushed her cloak behind her. "Who are you? What do you want?"

The woman's clothes and boots were perfectly clean, which Cera found strange outside for the hour... or any hour. She spun Cera's knife in her hand. Cera thrust her dagger at the woman's midsection. Her target shifted aside. Cera stabbed, and the woman shifted the other way.

She lunged at Cera, who dodged, moving her body into the woman's. Cera dropped her shoulder, rolled to the ground, and threw the woman down the riverbank. The woman landed on all fours like a cat, with Cera's dagger between her teeth. Both arms out, she pounced atop Cera, pinning her wrists to the ground.

The woman jerked her head aside, flinging Cera's knife from her mouth. "This is fun!"

Cera strained, trying to move her arms.

"You fight well in a gown." The woman loosened her grip on Cera, who ripped her wrists free, rolled over on top, and forced the woman's shoulder down.

Cera held her dagger point at the strange woman's throat. "It doesn't matter what I'm wearing."

The woman shrugged her other shoulder. "Seems not."

Cera pushed her down hard. "Who are you?"

"I am Nimue."

Cera loosened her grip. "The Lady of the Lake."

"Her too."

Cera let go. "Why...?" She motioned across Nimue's body.

"Why no flowing gown?"

"Yeah."

"I do enjoy a nice flowing gown." Nimue poked Cera's nose with her finger. "But they're not very practical for tumbling in the grass."

Cera swatted Nimue's hand and got off her. "We might not have been tumbling if you *had* shown up in a gown."

"And hadn't stolen your knife," Nimue added.

"Exactly!" Cera retrieved it so that she held both.

"Guess I was looking for a fight." She stood, and for the first time, her face fell. "I am sorry about your mother."

"You... you're real. My mother spoke of you a few times over the decades but not for a while. She told me the story of you giving Excalibur to King Arthur, but I always wondered if it was true."

"Yes," Nimue said. "I gave Arthur that sword to reassure

77

his countrymen, after the one he pulled from the stone broke in a rare lost battle. Arthur, though ever respected by his companions on the field, did not descend from nobility. Excalibur, chief among all swords, was meant to convince the nobles to believe in Arthur and to ensure that his reign endured in that pivotal moment and, I'd hoped, for far longer than it proved to. I met your mother when visiting Josephus, long before that, in Paris. Then on occasions after, I visited Diana with counsel and sometimes just as a friend."

"Merlin killed her." Cera gripped her daggers tight. "I *know* it was him."

Nimue nodded. "It was him."

"You know? You're certain?"

"I am."

"How do you know?"

"I know what I need to know when I need to know it," Nimue said. "Like I knew when Arthur took his last breath in his castle and that I had to race to him and retrieve Excalibur before Merlin could take it. And that's what I did, but I could not undo what the sorcerer had done to Arthur."

Cera had so many questions. "You went to the castle? You can leave the water?"

Nimue spread her hands toward the river as if to measure the distance between it and herself. "On occasion, for short stretches."

"I suspected Merlin killed Arthur," Cera said. "When I learned he'd aligned himself with King Hengist. But *why* did he kill him?"

Nimue shook her head. "That I do not know. But I do

know Hengist's rule is a hard one, and with Merlin setting the strategy, he's overtaking the Angles and the Saxons in Britain."

"Is Merlin… they say he was once a druid and that he's lived unnaturally long. My companions speak of him like he's been out there for ages."

"He has been on this earth for many generations of men."

"How?"

Nimue crossed her arms. "I don't know. However…" She raised a finger. "I do know that the fire he wields is not natural."

Cera recalled the exploding church roof and her mother, burned and lifeless, unable to drink the grail's water and be healed. She sheathed a dagger on her leg and wiped a tear from her cheek.

Nimue pulled a tiny blue square from her pocket and unfolded it until it became large. "This cloak will protect you from that fire or any."

The soft medium-weight fabric shouldn't have been able to be folded so small. The cloak had a hood, and up close, the material shone in the moonlight as a royal shade of blue. A silver clasp sewn into the ends would fasten it.

"If Merlin returns," Nimue said, "you will not suffer the same fate as your mother."

"Will he return?"

Nimue shook her head. "I don't know."

"Would you know before he did? Could you warn me?"

Disappointment filled Nimue's face. "Cera…" She grasped her shoulder. "I am sorry, but I don't know. I knew to meet you here and give you this gift, but of Merlin and you, nothing more."

"What are you?"

Nimue's face went blank. Then she steeled herself and squeezed Cera's shoulder. She walked to the river and waded into it.

"Do you have free will?" Cera called.

Nimue was waist deep, light blue glowing around her torso and deepening as it rose up her body. She turned around to Cera. "Don't give up on Perceval. Fight on as you urged him to in your letter, which he did receive."

"I will."

"Convince your order to invite him again. And think also of what you mean to ask of him if you manage to convince them and he succeeds and achieves the grail. If you are set in your course of action, if you truly believe it is what must be done, write Perceval another letter so he is better prepared to hear you."

The dark-blue glow washed over Nimue's face, which dissolved into mist, running from her neck to her chest and torso, until nothing remained but a ripple spreading in the water.

6

Hot, rotten sulfur stench seeped into Roan's nostrils. He inhaled, and warmth sank into his chest—heavy, thick heat. He opened his eyes and lifted his head. Fire roared before him, to the left, to the right, and all the way around. Roan was lying facedown on red-orange stone, which warmed his skin everywhere because he was naked. His chain necklaces were gone.

Roan stood. "Ah!" His feet burned on the stone. He fell back to his knees, which tolerated the temperature, having already been against the ground when he awoke.

Intensely orange and red flames raged in every direction. Above was nothing, blacker than any night sky he had known. Roan recalled the fight in the tavern in Dover. *Perceval, gha.*

Except Perceval hadn't slit Roan's throat. Drunk and exhausted, Roan had lain on top of the knight, and someone else had pulled his head up by his hair and cut a blade deep across the front of his neck. He didn't know who.

Roan held his neck and could feel the blade as he had then. And blood rushed out of him again. He squeezed with both hands, and blood oozed between his fingers onto the ground, a puddle of red growing. He clenched his neck tighter, cutting off air to his lungs, but the blood flowed faster until the puddle neared the encircling fire then reached it.

Flame roared over Roan's blood, racing toward him, flaring high. Roan turned aside, but it burned everywhere, and the fire ripped through him. "Agh!" His skin and insides blazed. "Aghhh!" Roan screamed, and his world went dark.

Roan inhaled rotten sulfur, and heavy heat sank into his lungs. He lifted his head. Fire roared high, encircling him. The black void loomed above. As before, he lay facedown on red-orange stone, naked.

Instead of trying to stand, Roan got straight to his knees. His neck hurt, aching from the slit of a freshly opened wound. He reached for it—but stopped, thinking that perhaps his grabbing it before had caused the blood to gush. He would not risk it again.

Roan didn't know who had slit his throat in Dover, but if Perceval had left him alone, it never would have happened. *Perceval... Perceval.* Roan loathed the Welshman's name in his mind. *Perceval, you have sent me to this torment.*

Fire towered before Roan, consuming a base of thick tree trunks and branches with loud cracking from its depths, yet when a log broke or burned out, another rose from the pile beneath, replaced by one emerging from fissures in the ground, ensuring fresh fuel for the inferno.

It was not the underworld in the stories Roan had grown up with, but Madeline had told him her people's stories. He saw that she'd been correct in describing the fire and the pain. Hell awaited those who—

Boom! A ball of flame's heat knocked Roan backward onto the scorching ground.

Aedre! Above him in the void, Roan saw his first wife, with her short raven hair and fair freckled skin, as clearly as ever. His back burned against the stone, but he wouldn't move an inch lest that inch cost him his view of fierce Aedre, sword and round shield in hand at the front of their line before the first day of battle outside Kent. On the grassy field Roan remembered well, she raised her sword and let loose a shrill cry of war.

"Aedre!" Roan called into the void as her countrymen and -women answered with their own eager cries before the havoc that awaited them.

She started for the British lines, and the rest of their side began a step behind her. The lines neared, all charged hard, but Aedre would not be caught up to. She would reach the enemy first and strike the opening blow.

A hulking British axman slashed clean through Aedre's neck on his way by.

"No!" Roan cried, his heart racing. She didn't die like that. "No! Aedre!"

A booming voice rose from all directions, "You'd rather see it this way?"

Up in the void, Aedre lay on their bed in their home, gaunt and frail.

"Stop," Roan called out. "Stop this, please!"

Aedre coughed, and her face strained. She moaned. That was how she'd died, Roan vividly remembered. A warrior stricken with some illness, confined to bed, her energy sapped, her fighting spirit broken.

She moaned, and Roan shut his eyes—and saw the same scene, but at the end, when she didn't have the strength to lift her head for a sip of water.

Why? Why did she have to die like that? Oh, Aedre. Poor Aedre. Roan cried, "Who are you?"

The booming voice did not answer, but Roan recalled what Madeline had told him of the rebellious angel thrown down from her God's heaven, and he knew. Aedre twisted her face and groaned like he'd watched her do for weeks in that room, and Roan had no doubt who tormented him.

Aedre disappeared, along with the house, and emptiness spanned the space above. Roan sat up, his charred back throbbing. In the flames before him, the melee in the field outside Cruchester materialized. A broad-chested man in a dented silver helmet and a white tunic pulled atop a black one held two swords crossed over the neck of his fallen opponent.

"I yield!" The defeated knight raised his hands in surrender.

The man above the knight—Roan—sliced both swords through his neck.

"I…" Roan stared into the flames, held the sides of his head, and said softly, "I let the next one go."

"I yield!" The knight's cry came from behind. Roan

turned and, in the fire, watched himself behead the defeated man again.

"I yield, I yield, I yield." Everywhere in the circle of flame, Roan ended that man's life.

Roan wept. The fire's cracking and breaking wood intensified. *I deserve this hell. Unquestionably.*

He could see Lady Tadman weeping. Roan heard her whimpers like piercing wails after he drove his sword into her husband, the morning after he got out of bed with her, when Roan had sent word for the lord to come home to ensure the encounter. Roan didn't know whether his tormentor had put that vivid sight and sound into his mind or if he had done it himself. And there had been many like Lady Tadman.

But he'd lost everything before any of that, Roan reminded himself. He had been part of so much good. Twice.

Above, he saw Madeline, plump and round with their son, in their home in the north of Francia, her homeland.

"No," Roan said. "Please no."

Madeline, the kindest woman he'd ever met, smiled down at him. Roan's spirit cratered, knowing what a strained failure his smile back amounted to.

"Yes?" Madeline called and headed for their front door.

"Madeline!" Roan reached for her, but she kept going.

Madeline pulled open the door. Lady Stanton, the woman Roan had seduced in Dover, stood there. She raised a long knife.

"No!" Roan cried.

Lady Stanton stabbed Madeline's neck.

"That isn't how it happened! She died giving birth." *To a son who never took a single breath.*

Lady Stanton stepped over Madeline's fallen body and pointed her knife at Roan. "My husband cast me out. You ruined everything!"

"No." Roan squeezed his head with his hands.

"I miss my children," Lady Stanton said.

Roan had never considered the possibility that he would not even meet his. "Grah!" he roared, and images shot to mind of the other women he'd hurt, and the men he'd killed in his rage. Roan searched for the voice that had spoken earlier—the Devil, or a devil in his service, no doubt. "How long will this go on?"

"Time is lost to you, Roan," the voice boomed. "An hour for you here could have been a year or a single second up on earth."

Roan gritted his teeth at the void and the raging fires all around. If Satan tormented him, that meant his adversary, Madeline's God, really did reign on high.

Roan stood, the soles of his feet burning. "I care not!" he screamed. "Show me your visions if it pleases you. They are nothing. I was in hell up there, all alone. God saw to that!"

The inferno blazed and cracked. Thick black chains shot up from fresh fissures in the ground then wrapped around Roan's wrists. They pulled tight outward and downward, slamming Roan's back against the scalding stone.

"Agh!" Roan's charred flesh burned anew.

Thick smoke filled his nose. From the wall of fire, it crept toward Roan, itching his eyes, so he closed them. And in his mind, he saw Aedre, sickly and bedridden.

Roan opened his eyes. The smoke stung. He closed them and saw Madeline the moment after she'd stopped breathing.

He opened his eyes. Aedre had been his world. When she died, Roan assumed his happiness had died with her, utterly and forever. But Madeline had proven him wrong. It had been *so good* again.

Until God took her too. *Damn you, Lord.* Roan pulled against the chains.

"Grr!" He pulled with all he had... to no effect.

Damn you, Perceval, for not leaving me alone. Staring into the disgusting smoke, Roan inhaled deeply and let his breath out slowly.

Damn me for all I did. Roan let his eyes burn, because he couldn't bear to see Aedre or Madeline in his mind. He feared that in whatever awful visions of their deaths played out, they might open their eyes and see what he'd become.

7

Perceval's horse, Ociel, chomped at the bit. Opposite them down the list, Sir Padgett's mount wildly waggled her head but focused when the knights started toward each other, white wooden lances held upright. Slowly, they made their first steps of that final tilt of the tournament held to celebrate spring at the start of Lyon's tournament season in 525. Colorfully dressed and finely jeweled lords and ladies sat in the box alongside the center of the dirt track, while common folk from nearby stood in the trampled grass in their simple soiled clothes, cheering and pumping their fists. The other tournament knights had congregated at the end of the track past Sir Padgett. Perceval urged Ociel faster.

After finding the caves in the Ardennes Forest empty of the grail and of everything, as expected, Perceval had spent the rest of the year and the winter traveling between towns in the Kingdom of Burgundy, southeast of Francia. Lord Hicquet invited him to his tournament, and Perceval did not pass up the chance to once more prove his quality in combat.

Dirt kicked up at the hooves of Sir Padgett's mare. The onlookers hooted and hollered. With his large jousting shield held firm in his left hand, Perceval lowered the lance in his right to a horizontal position. Padgett lowered his. The match was tied, and that run would decide it. Perceval held his lance tightly against his arm. Padgett's shield—Perceval's target—rose and fell with his horse's charge. Padgett's full helmet, like Perceval's, hid every bit of human emotion, but nothing concealed the determination on his animal's face.

The crowd grew quieter. Their clapping slowed then stopped. Sir Padgett's shield bobbed. Perceval aimed his lance at it. Padgett aimed at Perceval's.

Into Padgett's shield, Perceval jabbed his lance. Padgett's hit Perceval's. Perceval rocked back in his saddle and squeezed his legs around his mount. Padgett flew from his horse to the ground. Perceval settled into the center of his saddle, imagining word of his victory reaching Cera and her company of knights.

"Perceval!" The crowd erupted in applause and cheers.

Ociel slowed. Perceval dropped his lance and shield to the ground and patted his horse's neck.

"Well done."

They spun around to face nobles standing, clapping, and smiling from the central box, while townspeople raised their arms and shouted, "Per-ce-val! Per-ce-val!"

He pulled off his helmet, smiled to them, and waved.

"Whoo!" cheered the crowd.

Sir Padgett, covered in dirt but back on his horse, and Perceval rode toward each other and the lord's box.

"Good match, Sir Padgett," Perceval said in the local Frankish, speaking loudly to overcome the cheering.

"It is my honor to hear that, Sir Perceval, from a knight of King Arthur's Round Table."

"We could have used one like yourself," Perceval said. "If only Arthur still called us to gather at that table."

"Well fought, good sirs…" Lord Hicquet began loudly, and the crowd's yelling quickly died.

Padgett and Perceval both nodded to the lord, his lady, and their daughter—a teenager, Perceval thought—who beamed at him.

Lord Hicquet called down the track to the other knights. "And well fought, everyone!" He motioned to the victor. "Sir Perceval of Wales is your champion!"

Cheers erupted.

Lord Hicquet held out a small sack of coins.

Perceval shifted in his saddle before taking it and nodding respectfully, feeling uncomfortable, as always, with that part.

"And now…" Lord Hicquet announced to the crowd. "Let the celebration begin!"

The cheering spectators rushed to the large open tents set up a little ways from the track. The lord's box began to empty in orderly fashion. Sir Padgett started away, and Perceval followed him to where the other knights had their gear. They, too, were making their way to the tents for food and drink. Perceval dismounted, threw the sack of silver on the table, and filled a mug from a pitcher of water. He gulped it down.

"Sir Perceval," Lord Hicquet said from behind him. "What a masterful strike in that last tilt."

"Thank you, m'lord."

"You were wonderful," his daughter said. "Simply wonderful." She wore lavender, and her straight brown hair was in braids layered on top.

"This is my daughter, Ogiva." He motioned to her.

Perceval nodded. "Pleasure to meet you."

She smiled.

"We hoped you would join us for dinner tonight," Lord Hicquet said. "When all this is done."

"Yes, that would be my pleasure. Thank you. And thank you again for inviting me to this fine tournament."

Ogiva took Perceval's arm. "First, would you escort me to the party?"

Perceval expected Lord Hicquet to object, but he just stood there.

"Uh, sure," Perceval said.

"Splendid." Lord Hicquet clasped his hands. "I have other matters to attend to. You will see her home with time to prepare for dinner, yes?"

"Of course."

"Wonderful." Lord Hicquet headed back to the box, where a servant waited with a horse.

"Come on." Ogiva tugged at Perceval's arm so hard he could barely grab the sack of coins before following. "Are you married?"

"No."

"You are very handsome, and you fight well. Do you wish to be married?"

Perceval pictured Cera smiling, her blue eyes radiant,

holding out before her the Holy Grail. "There is one who has my heart."

Ogiva let go of Perceval's arm halfway to the tents. She huffed.

"What?"

"It's not fair." She crossed her arms. "*I* want to be married."

"How old are you?"

"Fifteen."

"You're so young. And you don't want to pick your husband because he landed a lucky lance blow."

"You won the whole tournament!" she said.

"Even so, the man for you is someone who inspires you and who you, in turn, inspire."

She raised an eyebrow. "Your love, she inspires you?"

"She does. I failed her once, but I will not again. She inspires me to be a brave knight and to fight well." Perceval lifted the sack. "And also to be generous and caring."

Ogiva looked at the tents.

"It's for them," Perceval said.

"You're going to give your winnings away?"

"Money is not why I fight," Perceval said. "I have plenty for food and the occasional bed to sleep in. That's all I require. Their need is far greater than mine."

Ogiva squinted. "My father will hate it when he finds out."

"Help me disperse it evenly?"

"Sure." She shrugged and retook his arm. "Why not?"

In Lyon, like most of Burgundy by that time—and of course, like Francia—fellow Christians were common. When people asked Perceval's purpose during his travels, and he answered by explaining his quest, he heard numerous stories affirming that the Holy Grail was out there somewhere, hidden, waiting to be found. One innkeeper said he'd hosted three knights and a gorgeous young woman for an evening twenty or so years before. They'd guarded a small chest like it was the most precious cargo in the world. The innkeeper later heard a story about the Holy Grail moving around Francia and wondered if it could have been in that chest. Without divulging anything he'd seen in person, Perceval told the man he believed he might indeed have hosted the grail and its bearers in his inn.

Farther south, in the Kingdom of the Ostrogoths along the Mediterranean Sea, a different kind of Christianity reigned. The Arians believed Jesus to be a son wholly separate from the Lord, his father—unlike Perceval's belief, to be sure, but the difference did not seem dramatic. Regardless, his mention of the Holy Grail did not pique the same interest as in Francia or Burgundy. No one that he spoke to in Ostrogoth land had stories of the grail passing through nearby.

To the west of Francia, in the Kingdom of the Visigoths in Hispania, Perceval experienced much the same with regard to religious differences and the grail. And such a distance from Britain, he also found rarer knowledge and stories of King Arthur, the Round Table, and what Camelot had been like. The most interesting thing about the Holy

Grail came from a baker's daughter, who said her late grandmother told her the grail lay hidden in a secret, yet somehow towering castle in Francia. Not long after that, back to the northeast, to Francia was where Perceval returned.

Once there, in Toulouse, a merchant noted Perceval's accent as foreign when the knight asked the price of an apple. She correctly pinpointed it as British then asked if he had any news of the wars raging on the island. Not for months, Perceval told her, except for slight variations of the same story: that King Hengist had repelled King Constantine's surprise attack in the wake of Arthur's death. A great many Britons fell, and though Constantine escaped, his fighting turned defensive after that. Hengist, with that threat to the west muted, had shifted his focus to conquering Angle and Saxon land.

The merchant claimed to know that King Hengist and his brother Horsa descended from Woden, a prominent deity in his Germanic people's pagan religion. She had also heard that the king himself had cut down, with his giant axe, Perceval's fellow Round Table knight, Sir Sagramor, but her source of the rumor left Perceval uncertain of its veracity. Perceval considered returning to Britain to find out for sure and to reunite with other of his brother knights, but the greater part of him understood that those things would have to wait. The war there did not feel like the path that would lead him to the grail.

On a warm summer evening, Perceval was dining on bread and chicken at a rowdy tavern in Bourges, in central

Francia. He stuck to water in his mug in case of any sudden incident that he could best meet with his full wits about him. Two men at the next table were on their third ale each, that Perceval had seen, and their talk turned to witches and wizards and tales of mysterious druids and other pagan things. In truth, they both had a knack for telling tales, and Perceval understood why, as they attempted to one-up each other with each successive myth or story, they enjoyed each other's company—for they did seem to be good friends.

"And of Merlin, you surely know," the one farther from Perceval said.

Perceval froze halfway into a bite of bread.

"The old wizard?" The nearer man widened his eyes. "The fire mage? Of course, I know of Merlin."

"He's older than you think. He's outlived kings and queens *and* their full-grown children and grandchildren."

Perceval finished chewing quietly, lest he miss a single word.

"I have heard such things," the man nearer said.

The other leaned forward. "But I know more."

His friend sat back, and Perceval froze again, holding the bread in his mouth.

The farther man continued. "Merlin began young, of course, and was educated as one of the druids. Then he grew old as we all do, older than you and me. But he gave up those ancient beliefs and became young again. He will live forever this way."

The nearer man rubbed his chin. "How can that be?"

The farther man leaned back. "I know not. A witch told

me the tale but ended it there." He raised a finger. "A beautiful witch, not like most witches."

Perceval finally swallowed his hunk of bread, and their conversation moved on to the specific physical attributes that made that particular witch especially pleasant to the eye. The voluptuous portrait they painted did indeed contrast sharply with the typical aged, wrinkly woman dealing in potions and herbs. But along with the image of a vibrant young woman, the potions and herbs remained in Perceval's mind, for every witch or wizard he'd ever seen practicing magic relied on those tangible things, if it was really magic.

When Perceval lived in the forest in Wales, his mother had explained that certain plants had different effects on people. Some, if eaten, could lower a fever, while others, placed on the skin, would soothe a bite or a burn. Perceval suspected wizards and witches used such knowledge to make their potions and balms that amazed others who did not understand the wholly natural ingredients in them.

He washed his bread down with water. *Perhaps the Lady of the Lake is magical.* Though he'd never met or seen her, he'd listened to tales of her told by Arthur himself. Perceval supposed whatever force held the sword locked in the stone against the efforts of so many, until Arthur had drawn it out with ease, might have been magical. He could not argue otherwise. But the people who called themselves wizards and witches did not strike him as so.

He set the rest of his bread on his plate. The one thing Perceval had ever actually seen that he could not explain away, and which spoiled his appetite for the rest of his dinner in that tavern, was the small ball of fire ever burning atop Merlin's tall wooden staff. Perceval had asked Arthur about it once when they spoke in private during a stroll around the castle. Arthur said that he himself had only asked Merlin about it twice. Each time, the wizard had simply smiled and told him it was magic, a secret of his art. Arthur didn't press the matter beyond that, so of course, Perceval didn't either.

He recalled the black-orange flame ceaselessly flaring and consuming itself above Merlin's staff. It had disturbed Perceval, but beyond that, it hadn't mattered. Yet scorches had marked Arthur's robe when he died. Arthur's knights had failed him by not concerning themselves more with Merlin's fire or the wizard's shrouded past. Perceval and the other knights had been blissfully blinded by Arthur's bright vision for the world, which Merlin's council appeared back then to be advancing. Perceval had wanted that world so badly—a world of peace, justice, fairness, and with all of that achieved, a world of joy, like that which permeated the court at Camelot when King Arthur presided. Perceval still wanted that world.

But without Arthur, can it ever come to be?

Perceval wondered if Gawain, Bedivere, and Sagramor had confronted Merlin as Galahad had said they intended to, demanding to know if he'd killed Arthur and why. But Perceval doubted they'd gotten the chance, Constantine having fared so poorly against Hengist in battle. Then Perceval thought, again, of riding to the northern coast of Francia and rowing home to Britain to confront Merlin himself.

A goblet of wine clattered to the floor across the tavern.

I cannot confront Merlin. Perceval drove the idea away. *Keep going,* Cera had said in her letter. Perceval would stay focused on his sacred quest. Nothing mattered more than proving himself worthy of her and the Holy Grail.

———————————

On a windy day that October, a young rider hurried to Perceval and Ociel on the path east. "Sir Perceval?"

He stopped. "Yes."

The rider held out a parchment folded into thirds. Perceval's heart beating fast, he carefully took the letter. A white seal closed it. The messenger turned his horse to go.

"Wait." Perceval reached into his purse for a few silver coins.

"No need." The messenger put up his hand. "The lady paid me too well for the task."

"She's near, then? You saw her? How is she?"

"Very beautiful. Also very intense. She was not near, though. I have been searching for you for some time. I am sworn not to reveal more."

Perceval held out the coins. "I insist."

The messenger took them. "Good luck, Sir Perceval." He rode back the way he'd come.

Perceval ran his fingers along the parchment to the seal… then broke the wax.

Sir Perceval of Wales,

He checked the end of the parchment whipping around in the wind. Cera had indeed signed it, thank goodness. Perceval grasped the letter with both hands and read on.

I am heartened to learn that you have returned to your knightly ways.

A blanket of shame wrapped over him. She knew he had faltered.

Ever the Lord's enemy seeks to sow doubt within us, but how we respond reveals who we are, and you have responded well.

The blanket tore and fell. He agreed proudly. He had responded well, with redoubled focus and conviction.

I eagerly await a time when you are able to see us again. Think not only of what you seek but also what it means.

Cera

And there it was, written plainly for Perceval to see. She couldn't mention the grail by name, but when he had proven worthy, he would see it again.

But will I prove worthy? Perceval lowered the parchment and read again:

Think not only of what you seek but also what it means.

The doubt creeping through him was not like when he'd run home to Wales. Giving up was the furthest thing from his mind. *But am I doing right? Do I understand the grail?* If he didn't know what it meant, even if he saw it again, he could not possibly achieve it.

Perceval urged Ociel forward, and they went slowly down the path.

In the Kingdom of Saxony, northeast of Francia, the people held pagan beliefs, and Perceval could not imagine Cera and her company there, so he did not venture into those lands. Instead, he turned back southwest.

Winter came to Francia, and while Perceval traveled less during those cold months, he did what good he could. He confronted thieves who routinely stole from lords and merchants. He tracked down a woman who'd murdered her friend over love for a man, and he delivered her to the authorities. Perceval chopped firewood for the elderly. Many days and nights, he read his Bible. The translation into their native language had been a gift from Arthur when Perceval accepted his invitation to become a knight of the Round Table.

The year 525 turned to 526, and Perceval's mind found a new depth with which to focus on the Holy Grail and Cera's most recent letter. Naturally, he wondered where she'd written from and how long that rider had been searching for him. Most often, Perceval thought of her fresh words about what he'd so long sought.

The grail was… divinity on earth, Perceval reasoned. He could not go back in time and history to meet Jesus. The Lord did not appear before Perceval as a man, voice, or burning bush as he had Moses. And Perceval did not require such proof of God. Perceval believed in Him. He *knew* He ruled on high above all. Yet to hold the cup that had held His son's blood… Perceval could not imagine a greater honor.

Perceval fought in God's name. His heart beat proudly whenever he declared it to himself. He confidently did his best in every endeavor, wherever he went. Perceval believed he did right in God's name. *But is that enough?* He could not help wondering if his path might have been tragically misguided.

A better knight would not dwell in such doubt and dread about his course and actions, Perceval lamented. Galahad, wherever his search for the grail was taking him, faced with whatever challenges, surely did not question himself so… as Perceval had not, on his renewed quest, until reading Cera's latest letter.

The grail would resolve all doubts, he assured himself. Achieving it would be the greatest possible validation that his efforts had been right and true.

That was where his mind had settled in March of 526, as leaves sprouted on trees and grass grew anew. Perceval sat leaning against the side of the Parisian shop where he'd just purchased parchment, a quill, and a small jar of ink. A few merchants sold their food and wares across the street. Two horses drew a carriage past. Mules pulled a cart up the hill. People strolled by in the midday sun.

Perceval set the parchment flat on his shield in his lap. If Cera sent another messenger, he would try to send the letter back to her. If she didn't... he decided to write her anyway. Perceval would start a conversation between them.

Dear Cera,

Since she'd signed with no title, he had no other way to begin.

Your letters

He paused. *Buoyed my spirits? No. Brightened my...*

Your letters lifted my soul.

Whatever else they did, they'd at first done that.

It heartens me that you speak of the time when I will again prove worthy. I eagerly await that day.

That day, he would also get to see her again, but Perceval dared not mention his eagerness in that regard. He watched a lone donkey pull a squeaky cart up the hill then continued, as she had, being sure to leave out specifics and avoid mentioning the grail by name.

I do think about what it means and that it represents

Perceval didn't want to write *proof* or *validation*, but those were the two words he'd always found his way to and gotten stuck on. Quill in hand, hovering above the ink, he had hoped writing would bring forth a new idea, one currently blocked by those fixed at the forefront of his mind.

An old beggar leaned heavily on his cane in the street, his hand out, approaching every merchant and passerby. *Life?* Perceval thought. If the stories of it were true, the grail did give that. The beggar sought money or food, Perceval supposed. The old man wandered into the middle of the street.

Snap! It came from up the hill. *Thadump.* The squeaky cart inched backward down the hill. Everyone watched it gradually gain speed.

Perceval stood, his shield, parchment, and quill hitting the ground. He sprinted toward the beggar. People pointed, some at the fast-approaching cart, others at the old man.

Screams rose. The beggar noticed the cart. Perceval pushed between two men. The beggar braced for impact.

Perceval leapt and tackled him out of the way. The cart nicked Perceval's boot as it passed. He watched it crash—*Cradack! Badoom!*—into the house at the bottom of the hill.

The old man groaned in Perceval's arms.

Perceval let him go. "Are you all right?"

"Grm." The man reached for his cane. "I am, thanks to you." He got himself to his feet. "Thanks only to you."

Some people cheered while others appeared shocked,

covering their mouths with their hands. Perceval considered where he'd been stuck with his letter, thinking about what the grail meant.

None of the people had tried to save the old man. Any of them could have, but instead, they did nothing. *Does that have something to do with the Holy Grail?*

Perceval finished that letter to Cera, including more questions than he'd anticipated. It calmed him to write regardless, to put his uncertainty to paper rather than only rolling it over in his mind. He prayed for the opportunity to send her the letter.

From Paris, Perceval headed west toward the ocean. On the way, a pair of robbers threatened him, and despite his attempts to talk them out of conflict, they pressed the matter. The skirmish did not last long before Perceval disarmed them both, and like the ones at Lord Yardley's on the way to Camelot, Perceval promised to take their hands if he caught wind of them stealing again. The prospect appeared to terrify them.

In those travels, Perceval did not come across any maidens or ladies in distress who needed rescuing. He hadn't wished the Saxon Roan dead back in Dover, but he wondered half seriously if perhaps him being gone left the women of the world better off. *Perhaps Roan is better off as well, pity the thought.* Roan had seemed so troubled, at the limit of reason. Perceval hoped that before his sudden end, he'd made peace with God.

Late one afternoon in August, in the northwest of Francia, Perceval reached the small town of Bevrée—what still stood of it. Fire had ravaged the place. Soot covered women, children, and frail old men huddled against half walls of roofless burned-out houses.

A woman approached Perceval's horse with a young girl. Perceval asked, "What happened here?"

"Fire," the woman said. "Burned everything."

"Do you have food?" The girl looked up at Perceval.

He dismounted, took two pieces of dried beef from his satchel, and handed one to each of them. Others left their husks of houses to head over. Perceval asked the woman, "Have you nothing to eat?"

"It burned," she said. "A week ago."

"Livestock?"

"Most left with Lord Girart. The rest stolen right after."

"He deserted you?"

The group of around twenty who gathered around him consisted of three young boys, a teenage boy, and two old men, and the rest were women.

A middle-aged woman explained, "Yesterday, he left with Lady Girart for Hispania, where he'd first met her. After everything *we* had burned, he said we weren't worth his trouble. It hadn't been a good harvest for any of us, and he said he couldn't spare anything. He took everything he had and his men, who were protecting our town with our husbands and older sons gone. We checked his house after. Nothing there's of any use."

"Where are your husbands and sons?" Perceval asked.

"Called off to war with the king."

King Childebert was fighting his brothers in the south to finally resolve who owned a particular patch of land. Perceval had avoided it in his travels, like he had avoided all the petty conflicts between the late King Clovis's four sons, since the great Frankish conqueror had died and left his vast territory split between them.

"Do you have more food?" the woman asked.

Perceval reached into his satchel. Then, changing his mind, he unfastened the whole thing from Ociel and held it out. "Here."

Everyone rushed over, wide-eyed.

Perceval lifted the bag high. "Wait."

They stopped.

"One at a time. Take only a bit so everyone gets some." Perceval lowered the bag, and the adults urged their children forward. They took a piece each, a few quietly thanking Perceval, the bravest making eye contact. Then the adults came, and most kept to a single piece. Others had walked over, and they ended up breaking the last few bits in half to ensure that everyone got something.

"Are you a knight?" the teenager with brown hair asked while he chewed. "You look like a knight."

"I am Sir Perceval of the Round Table." He chose to mention the table instead of Wales in order to bring some hope to the people.

"Arthur's dead," the middle-aged woman said. "Hengist rules Britain now."

"Not all of it," Perceval responded. "Constantine still

opposes him. Camelot has not fallen."

She clicked her tongue. "Not yet."

"Not yet." Perceval feared that her attitude was a realistic one. He looked around the group and debated whether he could find Lord Girart, considering his two-day head start, but he decided that even if successful, he would have a hard time compelling the lord and his men to return. "We'll need more food. Have you any money?"

"I took it all to Rennes," the teenage boy said. "On our only horse. What it bought didn't last long."

"What's your name?"

"Remi."

"Nice to meet you, Remi." Perceval was very glad to meet him, in fact, as he did not want to leave them all unprotected. Remi was young, certainly, which worried Perceval a little, but the boy had made the journey before. Perceval threw his purse to him. "Ride back tomorrow morning. Dried meat is what we want. Beef will be least expensive. And buy seeds of wheat we can plant for next summer's harvest. Don't mention where you're from or what's happened here." Perceval didn't want the thieving kind, or worse, to follow him back and take advantage of the mostly female group's relatively defenseless situation.

Remi nodded. "Okay."

Perceval pointed a few houses down. "Let's get a roof on that one. If we take the wood that's left from a few others and if we can find straw that's been spared from the fire, we can finish before nightfall."

Most of the adult women, a few daughters, and the two old men came forward, and they got to work.

———————————

They did finish that roof before nightfall. The following day, they gathered enough straw to put a few more up. They kept at it, and before long, though space was tight, everyone who wanted a roof to sleep under had one. Perceval stuck to his tent, and many others were content under the stars. But the children, especially, appreciated the security and the warmth of the buildings.

Remi made his trip to Rennes. They planted the wheat he returned with, and Perceval rationed the food, day by day, so it would last, he hoped, until their husbands and sons came home from war. It heartened Perceval that no one challenged him about the portions and no one stole. They took turns getting water from the stream, and everyone readily shared when they had. They were good people in Bevrée, he concluded. Lord Girart, aside from being a villain for leaving them, had been a fool to.

None of the townspeople had experience hunting real game. They had a few bows the men had left behind, but Remi, to Perceval's dismay, couldn't shoot well, despite the knight's instruction. Remi went out after rabbits with a knife or to fish, along with some of the women, but Perceval didn't want to leave everyone alone while he hunted larger animals. He feared what could happen to those in town with no one to protect them. He thanked God he had been the one to arrive, focused solely on seeing to their safety and survival until the men returned.

They got to rebuilding walls of homes next, which took longer, but they made good progress as the summer neared its end. Few visitors rode or walked to town, Perceval assumed because of spreading word that there was no longer a tavern in Bevrée to get a drink or meal at, or an inn to sleep in.

Those who did arrive hadn't heard of the fire and the lord abandoning the townsfolk. Perceval asked them for any food or money they could spare. Most didn't have any to give, but some gave a little, and all in town appreciated it and rationed the food to last as long as possible. Perceval eventually convinced one traveler of greater means to carry letters to riders who could deliver them to King Childebert and the husbands of the women of Bevrée. Perceval never knew if he found such riders, and no return letters arrived. Most disappointingly, no husbands or sons of townsfolk returned either.

By mid-autumn, despite the small animals and occasional fish the townspeople managed to catch, their food supply dwindled. When a traveler shared news that King Childebert's war would not end before winter and his army would remain camped in the south for fear that returning home would be interpreted as abandoning Childebert's claim on the land, Perceval decided he had no choice but to leave town and hunt for larger game. With Remi and three women eager to join him, they set off, taking turns between horseback and walking, to near-disastrous results.

They killed nothing all day. They spotted a few deer in the woods but could not get near enough for Perceval to take a shot before the animals ran away. As the group returned empty-handed, screams from town sent Perceval to his saddle and into a hard ride—his worst fear imminent.

Two burly men had shown up from the east and had a mother and daughter trapped in their house against their will, with the door locked shut. Other women and old men of Bevrée screaming outside had been bloodied and bruised, beaten back when trying to enter through the windows. Driving his shoulder into the locked door, Perceval burst inside and hacked at the men, injuring them badly. They fled, and the women they attacked, despite a terrible scare, had escaped injury or defilement.

Perceval never left town to hunt after that. Instead, he sent Remi north again to Rennes with the money they had collected along with his leather saddlebags, helmet, and mail shirt to sell. Perceval's armor was fine quality, so it would fetch a good price, and if any trouble came to Bevrée, he was confident he could defend its people perfectly well without it. They resumed building houses, and Remi arrived with what they hoped would be sufficient food to last the rest of fall and through winter.

Perceval spent those months as a guest of a woman named Joveta in a home they'd rebuilt, along with her two young children. Joveta cooked well and clearly loved her children dearly. She was quite pretty but never hinted to Perceval that she desired to be unfaithful to her husband. Perceval could not say the same of every other woman in town, but he explained firmly and politely that he had no interest. He told them the truth—that his heart belonged to another.

That winter, Perceval chopped the wood they'd gathered during the fall for fires. He visited every home routinely to ensure that it was warm enough. Never did long stretches pass before Perceval returned to his Bible. And of course, his mind wandered to Cera every single day. Yet all that time, over all those months, Perceval never ruminated about whether he was doing the right thing or on the correct path. The questions never nagged. He didn't seek validation. The people in Bevrée needed his help, Perceval knew he could provide it, and it fulfilled him to do so.

The year turned, and in February 527, three and a half years after Perceval encountered Cera and the Holy Grail, snow blanketed Bevrée. Lying beside the fire in Joveta's home, his closed Bible on his chest rising and falling with each breath, Perceval did mull over a different question. *Could the Holy Grail feed the men, women, and children of Bevrée?* The grail gave everlasting life to those who drank from it. They wouldn't age, or so said the generally accepted stories. But the word *nourishment* also popped up in tales about the grail. It wasn't clear whether that meant nourishment of the soul or of the body. They were getting by in Bevrée but only just. Everyone had grown significantly thinner since the day Perceval arrived, and in truth, they were hungry all the time. He wondered if the Holy Grail could help them.

Not a week later, another messenger from Cera found Perceval. Her letter urged him to consider *it*—the grail of course—as more than a trophy given at the end of a journey.

Perceval asked the rider, a young man named Tescelin,

111

to take Cera the five letters he'd written over the months since his first in Paris. He would have quickly written a new one, as well, detailing the situation in Bevrée and asking Cera to bring *it* to the town, and she would have known *it* meant the grail.

But Tescelin said he couldn't deliver any response to her. Cera had made clear that she would have moved on, and he did not know where to. Perceval begged him to try, but he said it was simply impossible. Perceval understood, but it hurt to hear regardless.

Fortunately, Tescelin did agree to find King Childebert in the south, to inform him of their situation and—whether or not he was actually allowed to see the king—to find the husbands and sons of the townspeople. To Tescelin's credit, he never asked for any payment, even as the line of women with names of husbands and sons for him to find grew. Perceval thanked God for Tescelin, wishing the world were filled with people like him, and wondered what the young man's future held, for surely it would be a bright one.

Before Tescelin rode off, Perceval told him that if King Childebert would send no one to their aid or would not permit the town's men to leave his army, he should come back and inform Perceval. What Perceval didn't say was that if it came to that, he would convince Tescelin to stay in Bevrée while Perceval risked leaving to pay King Childebert an angry visit himself.

By mid-March, no response had come, and their store of food was dangerously low. Perceval feared it would not last until the first harvest in May, so he sent Remi with his sword and shield to Rennes to sell. The shield was sturdy—it had never failed in battle. The sword had been a gift from the old knight who'd wandered to Perceval's home in Wales and had taught young, ever-eager Perceval the ways of knighthood and chivalry. Perceval borrowed an old but serviceable sword from one of the grandfathers in town in case danger came their way. Remi returned with plenty of food to last until the harvest.

And in late April, while Perceval carried two full pails of water from the stream, Joveta's daughter yelled, "They're back! Dad—he's back!"

From the hilltop, a dozen riders galloped toward town. Bevrée's women and children ran to them, but some stopped. They pointed and searched, then some ran on while the rest lowered their heads or dropped their whole bodies to the grass. Only half of the two dozen who'd gone to war had returned.

After the reunions, children and wives rode into town on horses with their fathers or husbands. Some walked holding hands. The unlucky bawled alone.

The men explained that Tescelin had found King Childebert and delivered his message to an advisor in the king's service straight away. But fearing the sudden loss of so many men, the king kept Tescelin prisoner and his message secret. Only when the king's encampment was overrun could Tescelin escape to share the information with the men, who raced home immediately.

They all thanked Perceval profusely and offered him money, which he refused. Remi told them Perceval had sold his armor and sword, so the soldiers offered Perceval theirs. He refused them all, though he did relent and agree to keep the old sword he'd borrowed. And when they pressed him on it, he accepted replacement saddlebags and a shield, and he did feel more like a complete knight strapping those to his mount's side.

And that feeling, especially, made Perceval eager to move on, with the townspeople able to restart their lives, either with those who'd returned from the war or without them, finally knowing their loved ones would not return. Perceval expected he would miss the people of Bevrée. They'd pulled together to rebuild homes. They stuck to the rationing plan without argument. Whenever doubt crept into their group, they met it with resolve. They were good people in a world that too often made it too hard for people to be good.

Perceval said brief goodbyes to each of them and promised to visit when his quest brought him nearby. He urged them to remember how strong they'd been since the fire gutted their town and their earthly lord abandoned them, though the Lord in heaven never did. By His grace and their strength, they'd survived the ordeal, and since they could manage that, they could manage anything.

Perceval packed his things, mounted his horse, and rode north.

Off the path among some trees in his tent the next morning, Perceval awoke thinking of Cera. The bearer of the Holy Grail had sent him a letter whose carrier had, in turn, found the husbands and sons of the women of Bevrée. God had presented quite a test in Bevrée, but then, God had also set in motion their salvation, for surely Cera, who acted in His divine service with the grail, was true to God's will in all things.

Perceval smiled widely. She would be proud of what they accomplished in Bevrée, he had no doubt. He wondered if the temptation of any of the women there would have overcome him had Cera not been so fixed in his mind and deep in his heart. He recalled her gaze into his eyes in the cave more than three years before, clear as if it were yesterday. It had pierced his soul, and her letters since then had poured through all of him.

A rider dismounted outside. Ashamed that he hadn't noticed their approach, Perceval unsheathed his knife and crept to the tent curtain.

"Sir Perceval."

Perceval recognized the voice from a cave mouth during a violent thunderstorm in the woods. He stepped out before the gray-bearded knight in gleaming mail armor and a white tunic with a red cross, who had shown him to the grail in the Ardennes Forest.

"Pack your things," Sir Berthold said in Perceval's language, as last time—a refreshing change from all the Frankish. "We've a long journey to complete before nightfall in order to safely cross the sand."

———————————

His tent packed, his small fire completely out, Perceval mounted his horse. "Where are we headed?"

"An abbey off the coast." Sir Berthold led them away.

"What's there?" Perceval couldn't help asking.

Berthold didn't answer or even turn to acknowledge the question.

Perceval risked another. "Why the production in the forest with the dogs the first time?"

"Awe and mystery," Berthold said. "We are a secret order, after all."

They rode north, and Perceval didn't ask any other questions. He'd hardly explored the northern coast of Francia, and Berthold's comment about crossing the sand was intriguing, but Perceval's mind mostly churned over three things: the grail, Cera, and what he needed to do to ensure the outcome his very being craved.

They rounded a bend and picked up their pace with grassy plains ahead. Air blowing through his hair, Perceval replayed the scene of the holy relics' procession over and over in his mind. *No more time to spare*, he kept telling himself. *What did I miss? Why did I fail?*

———————————

They rode all day, resting only when their horses needed to. Gentle hills turned to flatlands nearer the coast. Perceval ate a few bits of dried meat along the way, which after the hungry winter satisfied him. He noted the poor quality of the sword and shield he'd taken from Bevrée. He wore no armor. But Cera wouldn't care about those things, he decided, and he dwelled on them no longer.

Salty wind hit them with increasing force the last hour of

their ride as the sun sank to the west. They traced the route of the Couesnon River, which Berthold broke his silence to name, and then before them, a hill rose magnificently from the horizon.

As Berthold had mentioned, no cathedral topped it, only a long, plain gray abbey. Closer, the hill became clearly an island off the coast, with rings of leafy trees in between rings of low buildings. A low stone wall encircled the island's base, protecting the structures nearby.

At the river's mouth, Sir Berthold stopped. "Mont Tombe. We're in time." Surrounding the hill, flats of sand peeked out of the water. Berthold guided his horse down to the nearest, and Perceval followed. Hooves sloshing through the waterlogged sand, they rode at a steady pace.

Smoke rose from chimneys of buildings around the island's base. As they neared them, Perceval noticed people walking on paths a little up the hill. None paid the pair any mind. Perceval didn't see anyone at the stone-walled abbey at the top.

The main path coiled up the hill between the buildings and trees. The ends of the wall around the island's base didn't meet flush but rather left space for the path to begin in the sand, which was where they entered the trail. With Sir Berthold leading and the sun on the horizon, they ascended, the scent of burning fires from the houses filling Perceval's nose. Then people did glance their way as the two men passed homes, shops that surely doubled as homes, and even a small tavern—all stone with timber roofs, better suited to the climate than mud walls. Their conversations, which were in Celtic instead of Frankish, confirmed what Perceval's eyes told him—people from his island across the water had settled this little one.

Around and up they climbed the coiled path. Buildings became sparser and trees more plentiful, and the breeze stiffened. The grass plains on the mainland to the south felt a world away. Above the tops of the tallest trees, they reached the summit of Mont Tombe. All around, a long *whooshing* sound rose.

"Just in time," Sir Berthold said.

Wind buffeted Perceval's face. To the north, he noticed less and less sand peeking through the water as a low wave rolled in. *The tide.* The water level rose, hiding sand beneath it. To the east and west of the island, Perceval could no longer make out any sand. To the south, the flats they'd traversed disappeared, making the hill a true island separated from the mainland.

Berthold dismounted, so Perceval did as well and tied Ociel outside the abbey. Instead of opening the door before them, Berthold led the way around to the building's long side. In the middle, narrow stone steps led down to a small wooden door with a thin cross carved in the wall beside it.

Down the steps, Berthold knocked twice, a lock turned, and the door opened inward. Perceval ducked his head to follow Berthold quickly past a knight wearing the same red-cross tunic and into a dark stone-lined tunnel through the earth. With flickering light ahead, the door shut and locked behind them.

They rounded the corner, where a lamp burned and

another knight beside another door pulled a chain necklace with a key on it over his head. He unlocked and pulled open the door. Berthold descended the tight spiral staircase, and Perceval followed. Down they went into darkness, around and deeper. Then dim light seeped into the staircase.

Berthold and Perceval emerged into a square room where two small lamps burned, and a knight faced them, hands clasped, guarding an entranceway in the stone. On the four walls, painting begged for additional light. White, reds, blues, greens, gold… the entire rainbow of colors depicted the Nativity of Jesus Christ on the right. Jesus's acts and miracles during his life wrapped around the room, ending with his crucifixion to the left. On the ceiling, the archangel Michael stood triumphant atop serpentine Satan. Michael's sword was poised to strike down God's adversary.

Sir Berthold motioned past the knight. Leaving behind the spectacular scenes, Perceval entered a wide room with bare walls, dim as the previous one. Lamps burned in the far corners but left dark passageways on both sides. A single wooden chair sat vacant before Perceval, like last time but plainer. The scene was set.

Perceval steeled himself. He could not fail again. He knelt, bowed his head, crossed himself, and prayed, *Please, God, when the spear passes before me, and I see the crown that our savior was forced to wear on that fateful day… when Cera… when the Holy Grail is brought past, show me the way so I may stay in its presence, doing your will, living for you forever more.*

"Sir Perceval of Wales!" Berthold announced.

Perceval stood just in front of him. The same knight as last time entered from the passageway to the right, moved aside, and clasped his hands before him. And then came a second knight. *Sir Galahad!* At the other side of the passageway, he stood the same way. His auburn hair luminous even in the low light, Galahad's eyes shifted to Perceval, and he smiled.

Perceval returned the smile. He could not have stopped himself if he tried. *Of course* Galahad would have succeeded and found a place with the grail.

Perceval's smile disappeared when the middle-aged man, hunched, wrapped in a red cloak, wearing his crown, limped out alone past the knights. Anguish faced, he took a slow, small step toward the chair between the passageways, aided by a walnut-brown cane with an ivory handle and not the arm of the woman who'd accompanied him before.

The room's air seemed empty—frozen—like it had years ago. The king took another small step and grimaced. Perceval glanced at Galahad and the knight beside him then turned to Berthold. *Will none of them help the poor man? Will they stand by watching, like everyone watched the beggar in Paris when the cart sped directly at him?*

Perceval went to the king and offered his arm. "Please."

The king held Perceval's arm, and together, they walked to his chair. He leaned more of his weight on Perceval and seemed at greater ease.

"What ails you, Your Grace?" Perceval asked.

The king let go and stood tall. "I am well, Sir Perceval, now that you have asked."

Perceval's heart leapt. He understood. Enthralled by the holy relics last time, Perceval had not asked about the suffering of the man before him or whether he could be of assistance in easing it.

Perceval dropped to a knee. Galahad smiled at him.

"Rise, Perceval," the king said, so he did. "I am Josephus, King of the Order of Nolvan."

From the passageway, Cera stepped out in a white gown, as before, the Holy Grail held low in her hands, beaming at Perceval. Perceval choked up. Her fair skin and blue eyes, the dark streaks through her short blond hair—she *was* an angel.

Cera approached and raised the grail. Perceval's soul ached for him to take it in one hand, to hold her tightly with his other, and to bury his face in her neck and hair and cry because *her* letters, *her* words of encouragement and insight had brought him again before the Holy Grail and seen that he achieved it.

Josephus motioned to her. "Princess Cerise."

She must have been his daughter, though she seemed no less an angel when she bowed her head and held out the grail. Perceval reached for it, looking cautiously at Josephus, who nodded. Perceval touched the silver outside of the goblet. He wrapped his fingers around it where Cera's weren't. She let go, and Perceval held the Holy Grail.

"Thank you," he said to her.

She raised her gaze to meet his. "Thank you, Perceval."

Crystal-clear water half filled the gold-lined goblet. It felt lighter than expected, and Perceval wondered whether that was because of a divine property of the grail or merely the adrenaline coursing through him.

"Drink," Josephus said. "You have earned it."

Perceval rushed the grail to his mouth but stopped and took a breath. Cera smiled. Slowly, Perceval brought the cup's smooth edge to his lips. He tilted it and tasted the crisp water.

He swallowed, and a coolness ran down his throat with the liquid. He felt it moving from his core out to his arms and legs as a lessened sensation, bristling his fingertips and toes. Soreness from the day's hard ride disappeared. Hunger faded then vanished for the first time since August, when he'd arrived in Bevrée. The coolness subsided and left Perceval fresh and balanced, ready and eager for any challenge.

Cera reached for the grail, and Perceval handed it to her.

"You have a choice, Perceval," Josephus said. "We need knights like you in our order to guard the grail, the Crown of Thorns, and the Spear of Destiny. But to be part of this order is a commitment to secrecy and to a life of constant movement, for those are our chief strategies in protecting God's most sacred relics. If you stay, the grail will keep you young as you are now—you will not age. But you must commit to staying with the order for the privilege of drinking from the Holy Grail."

"I'll stay. Please." Perceval turned to Cera, and her smile widened. To Josephus, Perceval added, "It would be my life's honor."

"Good," Josephus said. "Swear to guard the Holy Grail and all of our relics. Swear to keep them secret and to protect them at any cost, even if that cost is your life. Swear now, before the Holy Grail, to do this for God and for the order."

"I swear."

Josephus nodded. "Thank you."

"Come, Perceval." Cera motioned to the passageway where she'd entered. "I want to ask you about your time in Bevrée."

She handed the grail to Josephus, and Perceval followed her between Galahad and the other knight then down the candlelit passageway. Off to the left in a small room, the brunette girls Perceval had seen last time were putting the crown and the tip of the spear into small chests and chatting with another knight.

"Will he join us?" one of them asked and glanced at Perceval as they passed.

Perceval wanted to cry out, "Yes!" but, hurrying to keep up with Cera, he only yelled it in his mind.

Cera! Perceval felt like he was in a dream. He'd drunk from the Holy Grail. *Thank you, Lord! My life, my true purpose is begun.*

At the end of the tunnel, Cera disappeared into a room on the right. She stuck her head out and motioned Perceval in. "Come on."

He entered the small square room, and quickly, she shut the thick wooden door behind him. A pair of wide white candles on the tiny desk provided the light. A drawn dagger lay beside them, a plain chair with a blue cloak draped over its back was askew before the desk, and a narrow bed abutted the wall.

Cera—her expression focused—turned to Perceval, raised a finger, and opened her mouth... but said nothing. She stepped past him and took another step but ran out of space, so she spun around and paced back his way. She was thin and only a few inches shorter than Perceval. She was so pretty.

"You wanted to hear about Bevrée?" he asked.

Cera shook her head. "Not actually."

"Oh."

"I mean, I heard what you did there." Her beautiful smile returned. "You saved those people."

"It was your letter that saved them in the end," Perceval said. "And your messenger. He got word to the husbands and sons of the townspeople, and they headed home."

She cocked her head. "I guess we make a good team, then."

Perceval could hardly believe where he was and who he was talking to. He'd longed for that moment. He treasured every second in case a sudden knock came at the door or Cera asked him to leave, and who knew when he would get his next chance.

Perceval had questions about the grail and the other relics. And the order. *When did it begin? Where did the name Nolvan come from?* He wondered how long Galahad had been with them. Cera spoke with a Frankish accent, giving him one answer.

"The other woman..." Perceval recalled her glaring at Cera. "The one with Josephus years ago, when I first came before him. Is she no longer part of the ceremony?"

"She died." Cera crossed her arms. "The wizard Merlin led an attack on our order, aimed at stealing the grail from the church basement where we guarded it. His men fought their way to the room holding the grail, and he closed in after them to take his prize, but—I'm told by those who were there—she charged him from behind with her sword held high." Cera looked away. "Merlin noticed, and before she could strike, with awful flame spewing from the palm of his hand, he burned her... horribly. Then more of our knights arrived and drove Merlin away. He fled without the grail." She turned to Perceval. "But my mother was dead."

"The grail could not help her?"

"I tried," Cera said. "I poured water from it on her lifeless, blistered body. We knew it wouldn't work. Josephus knew, we all knew, but we tried anyway." Cera choked up but fought off tears and firmed herself. "We loved her so much."

"I'm so sorry," Perceval said.

Cera shook her head.

"Josephus is your father?"

"No," she said. "My father was a Roman general who had been in our order a few hundred years. He died decades ago, also defending the grail."

Perceval nodded. "Certainly a prize worth dying to protect."

"It's not a prize, Perceval." Cera glared at him. "Nor am I. You, I thought, would understand that."

"I—"

"What is the grail?" She opened her arms. "The Holy Grail? What is it? You tell me."

"It's…" Perceval shrugged. "Proof that God—"

"You need proof?"

"No, I…" It wasn't validation either. Perceval had learned that.

Cera huffed and turned away.

Perceval couldn't say the wrong thing but feared that saying nothing would mean the end of their conversation. "The grail is validation that years devoted to—"

"No…" Cera let herself drop into the chair at her desk. "No, no, no!"

Perceval's chest tightened. He'd never imagined their meeting going anything like that.

Cera stood and resumed pacing then stopped, spun on her heel in its sandal, and pointed at Perceval. "Yes, the grail is those things."

Perceval breathed air into his petrified lungs.

"But," she went on, "it should be much more. In Bevrée, hunger was your chief concern, correct?"

"Correct."

"It showed when you came to us tonight but not as much since you drank from the grail."

"Since then, the hunger that has lingered for months has been quieted."

"In a few days, you'll be as strong as ever," Cera said. "Then stronger, so refreshed you'll be by the grail's water."

"What an incredible gift from God. We were all hungry in Bevrée. If we'd had the grail there, we could have—"

"Yes!" Cera rushed to him. "You do understand."

"I—"

She put her finger to his lips. "I will say more. The grail would have nourished the people of Bevrée. It can heal the sick and feed the hungry in Tours and in Nantes." She lowered her hand. "But Josephus does not allow it."

"Why not?" Perceval asked, sad that Cera's finger had left.

"He doesn't trust them. Men. He thinks they'd fight over it—that evil men would take the grail."

"They'd start wars over it," Perceval said.

The angel stepped back. "He says exactly that."

"I think—"

"You think." Cera pointed at Perceval. "But you do not know."

"I've watched men wage brutal battles and years-long wars over far less. Lines on a map, trading routes, a slight of protocol at a party. And this is the Holy Grail. Proof of God. We don't require proof, but others? This is *everlasting life*."

"Have you seen the people in Tours and Nantes?" Cera asked. "I know your travels took you there. How can you not want to help them?"

"I do. I just... I worry about what would happen after the grail did its work."

"You worry while they die," she spat. "What if you hadn't shown up in Bevrée when you did? Those people would have suffered much more. Many would have died."

"I was there in large part *because* the grail existed, hidden out in the world, only found at the end of a quest that meant years of doing good works in God's name."

"You saved thirty-four people," Cera said. "Thank God

you did. But right now, another thirty-four are suffering in the next town over, and you are not there to save them. If you were, you could not heal the very ill, and you could not feed the hungry—you have no more fancy armor or swords to sell." She came close again. "Hundreds suffer in Reims, thousands in Paris." Her hand went to his cheek. "With no Perceval there to help them. He could not, in truth, even though he is a great knight. But together, we *can* help them."

"How?"

Her other hand found Perceval's at his side. "We can take the Holy Grail away from this order and bring it to those people."

"Steal the Holy Grail?" Perceval whispered.

Cera nodded.

"No… I swore—"

"Yes, Perceval. It's the only way, and I don't think I can do it alone. You lived in Bevrée. You've been to those cities. *You* understand."

"I've seen the people, and I have seen their pain. I do understand, but I could never."

Cera let go of Perceval's hand. "Then you do not truly understand." She slid past him and sat down on her narrow bed. "And these years, waiting for you—twice—were more years wasted while people suffered everywhere." She leaned back against the stone wall. "It seems I will have to try to do it alone after all."

Perceval sat next to her against the wall and took her hand. "You're not alone."

Cera huffed then scooted over and laid her head on

Perceval's shoulder. She stared at the candles burning on her desk, so he did the same, taking in the sweet scent of her hair and feeling her body against his as he had longed for all those days and nights out there without her. Cera brought her other hand over and held his wrist.

In the light of the candles' flickering flames, Perceval saw the dagger on her desk—its gleaming blade and the simple cross etched in it. He pictured a strikingly different person from the Cera he'd imagined, wondering if such a thing could, or should, come to be—Cera, dressed in her white, was not a princess in a sacred ceremony. She was a fierce angel from heaven on the poor streets of Paris, rallying the people to come drink from God's Holy Grail.

8

The candlelight long burned out, Cera lay beside Perceval on her bed, still in her gown, him in his tunic and trousers, her head on his calmly rising and falling chest, their hands still held together. The increasingly frequent sounds beyond Cera's door meant dawn had arrived. The night had not gone the way Cera had expected it to. Perceval succeeded at the test and joined her order, but he failed her. He'd claimed to understand as she did, but he did not.

Cera opened her eyes and lifted her head. He wasn't the same as the rest, though. She could feel it more than ever.

Perceval's eyes cracked then quickly widened. "It's all right that I stayed here?"

The respectful knight, to be sure, Cera thought. She sighed, let go of his hands, and sat up. "It's fine. I'm sixty years old. Who I keep as my company is my business."

Perceval sat up. "Sixty?"

Cera shrugged. "The grail."

He nodded, and she wondered if he could actually be the man she had for so long prayed he would be. The man she needed him to be.

"They're readying things for our trip to Tours," Cera said. "We have a couple hours. I'd like to walk around the island before we go. Would you join me?"

"Of course."

"But first, the grail. We don't have to drink from it every day to remain nourished and keep from aging—every other day is sufficient. But we're leaving, and others will have the grail with them." Cera went to the door, pulled it open, and pointed down the passageway to the right. "Go freshen up. I'm going to do the same, and I'll meet you back that way"— she pointed left—"at the grail."

On Perceval's way past, he paused for a moment but then departed without saying anything. That disappointed Cera, but as her door closed, she felt relieved to have her space back to herself, as usual. Then as she went through her morning routine, the feeling faded. Her routine had been routine for ages, and Perceval had finally come, even more handsome in person than she'd remembered. She missed him.

She swallowed hard. If he couldn't really understand, she'd have no choice but to steel herself against attachment to him. What she needed to do on behalf of so many was infinitely more important than her personal loneliness.

Cera headed down the passageway to the chamber where four knights stood guarding three chests that sat on a ledge in the wall. One was open with the Holy Grail and a silver pitcher of water beside it on a white cloth, illuminated by the room's multitude of candles.

"Good morning, Princess," Sir Deverel said.

She leaned against the side of the entranceway. "Good morning."

Sirs Willard, Alan, and Porico added their greetings. "Morning, good morning, morning."

Cera nodded. "Morning."

Big Germanic Sir Hunald, the second knight ever to drink from the Holy Grail, walked past her into the room, and without a word, made the sign of the cross, drank, and departed. Mabyn entered next. They all said good morning to her, and another round of the usual pleasantries followed when Father Carlos came and went.

Cera smiled at the sight of Perceval returning, and his bright smile in response warmed her. She motioned into the room, and he entered.

"Welcome, Perceval." Deverel put out his hand. "I am Sir Deverel."

"Thank you." Perceval shook it. "It is my honor."

"We are all honored"—Sir Willard extended his hand, which Perceval shook—"to be among each other, who have found our way to these most holy relics."

"Truly." Perceval glowed as he greeted Sirs Alan and Porico.

Cera watched a man overjoyed at having found his people. And her stomach sank. They *were* good people—Sir Willard, Sir Deverel, all the knights, the priests, the other girls, and even Josephus. They were. But they were also wrong, and as Perceval drank from the grail, Cera thought again of how she needed him to see it her way.

He positively beamed when he finished and Cera went to take her drink.

"Sir Galahad," Perceval said behind her.

"Sir Perceval," Galahad responded.

Arthur's knights embraced, Galahad with a single arm around Perceval because he held a sheathed sword in that hand and fresh clothes of the order and a gleaming mail shirt in the other.

"For you." Galahad held it all out. "Welcome to the Order of Nolvan. I heard you could use a new sword, and I had no doubt you would succeed before Josephus, so I made certain to have a fine one here for you."

"Thank you, my friend." Perceval took it all. "I will always treasure having received these gifts from you."

"It is my honor to present them," Galahad said. "And we have good shields if you'd like to replace the one you brought."

"Thank you. But the one given to me in Bevrée is solid, and I cherish the reminder of those good people."

Galahad nodded.

"I look forward to catching up with you," Perceval said.

"As do I," Galahad said. "In Laval, halfway to Tours, surely we'll have time."

"We will not ride together?" Perceval asked.

"No." Cera stepped to them. "We split the relics up and take different routes to keep a lower profile on the road. You and I are with a few others and the spear. Sir Galahad is with Josephus and the group with the grail. We rendezvous in two days."

"In Laval, then," Perceval said.

"For certain." Galahad grasped his shoulder then went to take his drink from the grail.

Cera tugged on Perceval's new white tunic. "Get changed, then we'll go walk while preparations for our departure are completed."

———————————

From the abbey, Cera and Perceval headed down Mont Tombe's spiraling dirt path, the sun rising, the salty breeze gently brushing their cheeks. Cera wore the royal-blue cloak from Nimue over her white gown. Over the treetops, she could see to the water surrounding them. Sand flats had begun peeking out, which they would soon be able to traverse to the mainland. It had been years since the order's last trip to the island. When the tide rushed in, Cera had always hated how it separated them from the mainland and the people out there, even though one could easily cross the bay by boat.

"How long has your order been on Mont Tombe?" Perceval wore his new tunic, with its red cross at the center, over his armor, and he had his new sword sheathed at his hip.

"A week," Cera said as they strolled. "And it's *our* order." She immediately regretted making the quip, as she didn't actually want him settling into the idea.

"Yes," he said. "I'll get used to that."

Please don't, she thought.

"Do we ever go to Britain?" he asked.

"Normally. The order began in Britain. But we haven't been since the Romans left a hundred years ago. The warring between the Britons and the Angles and Saxons and now between Hengist and all others on the island is not a good environment for secretly moving holy relics around."

"Right," Perceval said. "And we're going to Tours next?"

"Yup. It's where I was born."

"Sixty years ago." Perceval smiled.

Cera raised an eyebrow. "Is that all right?"

"It's you. And it's wonderful. You are... I mean, I waited so long, and after all the letters, I wanted to have a conversation with you. To get to know you. So..." He shrugged. "It's a number of years, which is you, so that's wonderful. I'm making a mess of this, aren't I?"

Cera smiled, her cheeks blushing. "Not at all."

Woods lined the sides of the dirt path that crunched under their feet. Cera stole glances at Perceval, from head to toe. *Could he be even more than the man I've waited so long for?*

Eventually, he broke the silence. "How long will we be in Tours?"

"Not long," Cera said. "We don't get back there as often as we used to, and it's one of the places I really like to spend time, but it'll be a short stop to conduct the test for another knight. After that, we head southeast across Burgundy, and the Kingdom of the Ostrogoths, to Rome and Sicily."

"I've only been to Rome once. It's quite a journey."

"It's what we do."

"Why do you—we—move all the time?"

"Josephus," Cera said. "He wants the legend of the grail to spread throughout Europe and says stashing the grail away somewhere wouldn't accomplish that. I suppose he's correct."

"Makes sense. But harder to defend on the road, I'd imagine."

"It's more work to be always moving it, that's for sure. But I certainly wouldn't want to be stuck in one place with it."

"Understandable."

"And we've never failed—" Cera stopped herself.

"What?"

It was another wrong thing to say, but she had no choice at that point. "We've never failed defending it."

Perceval nodded, likely considering the implications of that fact as they pertained to her desire to take the grail from the order.

"It's mostly Britons here on Mont Tombe," Cera said, changing the subject. "Do you know anyone from Wales who settled here?"

"No. By the time I was old enough to have paid attention to such things, my mother had moved us out to be alone in the woods. I hardly encountered my countrymen. Then my focus was fixed on becoming a knight."

Cera stopped. "I read about your family. We compile reports on prospective knights. I was so sad to read what happened to them."

"I fear for my mother's soul most of all."

Cera touched Perceval's arm, but sharing his worry about where God would send a suicided soul could offer no greater comfort. She dropped her hand, and they continued down the hill. Homes became more common until, lower around the coiled path, homes and shops abutted each next one.

People emerged into the quiet morning air to grab fresh wood to rekindle fires that had died overnight. Others carried empty pails to refill with water. The Order of Nolvan's investigation had revealed that the islanders, like most people in the towns and cities they spent time in, regarded them as a group of devout Christian nobles. Those on Mont Tombe assumed they'd come to worship at the chapel in their famously located abbey. Some imagined they guarded treasure or even a holy relic, but none knew those things for certain. She planned to explain it to Perceval later.

A baby's wails grew loud, and a young boy ran out of a home and down the hill. A woman approached them in tattered clothes, holding a young girl's hand. "Spare any coin?"

"I'm sorry." Cera reached to stop Perceval's hand going to his purse.

"Any food?" the woman asked.

"No, I'm sorry." Cera pulled Perceval past her. "We can't," she said to him. "We don't have the food. If you gave her money, that would be our reputation, and you'd run out before long anyway."

"Then let me run out." Perceval produced two silver coins, went back, and handed them to the woman. He returned. "I can't just ignore her."

"Thank you for your kind heart." Cera took his hand and interlocked their fingers. "But as part of our order, you'll have to ignore people like her."

"I'll talk to——" He leaned close to Cera and whispered, "I'll talk to Josephus." He pulled away. "I'll explain it like you did. He has to let us do something."

"I have, Perceval. For years—for decades—I've taken my arguments to him and to my mother, and they were never moved to change. Since her death, I've tried again, but Josephus will not budge."

"I—"

"I've tried every approach, every possible line of reasoning. I've argued it passionately. I've presented things frankly and, in my opinion, extremely rationally. I've tried everything." Cera pulled them onward.

Smoke rose from chimneys, people strolled by, and Perceval gave coins to a man who approached and asked and to a woman sitting off the street, looking like she needed them. Halfway to the bottom of the hill, at a home on the left, the front door flew open, and a tall dark-skinned woman rushed out in a simple gray dress, speaking to the ground.

"He cannot die!" The African beauty held an empty water pail in one hand and her head with her other. "He cannot die." She neared, but her focus remained at her feet. "He cannot die," she chanted, heading down the hill. "He cannot die…"

Cera pulled Perceval toward the house then let go of his hand. A broad-chested, short-bearded Briton in a red tunic, who appeared older than the woman, peeked out then shut the door.

"Wait!" Cera called.

Slowly, the door opened.

"Who cannot die?"

The man gestured past Cera. "Her son. He is very sick."

Cera glanced at Perceval then back at the man. "May we see him?"

"Who are you?" the man asked. He had the look of a tired knight.

"We're passing through," Cera said. "We worshiped in the chapel in the abbey and are soon to depart. We would say a prayer for her son before we do."

"But who *are* you?" the man repeated.

Cera found herself tired then, of constantly using false names. "I am Cera, and this is Sir Perceval... of the Round Table."

The man raised an eyebrow. "A visit from Arthur might better comfort her son, but now, alas, that will never happen."

He pulled the door open wider, revealing a young man with caramel skin—lighter than his mother's—a gaunt face, and shoots of black hair sprouting from a head that had been recently shaved. He lay on a bed in the corner with his eyes shut. A simple cross hung on the wall above him. They stepped inside.

"He's dying," the man said. "Slowly."

"What ails him?" Perceval asked.

"Poison is our best guess. A week ago, on our way here, a robber shot an arrow into Arden's thigh before we killed the bastard—unfortunately, because we couldn't go back and ask if and how he'd poisoned the arrowhead. Since then, Arden's been getting worse, and now, in this bed, he lingers. The last two days, he hasn't said a word."

"He's your son?" Perceval asked.

"No," the man said. "I am Sir Gethen, in the service of his mother. She's a good woman who's had a hard life. Arden's father was a Welshman. He's been gone for a long time. I've helped care for the boy for every one of his seventeen years." Gethen walked to him, and Cera and Perceval followed. "He's grown into a strong young man in faith, mind, and body. He's a warrior, not this frail... what you see he is becoming."

Cera turned to Perceval. "I can't stand this."

"Nor I," he said.

Gethen shook his head. "He's her only son. He's all his mother has."

Out the open door, two mounted knights of the order led the pair of horses driving the first of their carriages, with Galahad and three more knights riding behind. The grail that could save Arden—and his mother's sanity—was so close.

So close but forever out of reach, the grail in the care of Josephus.

The commotion of the group of travelers fading, Cera turned to Arden. "No one should have to die like this. No one else."

"No," Sir Gethen said. "No mother should have to see this happen to her son."

"You say he's a warrior?" Cera asked.

"He has the heart and courage of a young dragon. I swear it."

"Then urge him to fight," Cera said. "And pray for him.

Tell his mother to do the same, to beg him to hold on and the Lord to keep him alive, until we bring something that will heal him."

"You know what poison afflicts him?" Gethen asked.

"No."

He squinted. "Then what antidote will you bring?"

"You'll see. It will be days, at least, before we can. Will you keep him alive until we return?"

"He's been a fighter his whole life. We will try."

"Do more than *try*." Cera looked at Arden. "Keep fighting, Arden. Don't give up. Whatever poison runs through you, be a dragon, powerful and desperate, fighting for your life—clinging to it if it comes to that."

Cera headed for the front door with Perceval following. She stopped and pointed at Sir Gethen. "Keep him alive."

He nodded, Perceval pulled the door open, and they left. Cera marched up the hill. "We can't take it on the road," she said. "You saw the numbers guarding it. Maybe in Laval, when we meet the others for the night."

Perceval stopped. "Cera, I don't know."

"I do." She stomped down to him. "I can't watch another one die. Arden's salvation drove past his front door in a carriage. All Josephus had to do—" Cera clenched her fists. "But he would not. So *I* will see it done. I need your help— I really think I do—but if I must, I'll try to do it without you." Cera headed up the hill to the abbey, and Perceval followed.

God, Cera prayed, *I'm sorry for waiting decades to act, but those days are near ended. Keep this young man alive until I return with your glorious grail to see him revived. Keep him alive! I beg you.*

A couple of hours later, Cera sat across from Perceval in their carriage, on the cushioned bench, facing the direction they traveled. He'd wanted to ride his horse, but Sirs Berthold and Alan both told Cera to ride in the carriage, and since she needed to talk to Perceval anyway, she figured not arguing with them was easiest. Once Cera decided on the carriage, as she'd hoped, Perceval agreed to join her. Sir Alan rode ahead, Berthold drove the carriage, and Sir Deverel led Cera and Perceval's horses at the rear.

Cera switched from her bench to sit beside Perceval. "We *could* try to take the grail, on the road, before Josephus gets to Laval."

Perceval pointed behind them.

"Berthold won't hear," Cera said. "I've been out front there, and I've been in here. I've been doing this a long time. If we keep to our normal voices, no one will hear."

"Okay. You talk of stealing the grail, but I swore an oath to protect it for the order."

Cera waved her hand. "Forget that oath. After all you'd been through, culminating in that moment, you would have sworn anything to Josephus."

He shook his head. "Even so, how could we take the grail while it is so well guarded?"

Cera pointed at where she'd been sitting. "The Spear of Destiny—the iron head where its power lies—rests in a chest

142

beneath that bench. With it, we would prevail against them."

"What power does the spear have?"

"Jesus knew he would die before he died and, in the time leading to that fateful day, acted accordingly with that knowledge. To hold the spear, or have it on your person, gives similar foresight."

"You know your future?"

"Essentially, but it's limited," Cera explained. "If harm is headed your way, you know of it with enough time to react. The holder of the spear sees their destiny, as Christ did. While He did not resist his fate, one with the Spear of Destiny may choose otherwise."

Perceval brought a finger to his chin. "Meaning, in combat, if I had it, I'd 'see' my foes' attacks ahead of time?"

"Yes. And knowing them, you could be ready with every parry and first to the next attack, to very effective results."

"But the knights guarding the grail are not my foes."

"Wrong," Cera said. "They oppose our effort to save Arden."

"They would die to protect the grail," Perceval said.

"Yes."

"You would kill them to take it?"

Cera folded her hands in her lap. "In our order, we kill when the cause justifies it. I've known no greater cause in my life."

"I won't kill them," Perceval said. "I can't."

Cera leaned back, pleased at her progress. Perceval hadn't recoiled the instant she mentioned taking the grail. Out the window to the right, plains were turning to forest. "Perhaps the road to Laval isn't the best opportunity, anyway."

"Why Arden?" Perceval asked. "In all your years with the order, why is this half-African the one you have to save?"

"He'll be the first, not the only one. And I care not where his mother or father comes from."

"Nor I," Perceval said. "I merely—"

"Whether my eyes are opened or closed"—Cera met Perceval's gaze—"I see Arden lying in bed, barely breathing, a shell of the young man Sir Gethen described. I can hear Arden's mother chanting that she can't lose her only son." Cera held Perceval's hand in both of hers. "He needs us, Perceval. He needs us now. And we, together, *can* help him. We can take the grail and save him. Isn't that enough reason to finally act?"

Schvth. An arrowhead pierced the carriage door. *Pfwt!* Fire burst from it as Cera raised her cloak to shield herself, and Perceval pulled her close.

Schvth. A second arrow lodged in the wall. *Pfwt!* Its fire set the side of the carriage ablaze.

"Merlin!" Cera cried as they picked up speed.

Cera rose out of Perceval's arms and kicked the carriage door open. From the forest, mounted men charged, dressed in green and brown, their faces painted the same for camouflage. An arrow flew through the carriage window to the far wall, and flames surrounded them.

"The spear!" Perceval called.

Two riders neared. Four raced ahead to Sir Alan, and a pair followed behind toward Sir Deverel.

"The spearhead is iron." Cera glanced at Perceval. "In an

iron chest. This fire won't hurt it."

She drew a dagger from under her gown. *Where is the old wizard?* His fire, from his staff, might burn the spear, though surely, he'd come to take it, not destroy it. One of the riders neared.

Perceval rose, elbowed open the carriage's other side door, and whistled loudly out of it. "Cera, I'll get you out of here."

She shook her head. "I haven't lived as you, Perceval, with the excitement of a next tournament melee, criminal to confront, or good deed to do ever imminent. I will not run or be 'gotten out of here.' I will make these thieves regret threatening you and God's holy relic, and I will cherish every second of it."

Perceval's jaw dropped as his horse galloped by the door at his side. Cera, leaning halfway out hers, focused on the nearest attacker, turning her dagger over in her hand. Then, stopping it, she held it downward. The long-haired rider held a sword high, out wide from his chain-mail-covered midsection. Cera squatted low.

"We came for your treasure!" he called in Frankish as he approached. "And I see *you* are exactly that."

Feet pushing hard off the edge of the carriage floor, Cera leapt at him, her shoulder hitting his chest before he could bring in his arm to block her. Off his horse, his sword flying from his hand, they fell to the ground. His back hit first with a thud. Cera held him as they rolled over and over, tangled in her cloak, until they slowed and she steadied them with her on top. She stabbed her dagger into his neck above his armor. His grip on her weakened, and his hands dropped to the grass.

"Predictable bastard." Cera withdrew her knife. "You couldn't have picked much worse to say to me."

She rose and set her cloak behind her. Perceval rode toward her as another of their attackers did as well. Sir Berthold had left the carriage burning to fight on foot alongside mounted Sir Alan, and they'd already dispatched two of their four foes.

"Help Sir Deverel!" Cera called to Perceval. The young knight had his hands full with two mounted swordsmen. Cera glanced at her oncoming attacker a few seconds away, his sword readied to swing down at her. She drew her second knife from her other leg and yelled again to Perceval, "Go!"

Perceval stopped, his new sword held low. Cera considered launching her knife at *him* for being stubborn but instead turned and threw it hard at her attacker, whose chest it lodged into, just left of center. His horse slowed as he drooped and dropped off its saddle, and the animal came to rest beside Cera.

She pulled her dagger from the dying man, wiped it clean on her gown, sheathed it on her leg, and mounted his horse with her other blade in hand. She scanned the scene for Merlin—no wizard anywhere.

Deverel still fought valiantly against two. Cera rode to Perceval. "Will you *accompany me*, then, to assist Sir Deverel?"

"Yes, I—"

"Ya!" Cera squeezed her horse's sides and headed to Deverel.

Perceval, his face finally focused, caught up, and because his sword would do better in the mounted engagement, Cera let him pass. He met the nearest attacker with a powerful sword stroke high and a fast one low across the man's unarmored stomach. Perceval smashed the back of his hand across his foe's head, and the man fell from his horse.

Cera leapt down to the face-painted man, who bled from his midsection. "Where is Merlin?"

The man coughed blood.

Cera dropped her knife, grabbed both his shoulders, slammed him into the ground, and screamed, "Where is he?"

"Me—" He coughed. "Merlin?"

She slapped him. "The wizard!"

"No wizards." His head rolled to the side, and he stopped breathing.

Cera let him go. Perhaps they'd merely been common thieves who also had a fondness for fire. Perceval helped Deverel take care of his other attacker. Sirs Alan and Berthold rode over, having finished off the last of theirs.

Alan called, "Are you all right, Princess?"

"Yup." She put her knife away and looked at her blood-and-grass-stained gown then cocked her head to him. "I'm fine. How are you?"

He didn't answer and instead turned to the burning carriage. "Let's retrieve the chest."

Cera's horse walked to her, and she mounted it. Perceval rode over.

"You'll get your wish," she said to him. "No carriage means at least we'll ride to Laval on horseback."

"Something tells me you'd prefer that, too, Princess."

A smile washed over her, and Cera let herself relax. She took Perceval's hand and squeezed it. "Yes." Then she forced a serious expression to her face. "But *they* call me Princess." She gestured to the battleground. "*You* can see I'm more than that."

"Yes, Cera." He nodded. "I am beginning to."

———————————

Without the carriage, Sir Berthold carried the spear sheathed like a knife off his belt and rode in the lead, the relic's foresight sure to alert him of another attack. With the knights around, Perceval and Cera didn't talk about anything of consequence, or much at all to each other. Perceval chatted with the knights. Talk of their travels to the great cities of Europe was what Cera overheard mostly. In her mind, she played out different ways they could steal the grail, imagining Perceval coming to terms with the fact that he would be aiding her in the endeavor.

When the sun set, they made camp around a fire Sir Alan started. Fortunately, Cera and Perceval's horses had been carrying supplies, so not all were lost when the carriage burned. Cera changed into a clean white gown. Since Perceval hadn't come to her tent, she went to his.

She pulled open the curtain and found him lying down, reading his Bible. "Would you like some company?"

"Yes." He sat up on his elbow.

Cera lay beside him, facing him with her head resting on her arm, and felt so good being back next to him. He turned to lie the same way, facing her, and she warmed, thinking about how far they'd come since the night before.

Perceval closed his Bible and lifted it. "I read this and am filled anew with wonder of the Lord, His love, and His promise of redemption, of death conquered by life everlasting in heaven, for the good and faithful. Yet that isn't enough for you, for His people."

"People suffer, Perceval, this night, on this earth, and they will tomorrow and the day after. Some are starving to death. Others are struck down by sudden afflictions. People want to work hard and provide for their families, but crippling injuries prevent many of them."

"God has a plan."

"God gave us the grail, the means to make a difference. That is his plan."

"He did give us the grail." Perceval set his Bible down behind him. "What does *Nolvan* mean?"

"Nothing really," Cera said. "Josephus figured anything with meaning—the Order of the Grail, the Order of the Sacred Relics, anything like that—would give away our purpose."

"How did it all start?"

"Are you comfortable? It's not a short story."

Perceval held her hand between them. "Take your time."

She smiled. "It started in Britain, like I said. But before that, it started with Josephus's father, Joseph, a wealthy man from Arimathea. He made up for his lack of creativity in the son-naming department by having the courage to ask the governor of Jerusalem, Pontius Pilate, for Jesus's body after our Lord had been crucified, in order to wash and entomb it. Pilate agreed and gave Joseph the body, which he took to his home and laid on a long table. While Joseph washed Jesus, hours after our Lord had died, blood suddenly trickled from where the Roman soldier Longinus's spear had pierced Jesus's side while he hung from the cross."

"The Spear of Destiny?"

"Yes," Cera said. "In his home, Joseph watched as more blood flowed from the wound and ran down Jesus's body. A warmth emanated from it, like blood pumped from a freshly beating heart. Then suddenly, in his haste to keep the blood from hitting the table or dripping onto the ground, Joseph reached for the nearest thing he could find. He grabbed the silver gold-lined goblet that you have held and drunk from and caught all the blood until the flow stopped.

"Joseph brought Jesus's body to the new tomb he'd prepared for it and rolled a large stone to cover the entrance. But the story of the Order of Nolvan does not follow our Lord's ascension to heaven. Joseph transferred the blood caught in the grail into vials, some of which he brought with him on his journey to Britain while the rest remained in Jerusalem. He brought the empty grail, too, though he did not know its power. Along with a dozen others, men and women who followed Christ—including his son Josephus— he made it to Britain, and in Glastonbury, he established the first church there. The group did not yet possess the Spear of Destiny or the Crown of Thorns, but they had other relics, though they celebrated the grail chiefly as it had held the blood of their savior. They never drank from it, however."

Perceval raised a finger. "The vials you mentioned... does that blood hold any special power?"

"Yes. Joseph gave most of the vials he traveled with to some of the first churches in Europe. The blood has dried inside the few vials we have, which we've kept sealed. But word from Jerusalem, from those who opened theirs, is that holy water mixed with the blood provides the same relief as the grail—one time only, as the blood is consumed in the process."

Perceval nodded.

"Over the years," Cera continued, "Joseph's church grew and became a frequent target of robberies. While other relics were taken, the grail, kept most hidden, never was. Eventually, at the end of a long life, Joseph died peacefully and surrounded by loved ones."

Perceval's face fell.

Cera shrugged. "They didn't understand the gift God had given them. Josephus led the church after his father passed, but before long, he grew ill. He had feverish days and restless nights full of coughing fits. He barely ate and struggled to hold down what he did. It was... not pleasant. I've heard Josephus describe it."

"I can imagine," Perceval said.

"Then I'm doing a good job telling the story." Cera squeezed Perceval's hand, and he smiled. "Josephus feared death, he told us. Despite confidence that he'd lived a good and faithful Christian life, he found himself full of doubt and ashamed of that. He grew weak, and when he sensed the end very near, he knelt before his church's most coveted relic of Lord Jesus—the grail. He took it in his hand, and it brought him joy to hold, as it ever did, and Josephus says his fear of death faded in that moment. Invigorated, he thought, *Before I die, why not drink from the cup that held our Lord's blood?* It was a fine goblet that his family had always cherished, so he would drink and thank God for taking away his fear.

"Josephus found common water nearest to him. He poured the goblet half-full and had a sip… and felt a surge of vitality inside himself. He drank the rest quickly, breathed deep, and with no cough in his lungs and a powerfully thumping heart, he realized he'd been healed."

"Even more than I experienced," Perceval said. "Considering his state and the total surprise at the grail's effect."

"Exactly. I remember, as a little girl, the first time Josephus told me the story of that drink. I still enjoy hearing him describe it…" Her eyes shifted then returned. "After that, Josephus shared the good news with the others, and when they drank from the grail, any ailment or injury that had afflicted them faded away, and their hunger vanished completely. From then on, they drank from the grail daily and revered it as the most holy of all relics. It took a while, but eventually, they understood that it also kept them from aging.

"But back on the day Josephus and the others first drank from the grail, some asked how they should share the news with the church's congregation. Of the sick and injured, who should they bring the grail to first? As you might imagine,

Josephus said no to it all. They'd been lucky the silver-and-gold goblet hadn't been stolen before, and if they shared its power, thieves would constantly seek it until one succeeded. They were not a knightly order at that time, you realize, so while keeping the grail to themselves didn't sit well with everyone, none could argue that it would become a target and ultimately be stolen. They agreed that if it were taken by someone with especially ill intent, the results could have been disastrous.

"Despite an oath of secrecy that the whole group swore, a few months later, that summer, a solemn, imposing knight came to the church, asking about a 'Holy Grail' that could heal the injured or ill and feed the hungry. Josephus asked which of those things afflicted the man. None, he said, but since hearing of the grail, he'd longed to see the goblet that had held his Lord's blood on the day of the Crucifixion.

"Josephus asked the knight if he deemed himself worthy to hold and drink from such a grail, if it existed. Had he lived a Christian life? Had he held to the ideals of chivalry? The knight said that he thought so. Josephus told him to return when he knew for certain, and then they would talk more on the matter.

"The knight thanked Josephus for the charge and departed. Josephus expected him back within days or weeks, but not until spring, nine months later, did the knight walk back into the church and tell Josephus of the chivalrous deeds he had done. The knight had considered himself 'good' before, but in pursuit of the grail, he found new meaning to the word and a deeper faith required to stay on the true path. Josephus retrieved the grail, and Sir Varden drank from it."

"Sir Varden," Perceval said, "who is still part of the order today, riding with Josephus, guarding the grail?"

"It is he," Cera said. "And there is a little more to tell."

"Go on, please. I'm sorry."

"Not at all." She smiled. "I never tell the story. If new knights of the order ask, I send them to someone else for it. But I enjoy telling you and watching your brown eyes and kind face take it in."

That kind face grew a little red.

"After his drink, Sir Varden crossed himself and was bowing his head in prayer when three armed men burst into the church and demanded he turn over the grail. Sir Varden did turn it over—to Josephus. Varden drew his sword and slayed two of the men, and the third fled. After that, Josephus decided the grail needed two things. First, faithful, chivalric knights like Sir Varden to protect it. And second, to be on the move lest the constant stream of would-be thieves materialized. And so started the Order of Nolvan."

Perceval whispered, "Four hundred and fifty years ago…"

"Mm-hmm."

He leaned close, still speaking softly. "For four hundred and fifty years, they've had the grail, part of an order—our order—upholding rules that have inspired the greatest knights in Europe and have kept it safe from the real threat of thieves, and you mean for *us* to steal it from them—from those greatest knights in the land? From that righteous king, Josephus?"

"He is *not* righteous." Cera let go of Perceval's hand. "I will be."

Perceval raised his eyebrows.

"Think of Arden dying in his bed," Cera said. "He's *dying*. Sir Gethen and his mother don't know what poison withers him, but his life will end. We could stop that, but instead, we're in this tent, discussing, wasting time."

"What if Arden's already dead?" Perceval asked. "He appeared so weak."

"He isn't dead."

Perceval rolled onto his back. "What you ask... I just don't know."

"Think of the people of Bevrée. And there are other derelict lords and kings everywhere. Think of the suffering, dying people who Josephus ignores. We would not ignore them."

Perceval stared at the top of his tent. With a huff, Cera rolled onto her back and did the same. Then she shifted over so her arm pressed against his—since she was no longer looking into Perceval's eyes, she felt too distant from him otherwise.

9

Flames flared at Roan's back. The infernal heat had long since burned his latest set of clothes to tattered rags, leaving most of him exposed. He slogged barefoot across the battlefield, uphill through blood and guts, while sharp edges of armor and weapons sliced into his feet and toes, and glowing coals burned them. He marched toward Aedre, being carried up the hill by enemies, deep into their endless lines of fighters—soot-covered humans, socket-eyed skeletons, and long-limbed demons.

"Roan!" his first wife screamed from afar, struggling against a skeleton and a man dragging her. Bone knuckles smashed across her face, and she slumped.

"Aedre!" Roan slammed his fist into a demon's spiked helm. The creature crumpled, and Roan's knuckles bled. He reached to the ground for a sword, but when he wrapped his hand around its handle, his fingers burned to bare bone, so he dropped it.

Roan spun around, his chest heaving, and the wall of fire seared his face. It was not real, he knew. He'd crossed the hellscape a hundred times—more, probably, but he couldn't keep an accurate count. He'd fought again and again through the lines of foes when there wasn't something else tormenting him.

"Roan!" Aedre cried.

But it was the only real he had, and it got worse for Aedre the longer it took him to reach her. "Grah!" Roan marched on.

———————

Black chain wrapped around Roan's throat, wrists, and ankles, pinning him to red-hot stone ground, where his fresh skin burned and blistered. Fire raged all around. Above him in the void, Lady Tadman slit his throat in the tavern in Dover. Roan had seen it so many times—occasionally, he'd see it just once before the next torture, but often, the vision repeated for days on end. Whether he kept his eyes open or closed, he still saw it.

Roan's focus shifted to that wretched knight of Arthur's who lay beneath him while Lady Tadman ran her knife. *Why couldn't Perceval have let me be? Perceval surely noticed my suffering, my anguish. Why couldn't he have let me suffer in peace?*

Madeline had warned Roan about hell, and she'd told him of the heaven that she and her Frankish countrymen believed in. Roan had listened to her and considered it and told her he believed, but in truth, the afterlife she described on high and in a pit beneath sounded impossible to him, illogical. What Roan had believed in with all his heart was her, on earth.

And earth had become as lost to Roan as Madeline had. Because of all Roan had done—he knew that—and also because of *that knight.*

Roan screamed, "Perce—" choking as his throat cracked open. Blood seeped out of him, boiling onto and burning his heaving chest. Roan could not fathom how that knight served a god who from His lofty throne in heaven let the hell Roan suffered in exist below.

Above Roan in the void, the scene started anew. He sat with Lady Stanton in the tavern. Perceval pushed open the door.

Nearly naked, Roan sat on a stone chair. Black chain bound his wrists together behind him. From the blaze before him emerged a throne raised on a platform, where a goat-headed demon sat. Instead of hands and feet, it had hooves. It banged one on the arm of the throne.

Roan got up from his chair—or as far off it as he could. "Satan!"

Chsh! Roan's chains pulled tight, slamming him down.

"A like-minded devil of his," the goat creature said plainly.

To Roan's left, a row of ten seated skeletons slid forth from the fire, and another slid into view beside them. Two rows of skeletons emerged behind them, seated higher, and more rows filled in around the goat's platform and higher behind other rows until hundreds of skeletons encircled Roan, staring at him. Roan had not experienced that scene in all his time in hell, however long it had been.

"You've been here three years." The goat creature pointed its hoof at Roan. "*Why* are you here?"

In unison, the seated skeletons shot their attention to Roan.

The goat crossed its arms in its lap. "Tell the truth."

"Or what?" Roan asked.

The goat smiled. Flames rose higher. *Perceval, that meddling knight*, Roan thought, but he didn't say it.

Roan recalled his own ways for the millionth time—the people he'd hurt and killed and the families he'd broken. It shamed him, and Roan hated thinking about it. But he wondered if that was truly the cause, the real *why* he suffered in hell.

A wave of heat smacked Roan. Empty skeleton sockets stared blankly at him. God had given him more than he'd ever dreamed of, Roan admitted, remembering life with Aedre and then Madeline, how good each day and night had been with them and how it felt to hold them and be together with them—to share every part of life with them and to be welcoming a new life, his son, into the world. And then God had stolen it all away.

The skeletons rocked to and fro in waves.

"Why are you here?" the goat creature repeated.

Roan considered his cruelty since Madeline died and, again, those blissful seasons before. Pulling his wrists upward against the chain with all his might, Roan got himself off the chair and screamed, "Because God is the Devil!"

The goat grinned. The skeletons wailed. Their demonic

cries pierced Roan's eardrums. They stomped their bone feet thunderously.

"Will they judge me?" Roan yelled to the goat over their wailing and stomping. "In this court?"

The creature furrowed its brow. "Of course not. You have already been judged and damned to hell." The goat and its throne receded into the fire.

Chsh! The chains snapped tight, pinning Roan to his chair. The skeletons left their seats and streamed to him, dancing, yelling, smiling, and circling.

Roan shut his eyes and still saw the skeletons, so he opened them to his pitch-black sky. Aedre appeared, strong and beautiful, with a smirk for him that he adored. And she faded in the sky, like she'd faded from his life. A tear welled up and seared Roan's skin the instant it left his eye.

Madeline appeared, and in that infernal pit, surrounded by raging flame and hollering skeletons, the sight of her filled Roan's heart with joy, like it had the day she'd come into his life and every day after. Above him, she was gone, just as she'd suddenly disappeared on earth.

Roan remembered how angry he'd been up there. He was still so angry. A light flickered in the void. Pure white, it solidified. Another tear welled in his eye. The bright light above Roan expanded.

The skeletons moaned. They hissed and retreated from Roan as the pure white grew. The fires around him sank lower.

The tear in Roan's eye trickled down his face. Cool air— he could hardly remember the sensation—accompanied the light. Roan had loved Aedre and Madeline so much.

The chains around his wrists and ankles loosened. In the light in the sky, the shape of a man approached, wings unfurled behind him. He reached out for Roan.

10

Near midday, Perceval rode Ociel southeast for the town of Laval, the midway meeting point in the order's trip to Tours, with Cera and their group guarding the spear. Sir Berthold still carried the relic on account of their carriage being destroyed the day before. The morning of riding had been a quiet one. Cera and Perceval had awoken together in his tent at dawn under a shared blanket, her head on his arm, her arm across his chest, and his holding her.

He should have kissed her when they awoke or before she left the tent, Perceval realized later. He didn't know if he could do what she asked—help steal the grail from the order. And it scared him to think about what would happen to his relationship with Cera if he refused. But he did know that he didn't like being apart from her, and he wanted her to know that.

He'd never seen a woman fight like she had against the fire-wielding would-be robbers from the woods. Perceval had noticed the dagger on her desk at Mont Tombe but figured it meant merely that she was a woman willing to take action after due consideration, as opposed to a passive noble.

When he'd pictured her fierce on the streets of Paris, it had been a fierceness of purpose.

Yet standing at the doorway of the carriage, a warrior's fierceness had flared in Cera's eyes, and when she threw herself into the first rider, she leapt with such force and conviction—and, yes, such purpose—that Perceval had been awestruck watching it.

Over the years, Perceval had seen men and even some women fight with wild eyes that matched their wild rage. Roan had been one such man, but there had been plenty in pitched battles as well. Perceval recalled Cera hurling her dagger into the second attacker, throwing with her whole body. With her passion came not wildness but precision—a perfectly aimed throw, a single stab of her knife before that—and control. She'd let Perceval ride past to finally assist Sir Deverel rather than forcing the issue with her weapons, which were worse suited to mounted combat.

Perceval remained awestruck as Cera rode up alongside him on the way to Laval, her face full of focus. Things had become much more complicated since he'd achieved the Holy Grail. He had expected that quest to end all quests for him, yet Perceval found himself on the brink of one that was perhaps greater and was certainly fraught with peril.

He thought Cera might say something, but she didn't. He wished she would reach out and take his hand. Then he would pull her to him and hold her and kiss her soft lips and only stop kissing to look into her blue eyes and see her warmly disarmed, in sharp contrast to her usual stern countenance.

"I've never seen a woman fight like you," Perceval said. "I apologize for sitting there during the battle, struck by it, doing nothing. It won't happen again."

"You're not the first to be *dumbstruck* by it," Cera said. "I've been at it for longer than you've been alive, you realize. You're twenty-seven? I trained with my father from when I turned ten until he died. I trained with my mother after that for a time—she was a powerful warrior, wielding her sword with such conviction…" Cera shook her head. "Anyway, I've had the teachers and the years of practice to hone my skills."

"It shows."

"And while I am sixty years old, I don't feel that age," Cera said. "My body has not weakened and worn. I've had the years to learn, but they have not been accompanied by fear or worry of an impending end to my mortal life weighing on my mind and soul. I feel as young as I look, and I know I look twenty-four."

"That shows as well."

"I appreciate the subtlety of your compliment, Perceval. Most of the new knights shower me with them because that is all they see of me."

Perceval yearned to tell her how pretty she was, how perfectly her hair fell around her face and hit her neck and shoulders—how, against her fair skin, her blue eyes cried out to him with a depth behind them. *Lean* or *thin* didn't do her body justice. The word *toned*—or *sublime*—came closer to what Perceval envisioned beneath the gown.

"None see me as a warrior," Cera continued. "Which has,

in truth, made it harder to find practice of late. In recent years, even my mother discouraged my training at the behest of Josephus, who doesn't think it's especially proper for me to be doing."

"They're mistaken, every one of them. Whatever else you might use those skills for…" Perceval gave her a knowing look. "The grail and the other relics, clearly, are safer with you aiding in their defense."

"I know," she said. "And I'm glad that you understand that, at least."

Perceval shifted in his saddle.

"One thing you mentioned yesterday that stuck with me," Cera said. "You spoke of the esteemed knights in our order."

"Yes."

"There are many. Soon after Sir Varden came, Sir Hunald and Sir Phelan joined the order. They, too, have been around since those first years. And in the centuries since, while we have lost exemplary knights defending the grail, we can, without a doubt, count many true heroes in our current ranks."

"Exactly," Perceval said.

"Heroes like *you*, Perceval."

He leaned away.

"Do not doubt it," she said. "You are one of the finest knights among us."

"Sir Galahad, surely, is a greater knight than I."

"Maybe. Though having followed each of your careers, I would choose you in duel."

"And Sir Lancelot—"

"Is not here," Cera said. "He is a powerful knight. His prowess is known. But we have not invited him to our order, and you, we have—twice. We've never done that before, you know. Offered a second chance before the king."

"I thank God you did. As I thank God for so much. Did you know I nearly died in Dover, years ago, on my way back to Francia?"

"Word reached us of a fight in a tavern with a Saxon, if that's what you mean."

"It is. Roan was his name. Second son of Osred. They called him Relentless once. But I encountered a troubled man. Older, tired, he appeared, until he fought with such rage..." *And a passion not wholly unlike what flares in Cera when she fights*, Perceval realized.

"Yes?" Cera prodded.

"He was a wild, desperate man—"

"And he did not vanquish you," Cera said.

"I know. He died but not by my hand." Perceval sat straight. "I know my skill in battle, my strength, and above all, I know my faith that has seen me through the hardest times. I know that I am a fine knight worthy of this order. But it would be foolish of me not to acknowledge the prowess of the others in the order. That is all I meant."

"That makes sense. I do not disagree." She leaned close and said quietly, "But do not forget, you would have the spear and its foresight aiding you."

Perceval supposed she would not let the matter of the grail rest until they'd settled it. The image of Arden, dying in his bed, flashed in his mind. Cera was right not to let it rest. "I would not kill them to do it. I could never."

"You won't have to."

After a moment, they both drew away. The conversation could go no further out in the open.

That evening, they reached Lord Rengault's home on the western side of the Mayenne River in Laval. For generations, his powerful family had been reliable hosts, when called upon, and guardians of the holy relics' secrets at all times. Cera had explained it to Perceval en route and also had told him how those families who betrayed the secrets entrusted to them were dealt with most harshly, just as God harshly enacted His vengeance.

And while the threat of death surely helped, faith in God and a desire to do His will kept most people in line. Lord and Lady Rengault had never given any hint of disloyalty, and the way they greeted Perceval's group with open arms certainly spoke to that.

Their home was a small castle. When the group entered through the central courtyard, after being shown the great hall where they would dine once Josephus and the others arrived, Lord Rengault, a stout middle-aged man, led Perceval and the knights to their shared room while Lady Rengault, who was leaner and shorter than her husband, took Cera to the private room prepared for her. After two solid days of traveling, Perceval enjoyed taking his armor off, setting his weapons down, stretching out on his back on a bed, and being still. Sir Deverel got similarly settled on the bed across the room, while Berthold and Alan went to ask Lord Rengault for a suitable chest to hold the spear in and a carriage for the morning, to replace the one that had burned.

Perceval's stomach growled, and he wondered whether they would eat first or be nourished by the grail. *Why eat at all, actually?* It seemed wasteful.

Sir Willard entered the room and then Sir Phelan, and they said their journey had been uneventful, which meant the Crown of Thorns had made it safely, wherever they had it stored at that moment.

Perceval's arm moved over his closed eyes, and his mind settled on the grail. He thought of the crisp water rushing to his core then spreading outward. He thanked God for giving His people such a precious gift.

Perceval did not require proof of God, yet now that he had it, his mind wandered further. *As a member of the Order of Nolvan, am I doing enough? Is the order doing right with God's powerful gift?*

If it would be used otherwise, Arden needed it to be soon, which presented a new challenge for Perceval. After King Arthur proclaimed the quest for the Holy Grail, Perceval had spent three years searching for it. While resolved in his purpose always, those years gave him ample time to think about both God and that purpose, and his resolve deepened. After failing before the grail, Perceval had months to contemplate his failure… for all the good it did. After he received Cera's letter and renewed his quest, another three years passed. For better or worse, he'd always had time, and with the grail, as a member of the Order of Nolvan, he would have all time.

Arden, on the other hand, had no time. Cera had been desperate to act for a long time. *Has the order done enough— for enough people—during their centuries with the grail? How exactly does Cera think we can take the grail without killing anyone? And even if we can, what if we're wrong?*

Perceval could guess what God would do to those so presumptuous that they would commit the high crime Cera suggested—which included condemning an entire order of His faithful to eventual death. He imagined spending eternity knowing he'd so egregiously affronted the Lord. His empty stomach churned.

"Perceval," Galahad said.

Perceval sat up to see him across the room. "Galahad." Perceval's heart warmed, as ever, at the sight of his friend. "Any trouble on the road?"

"None at all." He came over. "You?"

"Some, but we dealt with it quickly."

"Good." Galahad motioned to the room's entrance. "Rest later. It's time for dinner. The grail awaits."

Perceval followed him to the great hall, a big high-ceilinged room with tapestries in earthen colors hanging from every wall. A large iron cross had been fixed imposingly up in the far corner, the ends of its beam attached to each side wall. Dusk's light seeped through small windows near the ceiling. Thick white candles, arranged in black holders, burned up and down the U-shaped table's three long sides, augmenting the outside light and ready to take over when it faded completely.

Atop the table lay a spread of beef and venison, light and dark bread, and colorful vegetables. Lord and Lady Rengault sat at the far end of the room at the table's center, talking with Josephus and Cera, who sat beside them. Cera's gown was cut lower than her usual and was green, for a change, like an emerald. The bold color against her light skin melted Perceval.

"Are you okay?" Galahad motioned to two vacant chairs nearby at the side of the table, near the end. They sat as other knights and the relic-bearers Mireille and Mabyn filled in the rest.

Perceval gestured to the food. "We do eat, then, and not just drink from the grail?"

"Yes," Galahad said. "Seems wasteful, doesn't it?"

"It does."

"Yet that is our custom. We drink from the grail at the conclusion of the meal."

Thun—thun—thun. Lord Rengault smacked his palm against the table. "Welcome," he said loudly. "Welcome all." Everyone quieted. "Thank you for trusting us with this brief pause on your endless road. I hope you will be comfortable and find rest here, and if you need anything, ask me."

"Thank you, Lord Rengault," Josephus said.

He nodded. "Please join me in thanking God for this bounty before us. We thank Him for seeing us safely here together today. It is by His grace we are able to share this splendid feast. Amen."

"Amen," all repeated, and conversations resumed around the table.

From a decorated pitcher, Galahad poured water into the ornate silver goblet before him. "Water? Or there's wine and ale."

"Water, yes, please," Perceval said, and Galahad poured. "How long have you been with the order?"

"Nearly a year."

They took meat and bread from the central dishes onto their plates, though Perceval noticed both of theirs remained sparser than those around them. The others at the table loudly chatted. Laughter often rose or burst out.

Perceval wanted to ask Galahad's opinion of everything Cera had laid before him. He trusted Galahad's wisdom as much as his sword and heart, but he could not betray Cera's trust, so he only asked, "How have you found it here, among the order?"

Galahad beamed. "It is a dream come true."

Perceval smiled.

"For you as well, I'm sure."

"Of course." Perceval nodded. "Of course."

"I knew you'd make it," Galahad said. "I never doubted it."

They got to eating thin slices of venison and chewing fresh bread and talking about their travels before reaching the grail. Galahad spoke of his time with the order. He asked Perceval about Bevrée, and Perceval told the story of the sorry circumstances the people found themselves in when he arrived and of their survival through winter until the town's men returned. He did not mention Cera's letters.

They discussed home. Sir Sagramor, their fellow knight

of the Round Table, had indeed died in battle at the hand of King Hengist, Galahad confirmed. Gawain and Bedivere had, as Perceval feared, failed to reach Merlin—who had the protection of King Hengist's army—to confront him about what had happened to Arthur. With Merlin as his chief advisor, Hengist had conquered nearly the entire island of Britain south of Hadrian's Wall. King Constantine and his dwindling forces alone held out at Camelot in the southwest. Galahad had learned from knights of the order what Perceval had learned from Cera—that Merlin had killed King Arthur.

"Do you ever wish you could fight with Gawain and Bedivere?" Perceval asked. "To leave the order, defend our lands, and make Merlin answer for what he did to Arthur?"

"I don't. I miss our brothers, and I miss Arthur dearly, but that is not my fight any longer. I have a new purpose."

Perceval might have left it there, but instead, he leaned closer to Galahad. "Do you ever think about the people in the cities we don't let drink from the grail? The ones who need it—the ill and the starving?"

"I do." Galahad's face darkened. "It pains me. But imagining the chaos that would ensue if we did let them drink assures me in our course. We simply cannot."

Perceval nodded, ashamed he'd doubted that Galahad cared for those in need. But his mind didn't settle as he surveyed the scene of rowdy conversation and wine being poured and thrown back.

Cera stood. Perceval watched the angel in green stride over with her reddened lips, the dark-streaked golden hair he adored, and the Holy Grail she carried. She stopped behind him and held it out. "I've had my drink. Won't you have yours so I can steal you from this place?"

"Steal *you*," she'd said. Perceval replayed the request carefully, searching for any hint of another signal in her words, eyes, or actions. He took the grail, and Galahad poured water into the goblet. Perceval's eyes met Cera's, and he drank.

The cool hit him, and Perceval smiled. The crisp wind rushed inside, to every part of him, and he breathed easy. He bowed his head, made the sign of the cross, and in that moment, wished many more people had the opportunity to experience that heavenly drink. Perceval handed Cera the grail.

"Come," she said.

Perceval followed her toward the head of the table, where an open chest sat at Josephus's feet. While Josephus conversed with Lord and Lady Rengault, Cera placed the grail inside the chest on the white satin cushion and shut the lid. She led Perceval around the table.

"There they go," Perceval heard, but he wasn't sure who had said it.

"Why him?" Sir Varden, the first knight of the order, asked Sir Hunald, the second, beside him.

"Ignore them," Cera said, exiting the great hall. She headed through a long hallway and outside into the courtyard, where big candles burned, spaced along the wall, and four of Lord Rengault's knights stood guard. Only when they'd gone beyond the courtyard's main gate and started on the dirt path did she say, "We could not have taken it then.

You hadn't your sword or armor. Even if we'd made it outside, they would have ridden us down before we got far."

"I agree," Perceval said.

Cera took his hand and gently pulled him away from the home's candlelit entrance and onto the grass, and they walked down to a big leafy oak tree beside the river. Its quietly running water glistened in the light of the more-than-half-full moon.

She asked, "What are you thinking?"

"That it's ironic that the order's test is about compassion, when we reserve it for so few."

"It's maddening."

Perceval motioned back the way they'd come. "I think we wasted that food in there, which we did not need."

"Utterly wasted." She stepped close. "What else?"

He turned aside, unable to look at the angel. "That Arden lies dying while we all celebrate our immortality."

"He does. I pray he still clings to his life." She took Perceval's other hand and held both. "And?"

His eyes returned to Cera's. His lips were so near hers. "That after Arden, I would confront Merlin for what he did rather than leave it to the hope that another knight is up to the task."

She inched closer. "Help me steal the Holy Grail."

Perceval looked at the ground. "I swore an oath to the order."

Cera let go of his hand long enough for her finger to lift his chin. "Haven't you sworn other oaths? Before that one. To God, to do right in His eyes."

"I have. With my whole heart, I have sworn those oaths."

"Then your oaths are in fatal opposition. All cannot be kept, so hold onto your first oaths, those true oaths made over a lifetime, and not the one made in a moment right before being confronted with a fuller picture than Josephus offered."

Perceval turned aside. "What if you're wrong? What if I'm already where I'm supposed to be and what you ask would be a heinous crime against God?"

"What if the order is wrong?" Cera countered. "What if they commit such a crime every single day, and you can do something about it but don't? Help me do something. Help me steal the grail."

Perceval turned back to her and nodded.

Cera's lips curled up.

"I won't kill anyone," he said. "If it can be done that way, then I will help."

She pulled Perceval to her, and her lips met his. He dropped her hands and wrapped his arms around her as she held him. He kissed her, and his soul burned with a warmth that made the grail's water feel like ice.

Cera pulled away and rested her hand on his cheek. "You do understand."

"I do." Perceval moved her hand from there and held it. "And also that you are condemning them to an eventual death once they can no longer drink from the grail."

"They've lived long enough." She looked away. "They can live out their years like everyone else does."

"But not you."

Cera turned back to him. "I will use the grail as it should be used for as long as I am able."

"They'll hunt you," Perceval said.

"They'll hunt *us*," she corrected. "A small price to pay to be doing what must be done."

He nodded. "A small price to pay."

Cera leaned close, and he brought his lips to hers. She pulled him to her, he held her tight, and his heart raced. He wanted to never let her go.

And if they stole the grail together, he'd never have to.

"Come to my room?" she asked between kisses.

"Yes." He kept kissing her. "Please, your room."

"I'll tell you how we can take it," she said, pulling him toward the path to the house so hard Perceval had to hustle to keep up.

Once they were in the courtyard, they entered the home by a side door but heard from the great hall the singular sound of a woman singing, high-pitched and glorious. One of the relic bearers, Perceval guessed, Mireille or Mabyn. She finished to loudly clapping knights, then the dissonance of their conversations rose.

Cera led Perceval into her room, shut the door, and locked it. "We can't take the grail from here. I hate waiting, but we have to do it in Tours."

"Okay."

"Can I save the plan until morning?" she asked.

Perceval kissed her and pressed his body into hers against the door. His lips moved to her neck and his hand to her hair, and they breathed hard. Cera tugged his tunic up, and he joined her in pulling it over his head. He reached around her for her emerald gown's lacing while she kissed his bare chest. He untied the lace and let his hands rest there. Cera kissed his neck, and again, but he'd stopped kissing.

Gently, she pushed Perceval's shoulders away. "What's wrong?"

"We're not married."

Her eyes shifted away then returned. "Is it enough to say we will be, when all is done—when we have the grail and are away from this order?"

Perceval considered the question then raised a finger. "To accomplish that theft, surely, we risk a greater offense to God than making a vow to be married and consummating it early."

She nodded. "Surely."

Cera's hands went to Perceval's sides then slid to his belt, while he loosened her gown's lace until the gown fell down around her.

The next day, Cera and Perceval rode in the new carriage Lord Rengault had supplied, holding hands, listening to large drops of rain hit the roof. She rested her head on Perceval's shoulder often. Other times, their lips locked on each other's in deep kisses. When they weren't kissing, Perceval's mind vacillated between what had just happened and the task that lay before them.

He'd awoken that morning holding Cera in her bed, no clothes between them, no jewelry save her simple silver necklace and its cross pendant resting against her skin. *Oh, that this moment would never end*, Perceval had wished. If only dawn would not come and he would be left to hold her in peace forever. She smiled and nuzzled her head into his neck, and Perceval took it back. He wanted *that* moment to be forever.

When she fully woke, she explained how they could steal the grail from the order after they arrived in Tours the next day. As Perceval had seen, the grail was well guarded while in transit. When the order reached a destination, too many guards kept watch over it and the other relics.

But in the crypt beneath the church in Tours, Cera and the others would conduct the test, the procession of the relics, for a knight named Sir Turpin. For nine years, word had reached the order of his chivalrous deeds, and finally, he'd been deemed worthy of the invitation. During the ceremony, Cera would be playing her part, holding the grail while everyone's attention was initially fixed on Josephus moaning—for show—on his lonely throne and then on the first two relics that passed by.

The plan was for Perceval to wait in the passageway where the procession ended and take the Spear of Destiny from Mabyn once she finished walking before the king and reached him. Cera would hang back on her side while Perceval loudly stole the spear. As all rushed to him to see his brazen act for themselves and then to recover the spear, Cera would exit the other way with the grail, incapacitating knights who remained in her way, if any did.

With the Spear of Destiny in hand, Cera assured Perceval

that he would have such knowledge of his pursuers' attacks that he could beat them to any blow and strike them to injure but not kill. And the real trick, what could make it work, was that Cera knew a secret door to a staircase that led to a level below the main crypt. She didn't think any of the others were aware of it.

Since Cera had been born in Tours and baptized there, the local nuns had doted on her from her earliest years. Growing up always on the move, whenever the order's travels brought them near Tours, Cera begged her mom to take her to the church that felt like home and the priests and sisters who felt like family. She celebrated her ninth birthday there, and while members of the order and the church alike showered her with gifts, one nun—Cera's favorite, Sister Basina—gave her something truly special. When Cera's party had ended and the others held council in the crypt, discussing the order's matters of the day, Sister Basina showed Cera the trick to opening the door to the staircase farther down. After that, Cera had urged her mom to take them to Tours even more, so she could play in her secret lair, a level beneath the main crypt. No one used the lower level any longer, and she never saw another living soul there.

From that level below, Perceval could run back across the church and exit where Cera had, and she would be waiting with their horses. If the rest of the order didn't see them going, they'd be set. If they did, Cera and Perceval would have a head start and the grail and the Spear of Destiny to aid their escape.

It sounded like it would work, and Perceval couldn't

think of a better opportunity, especially not one soon, for Arden's sake. He played it repeatedly in his mind from start to finish. He thought he could draw the necessary attention his way to the west so Cera could escape on her side to the east. If the spear really offered the foresight she said it would, he figured he would succeed in repelling any who got in his way by injuring them only. And then if the passageway existed as described, Perceval didn't see why he couldn't get himself across the church to her.

What he couldn't be as sure about was how far behind them the order would be as they fled. But whether immediately or soon after, the order would chase them, so that seemed not the most critical detail. And the critical details did seem sound.

Perceval spent the night with Cera in her tent, and quiet as they could, they made love. He felt somehow closer to her than the night before. He felt in love, he decided. In the morning, they kept quiet again and continued kissing until they finally had to break down their tent so the others wouldn't be waiting on them.

Perceval and Cera rode that day in the carriage as well, arm in arm, hand in hand, speaking softly through their plan until certain they had it figured out and every detail committed to memory.

———————

That night, in Tours, Cera's room in the crypt beneath the church—the main-level crypt everyone knew of—was stone walled and candlelit. It was one of many small chambers that lined the long east side of the church. At the north end of the crypt, the procession of the relics would begin in the dark tunnel on the eastern side, proceeding westward in front of King Josephus. Perceval would be waiting on the west side for Mabyn to walk into the tunnel with the spear.

With Sir Turpin expected to arrive soon for his test, Cera and Perceval went over it all again in her room. "And you'll make a commotion taking the spear," she said, dressed in her usual white gown.

"Yes, yes." Perceval wore the uniform of the order: his mail armor and, over it, the white tunic with the red cross on its center. His sword and knife were sheathed at his hip.

"Mabyn will hand the spear to you, I'm sure," Cera said. "She'd have no reason to withhold it, but make it seem like a struggle. Make it loud."

"You don't think—"

"What?" Cera asked.

"Well, Jesus understood his destiny and embraced it. I'd be using the spear to know mine to change it."

"It's not the same," she said. "He was God. He knew the profound impact His death would have. The spear won't give you such far-reaching foresight. It's more like a sixth sense, so you can *chart* your destiny—to save Arden and so many after. I think we're using it exactly how He would want us to."

Perceval nodded.

"Once you have it," Cera continued, "you head westward to the tunnel's end and turn left to go south down the long side of the church to the marble pietà on the pedestal. It doesn't look like the sculpture moves, but you can get your hands behind it, and I assure you, it moves. That'll open the door in the wall—close it behind you—and head down to the lower level. Then come across, go back up, and meet me out the east exit."

"I've got it," Perceval said.

"I'll be waiting with our horses."

"Right."

Cera grasped the tops of his arms. "This will work because they're completely unprepared for it. Nothing like it has ever been tried. My mother carried the grail before me, and now I do. There's been no one else. They think I'm no more than a pretty girl in a play put on for them. They don't imagine I could, or ever would, do this, and by the time they figure it out, we'll be long gone."

"For four hundred and fifty years," Perceval said, "no one's tried this…"

Cera shook him. "Perceval…"

"I know." He wrapped his arms around her lower back. "We are in the right. I believe it. This order, even if it was once right or if there is virtue in its ways, isn't enough. Arthur sent us on the quest for the grail, and I achieved it. So did Galahad. We're both here, yet too many people suffer. For the world Arthur dreamed of to be real, we must chart a new path for the grail."

"And for us. As man and wife."

"I love you," Perceval said. They kissed, and he held her to him.

"I love you," she said.

They kissed deeper. His hand slid down to her leg to her dagger strapped to it. "You are indeed ready."

"I am. Ready for today. Ready to be away from here with the grail, to see Arden revived, and to help all those who really need it."

"Aye."

Thud—thud—thud. Someone was at the door. "Sir Turpin is upstairs."

Cera kissed Perceval quick. "Go."

Perceval pulled open her door and nodded to Sir Varden on the way out. North up the long tunnel, Perceval passed the room Mabyn and Mireille shared then passed one with bunk beds for four knights, where at present the girls were taking the Spear of Destiny and Crown of Thorns out of their iron chests.

On Perceval's right was the staircase. Cera would soon take it up to street level, with the grail, and then head outside. The guard at the staircase at crypt level, they reasoned, would likely rush Perceval's way, leaving only the one at street level for Cera to either deceive into rushing down the stairs after Perceval or to incapacitate so he couldn't follow her out.

Past the staircase, Josephus's room had its door closed, and then the tunnel turned left to the west. Perceval hurried that way, past the cushioned chair in the middle of the room where Sir Berthold would lead Sir Turpin to witness the procession of the relics.

If Turpin asked about the king's health early on, before the spear made it past him, they wouldn't be able to go ahead with their plan. Cera put the odds of that happening at one in four, based on her years bearing the grail before knights like him and what she'd read specifically in their research of his life and deeds as a knight. Based on Perceval's own experience, he deemed it likely that at least the spear would make it to him, even if Sir Turpin would, under other circumstances, eventually inquire about the king.

Perceval went five paces into the western side tunnel—not far. He turned to the empty room and the vacant chair.

Sir Deverel rounded the corner from the main room and headed his way. "Watching it again, Perceval?"

"I am. It is… such a sight, the relics presented like this."

Deverel smiled. "I watched a few times myself. You'll get used to it."

Perceval smiled. "We'll see."

"I'm happy for you and Cerise. Don't listen to the others. Some have become a little bitter when she was nothing but forthright with them. But she should have someone, and it seems she's finally found him."

Perceval nodded, and Deverel passed to guard the side of the church where the relics were supposed to end up. Perceval prayed Cera was correct that, with the spear in hand, he'd be able to injure the knights without killing any of them before he reached the secret staircase. They had only recently met, but Sir Deverel seemed to be a kind man.

Perceval crossed his arms and leaned against the wall. Before him in the main room, the chair sat vacant, and beyond it in the other tunnel, Mabyn appeared, holding the long wooden spear with the iron tip at its end.

Sir Alan stepped around her and rushed across the room into Perceval's tunnel. He nodded, saying, "Perceval," on the way past.

Perceval nodded back.

Footsteps sounded from the main room, presumably Sir Berthold leading Sir Turpin in. Beside Mabyn, Josephus stood tall. With the golden crown on his head, he nodded to Perceval.

Perceval returned the gesture then closed his eyes, crossed himself, and prayed. *God, what I'm about to do, I do for you, to serve you and your people in the way I believe you would want. The Order of Nolvan turns a blind eye to too many, and I know you would rather turn to those in need with open arms of realized hope, of prayers answered. I know because after your son, you gave us the grail. What I do—what we do—we do not for our glory but for yours and for the benefit of all those people. Give me the strength to see today through, and guide me so that I may do so without taking the lives of my fellow knights, for they do mean well.*

Perceval's eyes opened to Sirs Galahad and Hunald on either side of the far tunnel entrance, swords at their sides, hands clasped before them. He prayed also not to have to cross swords with his friend and that Galahad would understand his actions that day.

"Sir Turpin of Toulouse!" Berthold's voice boomed.

Josephus hunched himself over and limped out, one painfully slow cane-aided step after another. Perceval hardly breathed, waiting for Turpin to question the ailing king struggling before him, hoping for continued silence.

"Your Grace," Sir Turpin—it must have been—said.

Perceval's chest tightened further. Josephus grimaced and got himself into his chair. From the far tunnel, Mabyn emerged, the long wooden pole of the spear held before her. Perceval took a breath.

The rattling sound of metal moving might have been Turpin kneeling as Mabyn walked toward Perceval and the knight saw what Perceval had first seen—the brunette beauty beaming up at the narrow, worn tip of the spear. He did not relish the fact that in moments, he would ruin the blessed occasion for Turpin. But Perceval understood he was going to ruin a lot more than that.

Mabyn reached Josephus. Perceval would not hurt her, of course, but he did not look forward to even startling the sweet girl. She passed the king, and Mireille came out of the tunnel. Perceval couldn't see her well behind Mabyn, but he knew Mireille carried the Crown of Thorns on its satin pillow.

Mabyn neared. Josephus moaned. Metal creaked, but no words came from Sir Turpin. Mabyn lowered the spear to step into the tunnel. She smiled at Perceval. He peered around her to see Mireille reach Josephus. Cera would be expected to emerge into the main chamber shortly.

To Mabyn, Perceval put out his hands and whispered, "Could I hold it?"

"Of course." She held out the pole with the iron head attached at the end.

Perceval took the pole and couldn't help a sad look at her before ripping the iron head off.

"Sir Perc—"

"It's mine!" He dropped the pole and took his knife from his belt then dropped it, too, hating the pain he saw overtaking Mabyn's face. "Give me the spear!"

"But—"

"Give it to me!" He secured the Spear of Destiny in his knife's leather sheath.

Out in the main chamber, Josephus stood. "Perceval!"

Sir Alan is behind you, a voice said in Perceval's mind. *He's approaching quietly.* Perceval could picture it. *He's arriving.*

Perceval spun and smashed his fist into Alan's cheek exactly where the spear had told him Alan's face would be. Alan staggered.

He'll punch high.

Perceval dodged, and with his forearm sweeping across Sir Alan's chest, he threw him into the wall, where Alan's head rocked back into the stone. He slid limply to the ground, eyes shut but still breathing.

"Ayeee!" Mabyn screamed.

Away from Josephus and the main chamber, Perceval rushed west, farther into the tunnel, opposite the way Cera would be heading with the grail.

"It's mine!" Perceval cried, drawing his sword.

Sirs Berthold and Hunald follow behind you.

Sir Deverel approached, sword at the ready. "Perceval, what is this?"

"Out of my way!" Perceval swung his sword low, and Deverel blocked it.

He'll be ready for any sword strike.

Perceval drove his shoulder into Deverel and stomped on his foot.

Deverel jerked back.

He'll swing high.

Perceval ducked under the blade and slashed across both Deverel's thighs. The knight fell to his knees.

"I'm sorry." Perceval knocked the top of Deverel's head with the pommel of his sword. Deverel's eyes closed, and he crumpled. "I believe we would have been friends."

Behind you, Berthold cuts down.

Perceval parried the blow as he turned then kicked Berthold, who fell into Sir Hunald, and the pair hit the ground. Perceval hurried the other way and turned left toward the pietà—the sculpture of the Virgin Mary cradling the dead body of Jesus—on a marble pedestal against the wall.

Sir Phelan neared, angry faced, sword drawn.

He'll attack low, high, low.

Perceval met his cut low and quickly parried the strike high. He slashed across Phelan's sword hand. Phelan screamed as his blade clattered to the ground.

He'll punch at your head.

Perceval dodged and sent his elbow across Phelan's nose then his knee into Phelan's gut. He shoved the cringing knight to the ground.

Perceval rushed toward the statue.

"Perceval!" Sir Berthold yelled around the corner behind him.

"Perceval, stop!" Josephus called.

Perceval ran on. Sir Willard walked toward him.

He's uncertain what's going on, not ready to attack.

Perceval charged hard.

Willard put out his hands. "Perceval—"

Beside the statue, Perceval threw his shoulder into Willard, driving him tumbling to the ground. Perceval sprang to his feet, got the tips of his fingers behind the statue's edges, and pulled toward him. *Clunk.* A pair of vertical cracks in the wall appeared.

He pushed the wall inches inward. It must have taken all of young Cera's strength. On the right side, a gap opened that he could almost fit into.

Behind you, high then low.

Blindly, Perceval parried Sir Willard's sword strikes before turning to the shocked knight. Perceval drove his fist into Willard's face, and Willard reeled backward.

"Perceval," Galahad called from up the tunnel, kindness in his voice, sword held low, standing before Berthold, Hunald, and Josephus.

Forgive me, Galahad. Perceval pushed the wall far enough to hurry in. Then with his shoulder against it, he pushed until it shut with a *click*, and pitch black enveloped him.

The thick wall muffled cries of Perceval's name beyond it. He'd managed to avoid killing any of the knights—but he had no time to wait and celebrate that. He sheathed his sword and, head ducked low under the ceiling as Cera had instructed, with one hand on it and one out before him, Perceval descended the twelve straight steps.

He followed the tunnel directly to the east, his fingertips sliding along the coarse wall to his left except when they touched nothing but air, gaps that Cera had said were entrances to small rooms he couldn't see into, in the darkness. Perceval said to the Lord, *Thank you for seeing me this far. Please let Cera have been as fortunate in her efforts. And thank you for the Holy Grail and the opportunity to use it. If I'm wrong and our taking it from the order displeases you, forgive me, and I beg you, forgive Cera. Her heart is true. She means only well for your people.*

Perceval's hand in front of him hit stone—the east side of the building, Cera's side. The tunnel turned left, to the north, and he hurried that way. On his left, his fingers touched the stone wall until he hit gap number one. Then he felt more wall, with nothing but black in front of him. Then came gap two. He halted and felt for the wall on his right. Perceval took three steps—and found a gap on the right. There, he set his foot onto the staircase exactly where it should have been.

Three steps at a time, Perceval ascended, arms out, until his hands hit the wall at the top. He reached to the wall on the left, near his midsection Cera had said it would be, and… *There—the recessed edges of a square.* He pressed the block in. *Clunk.* Light seeped in at a crack in the wall atop the stairs. He reached into the two recesses in that wall and pulled it inward. Yelled commands and the commotion of men in armor grew louder, but they weren't near, so Perceval slid out into the hallway.

Before him was the staircase Cera should have taken to

street level. Cera, who his heart ached for more since he'd met her, who that day began her life's great adventure. Cera, his love, who wanted *him* along with her for whatever that adventure had in store.

Perceval smiled and hustled up the stairs, around as they bent. Illuminated by bright moonlight through small windows above the church's side door, Sir Porico sat slumped at the top, eyes shut, bloodied, head against the wall, but breathing. Perceval stepped over his outstretched legs, pulled open the door, rushed out—and skidded to a stop in the dirt.

Across the grass yard, Cera was on her knees before Sir Varden, dazed and weaponless, her face bruised and bloodied. Arrows were lodged into their fallen horses. Two knights of the order lay motionless on the ground.

Cera's head tilted, exposing her neck. With both hands on his long sword, Sir Varden, stone-faced, rested his blade inches up from her shoulder to measure his next cut. He raised his sword high.

Perceval drew his sword, stepped toward Varden, and let it fly.

Varden swung...

Perceval's heart beat.

Schvt! Into Varden's skull, Perceval's blade sank. Over Cera's head, Varden's swing flew. The old knight staggered and fell.

Lord forgive me. Perceval rushed to Cera.

"I'm sorry," she said, her lip cut and right eye swollen shut, the other half-filled with blood.

Perceval dropped to his knees before her.

191

She fell into him. "He knew." Her left arm bled from a bad gash exposed by her gown's sliced sleeve. "Seeing us together, he knew something was up." She wrapped her other arm around Perceval.

"It's all right." He held her tight. *But is it all right?*

"The other two... I had to kill them. I'm sorry. I know you didn't want me to. But I couldn't stop Varden."

"It's okay," Perceval said. *But is any of what we're doing okay?* "Where is the grail?"

Perceval noticed that Sir Varden's chest did not rise and fall with even the shallowest of breaths. Cera looked behind her across the grass to her slain horse, where a brown leather satchel lay on the ground.

"This way!" came a cry from the street at the front of the church.

Perceval lifted Cera to her feet and held her up in his arms. Blood stained her gown and down her leg where it and her thigh had been slashed open. Faint horse hooves sounded beyond the church's rear.

"You have to go," Perceval said.

She clutched to him. "*We* have to."

Their actions that night suddenly felt dreadful and wrong, but Perceval's heart plunged deepest at the idea of the woman he loved not seeing her dream come true. He backed her away and shook his head. "Without horses, they'd run us down. Take the grail and go. I'll hold them off as long as I can."

"Perceval, no." Cera took his hand, and focus filled her bruised face. "Let's go."

Limping badly, she pulled him to the satchel, which she strained to reach for. Perceval picked it up and brought its strap over her head so it hung on her shoulder across her body.

"Here!" The yell came from closer, and the hooves grew louder.

Perceval turned to the church.

"Perceval!" Cera pulled his hand.

He wouldn't budge. "Together we won't make it. But you can."

"I won't leave you!"

Perceval pulled her to him and kissed her bloody lips. "You must. The better world we fight for depends on it." He held out the Spear of Destiny. "Take it."

"They'll kill you without it," she said.

"They'll kill me anyway."

"Use it. Survive and find me." Cera pushed the spear back to him, and it pressed against his chest between hers when she kissed him deeply. "You promised you'd marry me."

Perceval said nothing as she backed away, because he did not want to lie to Cera. He re-sheathed the Spear of Destiny on his hip. From her satchel, Cera pulled out the Holy Grail in one hand and a small jar with a cork stopper in the other. She bit the cork and spat it to the ground then poured the water into the grail.

"There!" A lone knight, Sir Felix, ran from the church's front, pointing. "Hurry!"

Cera tipped the grail back and chugged the water. She

stood straighter, her swollen eye opened, the other cleared of blood, and her cut lip mended. She dropped the jar to the ground, and it shattered. She returned the grail to her satchel and, her limp gone, strode to Sir Guadulfus and pulled her dagger from his chest. She grabbed her other dagger from the ground and used it to complete the slit in her gown that a knight's blade had begun at her thigh.

Cera looked at Perceval. "I love you."

"I love you," Perceval told the fiercest, most beautiful angel he could ever imagine.

She glanced at oncoming Sir Felix then called to Perceval, "Find me!" She sprinted away from the church, down the street.

Perceval pulled his sword out of lifeless Varden's skull, nodded at his poor unmoving horse who had been with him through so much, then committed himself to living his last moments for Cera. *If we are damned, Lord—if our failure to escape together is your wrath for affronting you and your divine plan—spare Cera.*

Perceval headed for Felix, who rushed at him.

Punish me as you deem just, but give Cera the chance to find her way back to your light.

Sir Felix raised his blade.

He'll swing high.

Their swords met with a reverberating *clang!*

High.

Perceval spun to meet Felix's blade again.

Low, low, then high.

Perceval parried each strike, but they came fast, and he didn't see an opening.

He'll feign a swing then thrust.

When Felix thrust, Perceval slid aside and wrapped his arm around the knight's neck. Felix struggled to get free, but Perceval's grip tightened as he gasped for air.

"I'm sorry," Perceval said, looking at fallen Sir Varden.

Sirs Phelan and Galahad rounded the church's front, swords drawn. Perceval cringed, wondering what Galahad must think of him. Three horses rounded the rear of the church, charging at Perceval, ridden by Sir Hunald, Sir Berthold, and Josephus. Perceval let go of Felix's unconscious body.

Run away!

But Perceval wouldn't. Cera needed more time without those horses after her. *And what if she's right?* Bright light shone through his dread and doom. He'd prayed for God to forgive her, but he wondered if the knights of the Order of Nolvan should have been the ones seeking the Lord's forgiveness.

Perceval headed for the three horses and readied his sword. The knights rode in the lead, furious faced, swords out.

You won't defeat them all.

So be it, Perceval thought. He slashed Berthold's mount before the knight could strike.

Duck!

Perceval did, under Hunald's sword swing. Josephus's horse rammed into Perceval, sending him flying to the grass. The other knights ran over. The first horse lay bleeding on the ground. The other two walked to Perceval, who did not see Cera anywhere. *Thank goodness.*

Galahad reached Perceval and stood before him. Phelan and Berthold went behind, surrounding Arthur's youngest knight.

"What have you done?" Josephus called from his saddle as Perceval got up. Josephus pointed his sword, incensed. "Where is the grail?"

Perceval dropped his sword. "I know not."

"Give me the spear!" Josephus demanded.

Perceval unsheathed it and held it out.

Josephus grabbed it. "Where is Cerise?"

"Long gone," Perceval said. "Embarked on a holy quest."

Schvt! A sword thrust through Perceval's back and out his stomach. Sir Phelan held it.

"Perceval!" Galahad cried.

Perceval dropped to his knees and coughed blood. Phelan, his hand red where Perceval had slashed it during his escape, pulled out his blade and readied to swing it.

Cera, Perceval spoke to her with his soul. *I'm sorry I won't be able to find you out there on the run, to help you reach Arden and face whatever peril lies on your road to Mont Tombe. I couldn't wait to see the look on your face when you finally didn't have to stand by and let another one die.*

"Wait!" Galahad yelled, getting between Phelan and Perceval.

I am sorry, Cera, that we won't get to swear before God— whatever God thinks of us—to give and have each other's love, for all time, but know that I love you always, forever.

"Stop this!" Galahad screamed.

"I'm sorry," Perceval said, making eye contact with

Galahad first then looking at the enraged eyes around him. "I'm sorry for taking Sir Varden's life." Perceval lifted his eyes skyward. "Please, God, forgive me."

Sir Berthold shoved Galahad away.

"He may forgive you," Sir Phelan said. "But I won't."

Phelan swung his blade, and air from it hit Perceval's neck the instant before the steel sliced in and through, and all went black.

11

Cool white light descended upon Roan, at its center the shape of a fit man with wings wide behind him. The fires in the ring around Roan burned lower, and the skeletons scrambled away through it, retreating from the brightness. The shirtless winged creature reached down. The black chains on Roan's wrists and ankles loosened. Roan slipped his hands free and reached back.

The creature grasped Roan's wrist, and Roan grasped his. The creature smiled—his clean-shaven youthful face framed by long blond hair—then set his gaze above into the white. Down his wings pushed, up they rose, and low the wind from his wings blew the flames of hell. The angel—for what else could he be?—beat his wings, and they flew higher.

Unless it was a trick. Roan winced as they rose. Maybe it was another vision, a fresh scenario for him to suffer.

The angel gazed down, and Roan's heart leapt. The angel and what he evoked did not feel fake. Only when he faced upward did Roan look at his empty ring of fire below and see other rings of fire, with men and women at their centers, along with enormous red mountains that the flames around him had concealed. He also saw plains without flame, where men and women marched and wandered in all directions, to who knew where.

Roan grasped the angel's wrist with his other hand. The angel glanced at Roan, and joy radiated within him. Up they went, and Roan's spirit cried, *Yes! Higher. Let us go higher! Not back down there. I've seen enough. I have suffered enough.*

Dread shot through Roan. *Have I? After everything I did, can I ever have suffered enough?*

Pure white flashed everywhere, and Roan shut his eyes. A beat of the angel's wings sent crisp air rushing. With another beat, they glided downward until Roan's bare feet touched smooth, solid ground. The angel let him go, and Roan opened his eyes. He was standing in a square gray room, dressed in a clean black tunic and gray trousers.

"I am Uriel," the angel said, wearing only a white cloth wrapped round his hips and standing even taller than Roan with a toned body and lustrous golden hair.

"Are you an angel?" Roan asked.

"I am."

"Of... of God?"

"One of his archangels."

Tears welled up. "I never truly believed."

"But now you know," Uriel said.

In the middle of the room, on the stone floor, stood a flat stone bench. The walls and ceiling were the same plain gray stone, the air totally still. Behind Roan, a small section was cut out of the floor's corner, with pale red emanating from the opening. In the corner of the room diagonally opposite, white light glowed from a matching section missing in the ceiling.

"Where are we?" Roan asked.

"A place between." Uriel motioned to the bench. After Roan sat, Uriel joined him and brought his wings together behind him. "I lifted you out of there because God has a task for you."

"For me?"

Uriel nodded.

"A woman has just stolen a holy relic she was entrusted to protect. The order of knights she stole it from will hunt her to retrieve it. Others will try to steal it from her. God doesn't want any of them to have it."

"What relic?" Roan asked.

"The Holy Grail."

"It's real?"

"It is real," Uriel said. "The grail has been protected by the Order of Nolvan since the time of Christ. Now that the knights have lost it, God has decided it is too powerful for them, or anyone, to possess. You are to destroy it."

"Who stole it?"

"The grail princess. The bearer of the holy cup in the order's test of worthiness for would-be members of their ranks. Her name is Cerise. Cera, she prefers."

"Why me?" Roan shook his head. "Why doesn't God take it himself if he's all powerful?"

"On earth, He doesn't work that way these days. I would be honored to retrieve it for Him. Completing the task would fill me with an angelic joy incomprehensible to you.

But He will not permit me to go to earth either."

"But why me? I hate God."

Roan waited for Uriel to smash him flying into the wall or cast him back into the pit through the cutout in the floor.

Uriel smiled. "Apparently, God loves you regardless."

"He sent me to hell!"

"Perhaps He could love you," Uriel said, "and wishes for that version of you to come into being."

"And stealing the Holy Grail—destroying it—will do the trick?"

"No. The task is your price for a second chance." Uriel looked at the bright cutout in the ceiling. "God would not send anyone from the light of His heaven to earth, though countless souls who love Him completely would volunteer. He would find it cruel to separate them from His warm embrace." Uriel turned to Roan. "But for one who has fallen, He offers an opportunity. Complete the task to earn a second chance to live a good life."

"But He *is* cruel," Roan said. "He took Aedre and Madeline—and my son. I held his lifeless body!"

Uriel set his hand on Roan's shoulder. "God's world for mankind is not easy."

A tear rolled down Roan's cheek. "Are they in heaven?"

Uriel withdrew his hand. "I'm not here to talk about that."

"They must be. Tell me they aren't in the pit I burned in."

"Think of your life and theirs," Uriel said, "and decide where you think they are."

"Heaven!"

"Hold to that belief." He pointed at Roan. "And think of your soul if you wish to do better."

"For my soul's sake, I'm to destroy the Holy Grail?"

Uriel nodded.

"Why me? I'll see the task done, I assure you. But why send me, of all people, to do it?"

"They called you Relentless," Uriel said.

"Yes." Roan's heart remembered how to pound strong and proud.

"That is why. This is important to God. He would not send just anyone."

A spark lit inside Roan at the chance he thought had been utterly lost. He would complete the task but not for God. Not really. Roan would do it so Aedre and Madeline could once more be proud of him.

"Where is Cerise?" Roan asked. "What does she look like? You said she just now stole the grail?"

12

Legs pumping, leather satchel containing the Holy Grail and her folded-up blue cloak strapped tight across her body, Cera ran along the hard-pressed gravel streets of Tours under abundant moonlight. Between low houses, away from the church, she went south, figuring knights of the order would expect her to head north across the bridge spanning the Loire River to put it between her and them and to get out of the city as quickly as possible. And Cera did need to go north to reach Mont Tombe and Arden, but what she needed most immediately was a horse.

People watched her pass, some with questioning faces. Men yelled behind her—she skidded to a stop. It had to be the order. Cera couldn't make out the words. She didn't hear the clang of swords striking in battle. *Perceval, get yourself out of there...*

She turned west toward the tall basilica. Two horses stood tied outside an inn.

"Whose are these?" Cera asked the filthy man sitting slumped beside them.

He shrugged. If a lord owned one, she'd take it in a

heartbeat. But if their owner relied on the animal to earn their living, taking it could mean relegating them to the poor situation Cera aimed to help people escape from. Unable to spare the seconds to go in and ask, she ran on.

The basilica grew larger before her. Cera felt for her knife on her leg and spotted the other through her gown's cut slit, which made running easier, but she'd still need to find something else to wear. They would look for her at the basilica, she decided, and opted to go south again instead.

Horses galloped in the distance. "This way!" Sir Phelan yelled, his voice unmistakable, though Cera could not see him. "You two, that way! And you two, ride east."

With houses left and right and no horses to take, Cera headed for the city wall. She had to get farther from the knights. *Perceval, what happened to you back there? Are you running these same streets, or are you on a horse, already outside the city?*

"A woman dressed in white!" Phelan called out from around the corner behind her. "Have you seen a woman in white?"

Cera wouldn't make the wall. And if she did, even with a horse, they'd be close on her tail. Every house had smoke rising from its roof. The one two down on her left had its windows closed and front door cracked open. She rushed that way at the young boy who came out. Cera grabbed him, went in, and quietly shut the door behind them.

With one hand around him and one covering his mouth, Cera knelt with her back to the door. Looking at his shocked mother and young sister—presumably—at the table, Cera raised a finger to her lips to ask for their silence. Hooves hit the street hard outside.

"Cerise!" Phelan cried. "Where are you?" The hooves faded.

"He's after me," Cera said softly. "He'll kill me." She uncovered the boy's mouth an inch and, when he didn't scream, let him go.

He ran to his mother. Behind her, a cross hung on the wall.

In the corner of the room, a man lying on the ground strained, lifting his head to see her. "Who are you?"

Not a princess, Cera realized. *Not to these people.* And she didn't even consider herself a member of the Order of Nolvan any longer.

"A woman set on doing what good I can," she said. "If I can escape from those men."

The man in the corner grimaced, getting himself up onto his elbows. "And what good is it that you aim to do?"

"The kind they never would." Cera heard yelling outside but nothing near. She stood. "What ails you, sir?"

"His back," his wife said. "He's a blacksmith. He wrenched it a couple years ago. Now he works his forge all day through the pain."

"It's fine," he said.

His wife raised an eyebrow. "You can see it isn't. He lies flat on the ground here because the bed makes it worse."

"Let me help you." Cera stepped toward him.

His wife put out her hand. "Are you a witch? What's in your bag?"

"I'm not a witch. I have—" Cera wanted to explain, in

glorious detail, all about the wondrous relic she carried, but blurting it out seemed risky. "I believe our Lord would rather see you well than suffering all day while you work, all evening when you should be enjoying time with your family, and at night instead of sleeping peacefully."

"I wish I could believe that," his wife said.

Cera set her hand on her shoulder. "Let me show you the truth of it. Could I have some water?"

The boy slipped out of his mother's grasp, climbed onto a chair at the table, and filled a low cup with water from a jug. He brought it over.

"Thank you." Cera smiled to him and took it, then she went to his father and knelt.

"What will you do?" his wife asked.

Cera unlatched her satchel and from it brought out the smooth silver grail. "Merely share God's gift." She poured the water into the grail and held it out.

Slowly the man took it and examined it. "What is this?"

Again, Cera wanted to explain but found herself holding back. "Please, drink, and you will see."

He glanced at his wife.

"It's water," she said. "What's the worst that could happen?"

He grimaced, turning himself to the side to balance on one arm. He looked at Cera, who smiled. He brought the Holy Grail to his lips and tilted it.

His eyes widened, and he tipped the grail farther, finishing the water. He breathed deeply and held the grail before him. "My God."

He sat straight then stood, twisting from side to side, smiling.

His wife gasped. "Herbertus…" She crossed herself.

"No pain." Herbertus hopped into the air and landed. "No pain at all. What is this?"

Cera rose and reached for the grail.

"Who are you?" he asked. "Are you an angel?"

"My name is Cera." She grasped the grail, and he let it go. Cera returned it to her satchel, which she latched closed. "I am a woman set on sharing this gift from God with those in need." She pointed outside. "Those men are after me and would kill me if they caught me. May I stay here while they spread out searching for me? I'll be gone before morning."

"It would be our honor," Herbertus said.

"Thank you."

"My name is Faregildis." The woman held her children close. "This is our son, Hugo, and our daughter, Frotlina."

"Nice to meet you all."

"Can *I* see it?" Frotlina asked.

"It's not a toy," her mother said.

"It's fine." Cera unlatched her satchel and crouched. "Just for a second, okay?" Cera handed her the grail, and Frotlina held it, smiling, while her brother looked on.

"Those men after you," her father said. "Who are they? What do they want with you?"

"The grail," his wife said. "I've heard stories about it but never really believed them."

"The grail is true." Smiling, Cera reached to Frotlina, and she gave it back. "The men after me are knights. I expect most will ride out from Tours in search of me, and they'll leave a handful here in case I remain. The injured, most likely."

"Injured?" Herbertus asked.

"In my escape," Cera said, wondering where Perceval fit into the scenario she'd laid out. She swallowed hard, praying he fit into it somewhere.

"What if they come here?" Faregildis asked. "Looking for you."

"I'll keep watch." Cera pulled her dagger off her right leg and twirled it in her hand. "No need to worry."

Faregildis glanced at her husband.

He shrugged, twisting. "I'll give you refuge from your pursuers and would give you more if you asked for it."

"Thank you." Cera went to the table, spun a chair around from it, and sat facing the front door, with her dagger in her lap.

———————————

Outside, horses occasionally rode by, but Cera didn't know if they belonged to knights of the order. She heard commands yelled from afar. They sounded like Sir Phelan most often, the third knight ever to drink from the Holy Grail.

Cera decided waiting until near dawn made sense, to let the riders searching beyond Tours get farther away and those in the city grow wearier, either from injuries Perceval inflicted or merely at the lateness of the hour. Cera said a prayer, asking the Lord to see to Sir Guadulfus's and Sir

Menendo's souls. While Cera had been ready to kill to ensure her escape with the grail and had not hesitated when it became necessary outside the church, she didn't enjoy thinking back on it. She'd known those two misguided but not evil knights her whole life.

Early in her vigil, Herbertus lit a candle and pointed at the spot where it would burn to, halfway down, an hour before dawn. His wife asked how he could be so precise, but he waved his hand and told Cera to ignore her. He was sure.

Other than that, the two seemed nearly giddy with each other before going to sleep, his back free from pain. They offered Cera food, but she declined, having drunk from the grail before running from the church. Herbertus and Faregildis asked more questions about Cera and the grail, but she didn't reveal anything else. She'd always imagined herself wielding the Holy Grail like a beacon, proclaiming it as proof of God's love on earth for all to see and share. But in that house, Cera considered what would happen if she actually did that. The family seemed like good people, no threat to her or the grail, but she didn't know who they would tell and what effect that would have on Cera if she went on and on about it. Cera recalled her failure before Sir Varden. She'd defeated two knights of the order, but only Perceval had saved her from dying before helping a single person with the grail.

The family had already seen the relic's power. Cera deemed that enough information for them. She waited with her cloak around her, watching the door and worrying about Perceval as they slept. *Did he suffer a horrible fate at the hands of the order?* She shivered and shook her head, driving the notion away. *Of course not. Not Perceval.*

Cera wondered if he waited nearby outside the city or was riding for Mont Tombe already. If she didn't run into him around Tours, she'd look for him in the towns along the way, but if he'd taken a circuitous route to throw off pursuers, she realized she might not see him for a while. She smiled anyway, thinking of them together at Arden's bedside after he drank from the grail and was healed and well. Then she thought of her and Perceval making their way west along Francia's northern coast, sharing the gift of the grail with all who needed it.

When the candle had burned halfway to where Herbertus had pointed, and Cera felt the night's long hours starting to catch up to her, her mind wandered to visions of her and Perceval uplifting the ill and the hungry in Paris. She imagined, their day's work done, time alone with Perceval, her in his arms and him in hers, together as man and wife. There she lingered with Perceval, her heavy eyes sliding shut...

She shook her head, snapping out of it. Like those nights with Perceval, sleep had to wait. While a drink from the grail nourished and healed the body and could provide a burst of energy, the grail could not replace sleep. The human mind simply needed rest.

Someone knocked softly on the door. Cera sprang to her feet and froze. Knights of the order would not be so quiet.

Behind her, Hugo and Faregildis slept in their bed and the children slept on the other side of the room. A white parchment slid under the door. Cera went and grabbed it. No seal closed the single folded piece.

Cera,

Arden has two days. By this time Wednesday, if you have not reached him, he will have taken his last breath.

Hurry!

Nimue

Cera cracked open the door and saw blue droplets in the air. She opened the door wider and watched them shrink and fade to nothing. Cera shut the door and reread the Lady of the Lake's letter, which didn't take long.

Two days... how does she know? And why didn't she stay to deliver the message herself?

Faregildis sat up in bed.

"I have to go," Cera said quietly, walking to the candle. Two days meant riding straight through to cover the distance to Mont Tombe in half the time it had taken them to reach Tours.

Faregildis came over.

Cera set the corner of the letter on fire and held it while it burned.

"Where will you go?" Faregildis asked.

"To save a young man."

"A friend?" she asked. "A husband?"

Cera shook her head. "I know him only as I saw him the once, lying in bed, weak and dying."

"Is he a nobleman? Why him, of all people?"

"Perhaps because he's not noble and I know so little about him. Perhaps that is why my heart yearns to save him. For so long, I've been idle while people died all around me. I *can't* know he died too. His mother agonized seeing him suffer. I don't know her, either, but I can't bear to think of her grief if I don't save her son. And I *can* save him. Finally, I can save someone." Cera stared at the half-consumed parchment. "Then so many more."

"You are an angel," Faregildis said.

"No. I'm just doing what should be done. And it seems I have an ally in my efforts." Cera dropped the remaining edge of the letter, and it burned out.

Herbertus awoke and came over. He rubbed his eyes and looked at the candle. "You're early. The candle is not wrong."

"Close enough," Cera said. "Thank you both for letting me hide here."

"Thank *you*," Herbertus said. "I'd tried everything, but my back ached every day I worked and screamed at me all night. You've given me a peace I gave up on ever having again."

Cera smiled. "I'm glad I could."

"Is there anything else we can give you?" Faregildis asked. "Some food for your journey?"

"No, but thank you."

"Where are you headed?" Herbertus asked.

Faregildis put her arm on his. "She needn't say."

He nodded.

"God be with you both," Cera said.

"And with you," he said.

Cera went to the door. Dagger in hand, she pulled it open and peeked out into the quiet street the moon still lent some light to. She looked left and right and saw no people—knights of the order or otherwise. Cera turned around, brought her cloak's hood over her head, and nodded to Faregildis and Herbertus, who waved as she left. Cera softly shut the door.

The air felt cool but not cold, and with her cloak wrapped close, she was comfortable and better concealed by the blue than by her gown's bright white. Cera walked east, scanning all around for any sign of knights. Houses remained quiet, their windows shut. Behind her, no one followed.

She envisioned the two-day journey to Mont Tombe, riding through the night, having to change horses along the way rather than wait and lose time while they rested. She figured that trading her own horse plus the gold in her satchel would be enough to pay for it. It had to be.

White tunic—far ahead. Cera ducked behind a house and peered around. It might have been a knight. Cera didn't want to go that way, anyway.

She darted to the house across the street, crept around it, and continued north past the next house. Staring down the street from there, she saw no knights' white tunics—no anyone. Time would be tight to reach Arden. Nimue had gotten word to Cera without much time to spare. *And why did she?* After they'd rolled around in the grass by the river in Würzburg, Nimue had told Cera, "I know what I need to know when I need to know it." *Does she know of Arden's importance to me?*

Cera headed right, to the east, until reaching the main north–south street. She crouched low, close to the wall of the shoe shop on the corner. There was no one to the south. To the north were two white tunics and horses. Cera made out a red cross on one of the knights. They guarded the bridge she had to cross, and one of their horses would suit her needs perfectly.

But she skipped the main street and went back and around the building the other way. In between houses, Cera made her way north, unable to see the knights, who likewise would be unable to see her.

At the last home before the street running east toward the bridge, she squatted. As slightly as she could, Cera peeked out. At the edge of the bridge, Sir Radulfus stood, fingers tapping on the pommel of his sword handle, looking into the city. Sir Deverel sat against a fence post, legs extended, gazing outward, blood on the bottom of his tunic. Their horses were tied nearby. Cera checked in the other direction, away from the bridge—no one.

If she could take care of Radulfus and Deverel quietly, she could ride away without further fuss. That would mean killing them, which wouldn't have been her first choice, but Cera had to be sure to escape and had already killed two knights leaving the church.

She lowered her hood, switched her dagger to her left hand, and from the ground, grabbed a stone half the size of her fist in her right. Pushing open her cloak, Cera moved away from the building and threw the stone past the knights onto the bridge.

Crack! It landed and clattered. Both shot their attention that way.

Cera ran for Sir Radulfus's back.

He pointed toward the stone down the bridge. "There."

Cera closed in. Deverel peered where his companion pointed, but he didn't stand. Cera wrapped her arm around Radulfus and slid the dagger in her other hand across his throat.

Dropping him, she rushed to Sir Deverel, who yelled, "Phelan!" just before Cera stabbed her blade into his gut.

He slumped to the side. "Cera…"

"Perceval!" Cera withdrew her knife. "What happened to Perceval?"

Deverel whispered, "Dead."

Cera gasped and backed away.

Sir Phelan rode furiously up the street toward them.

Cera swallowed hard. "Who?" It was supposed to be her and Perceval together.

Deverel, whose thighs had been slashed—likely the reason he hadn't stood—looked at Phelan half a block away.

Phelan drew his sword in a bandage-wrapped hand. "Traitor!"

Cera drew her other dagger and hurled it at his horse's

chest. It sliced in, the horse reared, and Phelan tumbled off.

The knight got to his feet. "You Judas!"

"What did you do to Perceval?"

Phelan grinned, walking to her. "I ran my sword through him then cut off his traitorous head."

"No!" Cera cried. "Bastard!"

"Before the end, he whined about how you tricked him into your thieving plot. How you lured him into your bed of sin."

"He did not!" Cera screamed.

"Give me the grail," said Phelan, "and I will make your end even more swift."

Cera set her dagger at the ready. "Come and take it!"

He charged, and she half turned, bouncing on the balls of her feet, squatting slightly. Phelan raised his sword high. Cera jab stepped as if she would go at him. He cut downward, but she dodged and slashed his passing shoulder.

"Agh!" he screamed.

Cera twirled her knife. He thrust his sword, and she parried with her shorter dagger, angling her body to help. Phelan swung high, and she parried. He went low, and she blocked him.

He slashed over her, and rising from her duck, Cera stabbed at his gut. He knocked her aside, her dagger sliding harmlessly across his chain mail.

But she hooked out her foot, catching his leg as she flew away. Phelan fell to the ground. Cera landed and jumped to her feet. Pouncing atop him, she avoided a wild swing of his blade and slashed that wrist.

He dropped his sword and shoved her off with both hands. Phelan scrambled to his feet, but as he reached for his sword, Cera threw herself at him, tackling him back to the ground beneath her. She plunged her dagger into his neck.

He gagged and strained, then his struggle lessened.

"For Perceval." She held the knife firm.

Phelan's head rolled aside, and his body went limp. Cera took a deep breath then scanned the streets. No one else was coming. She got off Sir Phelan, wiped her blade on her gown, and sheathed it.

Phelan's wounded horse had calmed enough for Cera to approach.

"Shh…" She set her hand on his side. "I'm sorry about that." She pulled her dagger from his chest. "And that."

The animal seemed relieved.

Cera hurried back up the street, to Sir Deverel, who'd gone pale and held his stabbed stomach tight.

Cera asked him, "Did Phelan kill Perceval?"

"Y… yes," Deverel managed.

She crouched to the knight she'd ridden with for a decade, protecting God's holy relics. "Did Perceval say those things before he died?"

"No." Deverel shook his head. "He said you were on a… a holy quest. He asked forgiveness for killing Sir Varden. I wasn't there. Galahad told me."

"Where'd the rest go?"

"They rode out from Tours in all directions, searching for you."

"How about you?" Cera asked. "If I let you drink from

the grail so you don't die here, would you pursue me?"

Deverel met her gaze firmly. "I would. I swore an oath to Josephus, to the Order of Nolvan, and to God to protect the relics, the grail above all."

"I swore no oath," Cera said. "Maybe everyone assumed I did. Or maybe they figured it didn't matter whether I had or not." She stood. "I don't take pleasure in leaving you like this, but I will not knowingly set another foe against me."

He nodded. "I understand, Princess."

"You're a good knight, Sir Deverel." Cera sheathed her second dagger. "You were always kind to me. Thank you for that."

"You deserved kindness," he said.

Cera nodded then went to his horse—the darker of the two—untied it, and mounted it. She grabbed the reins and called to Deverel, "Rest in peace." Cera clicked her tongue and started north across the bridge.

They picked up speed and broke into a hard ride, a pace that Cera intended to continue until she'd put some distance between her and Tours. Then they'd push on as fast as her horse could manage over the long journey, until short breaks wouldn't cut it. When he was utterly spent, she'd find a new horse to keep going.

Cera asked God, *Please give me two good days of riding. If the Order of Nolvan is to find me, and I have to fight them off, let it be later. Give me safe passage now, and I will reach Arden with the Holy Grail. I will not fail!*

As Cera left Tours, her eyes watered, and she prayed for poor Perceval's immortal soul.

13

The bartender set a mug of ale on the table. "Here ya go," he said in Frankish.

Roan nodded, though he hadn't remembered ordering it. The bartender grunted and walked away. Roan didn't remember the table he sat at, the tavern it was situated in the rear of, or the people at the other tables talking, drinking, and eating.

He remembered Uriel and gruesomely hot hell. Roan's hand shot to his neck and felt a raised scar where it had been slit. Mercifully, the wound didn't gush with blood.

Roan wore his old black tunic, coal-gray trousers, and boots, which were free of the cuts from Perceval's sword. *Gah, Perceval...*

Beneath Roan's tunic, his two chains once again hung to his chest, one for each lost wife. His long sword and knife were sheathed on his hip. Roan ran his fingers along the tabletop. It felt real. He rotated his right shoulder—tight as ever. Uriel had actually sent Roan back.

Roan closed his eyes and could feel the roaring oven of hell, so he opened them to the crowd before him. The people merrily chitchatted away while below them, Satan and his devils were real, and above them God reigned and at least the one angel dwelled—but of course, there were surely more. Madeline had been right about it all. *Sweet Madeline.*

Uriel had said he'd send Roan to Francia, meaning the Christians in the tavern purported to believe in those divine things. Yet Roan *knew*. He knew the horror of it all.

Beyond the windows at the opposite side of the room, the light was dim. That plus the liveliness around him meant it was nighttime, likely soon after sunset. Roan scanned the crowd for a dirty-blond woman in white, with a royal blue cloak and leather satchel. He did not see Cerise.

Cera. Uriel had mentioned that she'd be going by that name.

Roan lifted his mug of ale but took only a sip. She would come to the tavern, Uriel had explained. And when she did, Roan's task was to take the grail and see it destroyed. After that... he set the mug down. After that, he'd be alone in the miserable world again.

But Roan understood he could not do as he had before. Throughout his life, Roan had never believed that Woden, or any of the gods, cared about him or anyone. He couldn't imagine what difference people's pitiful animal sacrifices to deities would make. Thunor, with his axe and thunderbolts, was fun to imagine, but there was no reason he, or any gods, would have anything to do with Roan's little life.

Roan sipped his ale and wondered where his gods fit in with the hell that had tormented him for three years. He shuddered. It felt like more time—longer than any epoch of his life—since Roan had been in a place like the tavern and not surrounded by ceaseless fire. He could not go back there, he vowed. However cruelly earth treated him, Roan could not fall on earth, damning himself again to that even worse pit.

Except Perceval. Roan clenched his fist. Roan would find him and would have vengeance. *Damn the cost.*

The tavern door opened. *Cera.* The tall, gorgeous young woman in a bloodstained white gown and blue cloak appeared weary—in her eyes and all over—when she entered. The strap of her satchel, Roan's target, crossed her thin body.

She called out, "Who has a fresh horse they will sell me?"

Conversations slowed and stopped, and attention turned to her.

"I've no time to spare." Cera held out a handful of gold coins. "I must ride immediately, and you may also keep my horse, a fine one but spent from a long day's travel."

A man at a nearby table raised his mug her way. "I have a good horse."

Another got up from a table. "No, no. Mine is a finer mount."

Roan stood. Cera would never ride from here. Roan headed around the table while a handful of men approached her, going on about the horses they could offer and asking if she might want to discuss it over a drink—their treat.

"Just the horse!" She raised a finger. "And I only need one."

The persistent men surrounded her, and Roan neared. He reached for his knife but stopped, wondering how far he could go to take the grail from her. Roan would not delay in his task—that he knew for certain. He pushed two smaller men aside to stand before Cera.

"Hey!" one shouted.

Roan glared at him.

"All right, all right."

"You have a horse?" Cera put her hands on her hips. "Or did you force your way to the front to brood and glare before me?"

"I have a horse," Roan said.

"If it's nearby and ready to ride so I can be on my way, I'll take it."

"He's fit and rested," Roan said. "He'll serve you well."

Cera motioned to the door. "Take me to him."

Another man came forward. "I was first!"

Roan drew his knife, clenched his teeth, and readied to plunge it into the man's gut… but pointed it at him instead. "First and still too slow." Roan shoved him stumbling away, put away his knife, and pulled open the door.

Cera walked out into the fleeting light. "Is it far?"

"No." Roan pointed down the street he'd never been on in a town he couldn't identify. "This way."

Cera took two steps, and Roan grabbed her arm. She turned to him—so pretty, but that wouldn't help her now.

"I'll take the satchel," Roan said.

"You will not!" She pulled her arm away, but he gripped it firmly.

"You shouldn't have the grail," Roan said. "I've been sent to take it." She pulled her arm, and he lurched forward but held tight and regained his balance. "Give it here, and be on your way. I don't want to hurt you."

"Well…" Cera glanced at his hand on her arm. "You are."

Roan relaxed his grip slightly. "Give me the grail *now*."

"And you'll let me go?"

"I will."

"Fine." With her free right hand, Cera reached beneath her cloak for the satchel, turning herself a little while she did. She reached lower then threw her hand out at Roan, dagger edge slashing his forearm.

"Gha!" Roan let her go when she slashed at it again. He smashed his fist across her face, and she staggered backward, red dripping from her nose.

Roan stepped to her. "Give me—"

Cera lunged, thrusting her knife, and he barely dodged it. She lunged again, and Roan's cut arm screamed in pain when he deflected her attack with it. He backed up and blocked out the pain, which paled compared to what he'd endured in hell and, before that, on earth. He drew his knife. Cera formed a small smile.

Roan wouldn't kill her, but he would have the grail. They stepped toward each other, stabbing their knives downward.

They blocked the attacks then retreated. Patrons came out from the tavern to watch.

Roan and Cera thrust their knives and dodged. He faked a left jab, she started to avoid it, and he slashed that way— she shifted her body and sliced her blade across his side. She had anticipated his fake.

Cera moved beyond his reach, and her smile widened. "The Order of Nolvan will never get it back, however many thugs they hire to come after me."

Roan held his newest wound then brought his bloody hand up to see. "I'm not from any order." The pain dulled when he recalled the grisly gashes the army of the dead had inflicted, from his feet to the tip of his head, while he marched through their lines after Aedre.

Cera squinted. "Then who are you?"

"Roan." He licked his bloody fingers.

Cera's smile vanished.

Roan charged. Bravely—foolishly—Cera set her feet firm. He raised his knife high and cut at her shoulder. She dropped low while blocking, grabbed his arm, rolled, and kicked him away. Roan's back hit the ground, and she pounced on him. He stabbed, but Cera blocked and shoved him down with stunning strength.

Cera stabbed, but Roan blocked and threw her off. He got to his feet as she got to hers, and again, he charged. She slid aside, but he caught her, pulled her close, and sank his knife into her stomach… as her blade found home in his. The onlookers gasped. Cera twisted her knife, tearing Roan's insides.

Roan didn't turn his knife in her. He should have. In any other fight of his life, he would have, to worsen the damage, but Roan feared it would kill her, and he just didn't know what would become of his soul if he did.

Cera gritted her teeth. "Go to hell."

Roan gritted his. "Once is enough."

Her free hand moved low. Roan pushed himself away from her, but she held him tight. He punched her chin. Her head rocked back, and as she let him go, a second dagger slashed across his neck. Blood sprayed as Roan fell.

He held the gushing wound with both hands. She dropped to her knees, bleeding badly from her stomach and nose. Roan's head felt heavy, his eyes heavier. His blood puddled around him.

Cera unlatched her satchel and pulled forth a silver goblet. Roan reached for the grail but couldn't keep his eyes open. They shut, his arm dropped, he fell to the side, and everything went silent and dark.

14

Cera spat the cork to the grass and poured the small jar of water into the grail. On the ground between her and the tavern, Roan's eyes had closed, and his breathing had stopped. She sipped the water and, in the last of dusk's light, watched him lie motionless while she drank the rest. The cool sensation at her core rose and spread, and Cera's nose no longer hurt. She wiped the blood beneath it with her sleeve and checked her side under her tattered gown. The knife wound had healed, and Cera breathed deeply with no pain. *Thank you, Lord.*

Years had clearly worn Roan but hadn't sapped his strength in combat. If Perceval hadn't told her that the Roan he'd fought had been killed in Dover, she would have guessed the dead man before her to be the same Saxon, based on the description Perceval had given.

Cera wanted to shut her eyes and keep them shut, to sleep after the night awake in Tours and the day's riding. But Arden needed her, and the town had proven dangerous. She certainly couldn't count on it to be safe after that encounter.

She turned to the crowd of murmuring onlookers. "Someone sell me a horse *now*."

———————————

Cera rode northwest for Laval as fast as possible in the darkness. The horse she'd purchased did well in the low light. During the day, she'd traveled more than a third of the way to Mont Tombe. If she covered half that distance overnight and reached Laval near daybreak, she'd be in good shape to make it to Arden in time, arriving there the following evening, assuming Nimue's letter was accurate. Cera couldn't reason why the order would expect her to return to Mont Tombe, so she figured Laval, on the road there, would pose no greater danger than any other town.

It heartened Cera to know that Arden lived as recently as when she'd received Nimue's letter. It drove her onward, in fact. While God's grail had mended her body fully, Cera's mind still craved sleep, but she would not rest until Arden rose from his bed, healed and full of life.

As they gingerly navigated the path, Cera wondered how Nimue had found her. *Why did Nimue find me? What interest does she have in my mission? And most basically, what is Nimue?*

She was not an angel. Nimue had supported Arthur, who was, indeed, a Christian king, and she'd been a friend to Cera's mother and Josephus. But Cera had heard stories of the Lady of the Lake giving gifts and counsel to pagans before the birth of Christ and after. And there was no angel, arch- or otherwise, named Nimue in anything Cera had read. There were the archangels Raphael—the healer—and Gabriel, who'd revealed to the Virgin Mary that she would conceive and become the mother of Jesus. The archangel Michael led God's armies against Satan, and Uriel was the archangel of repentance. No Nimue among them. She seemed of this earth, though, most surely, not human.

And if Nimue cares for Arden, why doesn't she ask me for the grail to take to him? Cera would have trusted her and only her with it… probably. It would have been quite a risk. But Nimue had done no more than write a letter with a deadline.

The night was quiet, save for Cera and her horse. She kept vigilant for any sudden attack from members of the order lying in wait. She watched, too, for a Saxon in black— Roan—despite knowing that *he* would not actually attack. Her dagger had slit his throat. She'd seen him die.

"Once is enough," he'd said about hell. Perceval had described his Roan as wild, but the warrior Cera had encountered was crazy if he really believed he'd been to hell and back.

How did he know I had the grail?

If the family from Tours had told him, Roan would have been hard-pressed to get ahead of her, as fast as she rode. Cera decided it must have been a member of the order who'd sent him, hired as a mercenary, despite what Roan claimed.

In the darkness, her thoughts drifted to Perceval. She frowned and sniffled but did not weep, knowing it wouldn't do any good. Her tears would not bring him back or save her from being more alone than ever.

Was Perceval right? Could stealing the Holy Grail have been wrong and my convincing him to help tragically worse, and now I'm suffering the grim consequences?

Cera firmed herself, and as the night wore on, though she could not keep those worries from attacking the armor of her heart's resolve, that armor would not be nicked or blemished.

Half an hour after sunrise, Cera neared Laval. They'd made good time, so with the Mayenne River running calmly on her left, she let her horse walk. Cera's back had grown sore after the effects of the grail wore off, and her eyes grew ever heavier. She shut them and listened to the smooth sound of the water as her horse's consistent gait brought them into town.

Cera wondered if maybe she should sleep, if she could find a place and someone to wake her in an hour. She could spare that much time and likely make up the hour able to ride harder, more alert after the rest. The plan sounded good, and the river was so very calm...

Cera jerked, and her eyes shot open. She needed to find that safe place and a fresh horse first. No smoke rose from the chimneys of the first houses. No one was out at the early hour... except a woman down the street in dirty beige.

"It's you!" She started quickly toward Cera. "It's really you!"

Cera sat straight and halted.

"It is you!" The woman beamed at Cera. "I dreamt of you."

"You dreamt of me?"

"Last night, of a woman in white, wearing a blue cloak, riding to town with a miracle for my Lantsi, my daughter."

"And you came out this morning to see if I really was riding into town?"

"Praise God, yes! I woke in a fright, for the dream seemed real as we are talking now. I pray every day for my Lantsi, and always before bed, and I never have dreams like that. I had to come out and see, and here you are!"

Cera checked behind herself for knights in hiding. "It's pretty convenient."

The woman frowned. "Convenient?"

Cera scanned the town for white tunics with red crosses—for anyone peeking out from alleyways between homes and shops. "The timing, I mean."

"My daughter suffers," the woman said. "It's the leprosy on her face and arms. It's awful for her."

Cera looked the woman in the eye and saw pain—pain that she could cure. "I'm sorry."

The woman's face lit up. "What is it you bring?"

Cera held the satchel against her side. "It's here."

"Hm. Well…" The woman started down the street. "Come on!"

Cera rode behind her. "I have only a few minutes to spare, but I do think I can help her."

"Thank God!"

So Cera would not sleep in the town but instead would use the time for the afflicted girl. Her mind sharpened, and she felt more awake than she had in hours. "Is it far?"

"No." The woman pointed at a side street. "Just here."

"Is there a livery I might visit after? My horse needs to be fed and watered."

"Yes, of course." She pointed ahead on the main street. "That way. You won't miss it."

Down the woman's street, at the end of the block, Cera dismounted and tied her horse to the post.

The woman looked Cera over and squinted. "Is that blood?"

Her gown was a mess. "It is."

"Are you okay? That wasn't in my dream."

"I'm fine."

She shrugged then opened the door, and Cera followed her inside. The room was neat and sparsely decorated, with two beds. No one else was at home.

"They must be out." The woman closed the door. "My husband likes to take her with him to get water before the town wakes. When they see her, some are kind and pretend not to notice, but most—the faces they make, the snickering... and no one will go near her. It's terrible."

What she said made sense, but Cera didn't like standing still in the home, doing nothing, not even getting real rest. Every second felt like Arden moving a minute closer to his end. She needed to get back on the road.

"Will they be home soon?" Cera asked.

"Yes!" The woman motioned to a chair at their table. "Here, have a seat."

Cera did, unable to find any young girls' toys strewn about the place. "How old is she?"

"Hm?"

"How old is your daughter?"

"Ah, um, eight."

Cera stood. "No toys? No dolls or the like?"

"Oh." The woman furrowed her brow. "She's not the type. Takes after her father."

Cera pointed at her. "Swear to me your story is true. If it is, your daughter's skin will be healed, and she will be a leper no more. If not—"

The woman looked at the ground.

"Is this a trap?"

"He made me!" Her eyes shifted to Cera. "I do have a daughter. She's at my house with my husband, but she is no leper. A wizard came to us an hour ago and said he would turn her *into* a leper if I didn't bring you here."

"A wizard?"

"Old. He walked with a tall staff. Fire blazed atop it."

"Merlin!"

The house's door swung open. A stern-faced soldier—Cera assumed he had not earned the noble title of *knight*—in a gray tunic and mail armor stepped in with more of his kind following.

Cera drew a dagger and sprinted at the soldier. He froze, and the three behind him had to halt. Cera would not be trapped in that house.

He reached for his sheathed sword. Cera threw her shoulder into him, and he stumbled backward out of the house, into the men behind him. The lead soldier fell beneath Cera. She stabbed into his neck, and blood poured.

A soldier's boot into Cera's ribs sent her rolling, but she sprang to her feet.

"Stop," a strong voice boomed from behind the three remaining soldiers, who parted. The old wizard—the tallest, widest of frame, and leanest of the lot—came forward. His dark-green robe had its hood down, bunched at his neck. Floating an inch off the top his long wooden staff, a small ball of orange-black fire rolled and flared.

"Fiend!" Cera screamed. "Murderer!"

In the middle of his wrinkled face, he curled the corners of his thin lips. "Give me the grail, princess, and you will not suffer the same fate as your mother."

"You will never have it," Cera said. "I will not let you. God would *never* let you."

Merlin smiled. "God does not care."

Cera stepped fast and hurled her dagger at his chest. He swiveled his staff, and the blade's tip stuck straight in the wood.

Merlin pulled it out. "God didn't care when I helped King Alaric siege Rome and starve its people, before we sacked the eternal city, one hundred and seventeen years ago. Centuries before, God was not moved to do *anything* to ease the suffering of the thousands who perished each day over the years I watched in horror as Marcus Aurelius Antoninus's plague killed millions.

"I wondered, I really did, if God would stop me from ending good King Arthur's life. We were alone, the king and I, when I startled him with a huge fireball blazing at the center of his room then wrapped my arm around his neck and pulled it tight. Would someone rush in? Would an angel descend from heaven to stop me? Would an angel finally show interest in this world again? Or might God Himself lift a finger to cause some other miracle to save Arthur? So luminous was he, so celebrated... but then I laughed at myself, after all my years, to have wasted even the short moments on such fantastical hopes when Arthur's struggling ended, and his body relaxed, limp and lifeless." Merlin handed the knife to the soldier on his left. "Bring me God's grail."

The soldier flung the dagger at Cera's face. She turned, and it sliced her cheek. The three soldiers drew their swords and charged. She drew her other dagger and ran backward, around to the house's side and into the alley between it and the next house, but no farther. Cera wouldn't flee from the opportunity to put an end to her mother's murderer.

The first soldier rounded the corner, and Cera lunged, plunging her knife into his gut before he knew what hit him. The soldier behind him thrust his sword at her but missed. Cera twisted her knife in the soldier she held then kicked him away. In the limited space between buildings, the third soldier slashed his blade across Cera's left arm on his way past her.

Cera yelled in pain but steadied herself between the two soldiers in the alley. She faked at the one in front of her. He swung his sword, and she dropped and rolled into the legs of the soldier behind her. He fell, and she stabbed at his neck, but his arm blocked her. Cera stabbed, and he blocked, and she had to roll past him to avoid a sword thrust from the other soldier.

Cera stood. *Schvt*—across her ankle, from the ground,

the soldier slashed his sword. "Agh!" Cera dropped to a knee, holding the wound.

Merlin appeared behind both soldiers then stepped between them and tilted his staff, and the churning fire at the top, toward Cera. "You will suffer as your mother did after all."

The fire pulsed and burst, and Cera whipped her cloak over her. Warmth built. Stinking and rotten, it beat down. Beads of sweat sprouted on her forehead and everywhere, soaking into her gown. She pictured flame igniting her beautiful mother's clothes and hair and skin. Heat poured onto Cera, and she saw her mother charred and burned, blackened beyond recognition.

But Cera opened her eyes to flesh that wasn't burning. The cloak protected her, as Nimue had promised.

The heat died, and Cera limped backward, favoring her sliced ankle. She opened the cloak to scowling Merlin. Behind her, past another pair of houses, the alley opened to the street, but Cera couldn't move fast and didn't have time to drink from the grail to heal. If Perceval were there, this would be nothing. Together, they would have taken care of the despicable soldiers and killed wicked Merlin. *Poor, good Perceval.*

"No matter," Merlin said. "You'll die by the sword, then."

His two soldiers hurried past him at Cera. She kept limping backward, but it hurt so much. She wouldn't get far. She had to separate the soldiers as best she could.

Cera leapt feetfirst off her good leg, kicking the lead attacker, sending him stumbling into Merlin as she landed on her side, her ankle throbbing.

She got up and mostly hopped toward the other soldier. He swung, but she twisted her hips to dodge. Cera thrust at him, but he moved aside and swept his arm across her, throwing her hard into the wall of the house behind her. He raised his sword but flinched when it hit the house behind him. She lunged off the wall and stabbed straight into his neck, leaning on him for support.

He choked as blood ran. Holding him, Cera turned toward the last enraged soldier coming at her. Behind him, behind Merlin, another soldier in gray rounded the building. Cera admitted to herself, finally, that she should have run away earlier.

The oncoming soldier shoved his dying companion's back, sending Cera to the patchy grass beneath him. The soldier, standing above, thrust his sword at Cera's face—and she jerked her neck aside. He thrust again, and she dodged. She pushed up at the dying man on top of her, but the standing soldier stomped on the body, pinning her beneath it.

He set the tip of his blade against his companion's back and drove it down through. Cera pushed up with all she had, but the standing soldier's boot wouldn't budge. His blade plunged deeper into the corpse on top of her.

"Mmh!" It pierced Cera's stomach and sank in. She couldn't push as hard.

Schvt! A thrown knife lodged into the standing soldier's chest.

A hand reached for it—a pale woman's hand beyond the

end of a clean blue sleeve. Nimue, dressed to fight as she'd been on the riverbank in Würzburg, ripped out the blade. The soldier fell, and Nimue smiled at Cera on her way past, her sword in her other hand.

Metal struck metal, and Cera couldn't see the fight, but it must have been Nimue and the newly arrived soldier. Cera pushed against the body on top of her but didn't have the strength to move it. Her stomach screamed.

She coughed, and liquid filled her throat. Cera felt for the hole in her gut then saw the blood on her hand. A body hit the ground down the alley.

"Gah!" someone let out, probably Merlin. Footsteps sounded like they were leaving, and Cera couldn't hear any fighting.

Nimue stood above Cera. "You don't look good." She dropped her weapons, rolled the soldier's body off, and noticed Cera's cut-open stomach. "Not good!"

Cera got herself onto an elbow and reached for her satchel but fell. Nimue lifted her so she sat against the building. The Lady of the Lake opened the satchel.

Cera grimaced, handing the grail to her. Cera pulled out her last small jar, bit the cork, poured water in the grail, then dropped the bottle to the ground. Nimue handed her the grail, and Cera drank the water.

The coolness filled her. Cera breathed deeper until, at a full breath, she saw that her stomach had healed. She rolled her ankle around, and it felt fine. "Thank you, Lord."

"And thank me!" Nimue, her silver eyes wide, sat herself beside Cera against the wall.

Cera smiled. "Yes." She set her hand on Nimue's leg. "Thank you, Nimue."

"You're welcome."

"Merlin got away?" Cera asked.

"He did. I had to see to you."

"How did you know where I was and that I needed help?"

Nimue shrugged. "I just knew."

"It can't be that simple. You have to know more. You have to know *why*."

"I… it may be because Arden is dear to me. He must live."

"Why?" Cera asked. "I don't want him to die, but who is he to you?"

"He is my dear friend's son. He is heir to the British throne." Nimue sighed. "I don't even know if I'm supposed to have friends."

"Arden is King Arthur's son?"

"He is. I loved Arthur—I understand that now. I loved him for the light that he was and that he sought for the world. Aiding him brought me joy unlike anything I'd ever felt in my long life. After all I've seen—flickers of good but a torrent of darkness, pain, and evil—King Arthur brought hope with him for a new world, a better one for everyone. When he died, it felt like part of me had died too."

Cera yawned.

"Not interesting?" Nimue asked.

"No! I mean yes! It's very interesting, but I'm exhausted. I've been riding. I haven't slept since Tours. Does Merlin know about Arden?"

"Only since he killed Arthur. After that, Merlin sought him out, bent on ending him like his father. Arden's been on the run, hiding from Merlin's assassins. One got poison into Arden's body with an arrow to his leg. He and Gethen chased down and slew the attacker then fled in secret to Mont Tombe, Arden's condition deteriorating all the time. He should be dead by now. A weaker man would be, but Arthur and Ayodele's son is no weakling. Though he is running out of time."

Cera yawned again and held the Holy Grail out to Nimue. "Take it to him. If you travel by water, surely, you could reach him faster than I."

"I cannot," Nimue said. "My gifts may travel the water as I do, but the Holy Grail, as you well know, is not one of mine."

Cera returned the grail to her satchel. "Then I must be on my way." She started to get up.

Nimue held her shoulder down. "You should rest."

"Arden needs me." Cera's eyes barely opened.

"You'll make better time after you've rested." Nimue pulled Cera's head down so it lay on her shoulder.

Cera looked at the dead soldiers. "If Perceval were here, we would have been fine."

"Yes."

"Perceval is *supposed* to be here." Cera couldn't keep her eyes open any longer. "I wasn't supposed to have to do this alone."

"Perceval gave his life so yours could continue, but you are not alone." Nimue slid her arm under Cera's and held her hand.

"As long as I'm near water." Cera pictured Nimue rising from a river, sword drawn, ready for battle, and let herself rest harder against Nimue's firm body. "Don't let me sleep too long."

"I can't stay on land much longer." Nimue pulled the side of Cera's cloak so it better covered the princess. "I hate that I can do nothing about it, but in half an hour or so, my energy will be spent, my body will fade to mist, and I'll return to the Mayenne River."

"Wake me before you do." Cera imagined the blue glow overtaking Nimue, dissolving with her into droplets of water.

"No, I'll let you fall and hit the ground. That'll wake you."

Cera laughed and yawned all at once. "Who are you?"

"You know who I am." Her enunciation came as sweet notes. "I am the Lady of the Lake."

"But who *are* you? What are you?"

Nimue inhaled and let out a deep breath. "I don't know." She squeezed Cera's hand. "Rest now."

Cera fell asleep.

15

Roan's eyes opened, staring down through the cutout section of stone floor to hell's raging fire. He shuffled away and shot his hand to his neck—no blood, no open wound. Across the same gray square room as before, an angel was seated, its folded wings and back to Roan—an archangel, actually.

Uriel turned and motioned to the cutout. "You're free to return there, if you'd like."

"No." Roan marched to him.

"But you failed. You told me you would complete your task, yet here you are, dead again."

"I didn't know... I didn't expect Cera to—why didn't you tell me she could fight like *that*?"

Uriel shrugged. "You didn't ask. You gave the impression it didn't matter."

Roan went around the bench and sat beside him, marveling at the purity of the white light in the cutout in the ceiling. "Who is she?"

"I told you, she was the grail princess. She had help stealing the grail, but she hatched the plan, and when she set it in motion, and three knights of the Order of Nolvan tried to stop her, she killed two."

"How'd she escape? What happened to the third knight?"

"Sir Perceval of Wales took his life."

"Perceval! Where is he now?"

"Dead," Uriel said.

"What? *I* was supposed to kill him."

Uriel shrugged. "Gave himself up outside the church in Tours to buy time for the princess to escape."

"Meddlesome knight." Roan crossed his arms. "What else should I know about Cera?"

"You'll go back and complete your task?"

"Yes! I underestimated her. I didn't plan anything. I rushed it, figured it'd be easy. I told you I'd destroy the grail, and I swear, I will."

"You'd better."

"I know." Roan ached up and down, recalling torturous years of fire. He remembered the goat-led court at the end. "My soul is damned as things stand. I need to see Aedre and Madeline again." He looked at the bright light in the ceiling. "If He would ever have me." Roan clenched his fist. "Do you know what happened to them, Uriel? On earth, their lives ended horribly. And my son's never really started at all."

"I know," Uriel said.

"How can the god of that"—Roan pointed at the light— "preside over such misery?"

"You lived happy years with them—Aedre, then Madeline."

Roan slammed his fist on the bench. "Only for my life

with them to be ripped away while they suffered the ultimate fate."

"If they are in heaven—"

"If?" Roan stopped him.

"If they are, their fate is a glorious one."

"But I still suffer."

"That is your choice."

Roan looked closely at Uriel's face full of perfect features and at the white-feathered wings past it. "It's not easy for us, you know." Roan shook his head. "I will never forgive God. I hate Him!"

"Yet you will complete this task for Him?"

"If I never see Aedre and Madeline in heaven—if they're in heaven—when they look down on me, I ought to be doing something for God. Let them be proud of me, at least."

Uriel nodded. "Then I will tell you more about your target to better prepare you. For starters, she is sixty years old."

"Sixty? No way."

"The Holy Grail keeps her body young. But she's been training for what she faces now for longer than you were alive. As you experienced, her preferred weapons are a pair of daggers. Physically, the grail makes her a little stronger than a typical human."

"I noticed," Roan said. "Didn't expect it from one so lean."

"She is a fierce warrior, driven by the notion that she does God's will."

"Got it." Roan walked away as if an exit lay before him then spun to Uriel. "Anything else I should know?"

Uriel shrugged.

Roan pointed at him. "Can I kill her, if I need to, to take the grail?"

The archangel pursed his lips.

"I wondered before, and it cost me. With Perceval dead, I should have my revenge against his woman, and in battle, I can't be worried about what's acceptable and what isn't. I need to know so I can fight instinctively. Can I kill her?"

"God wants the grail destroyed," Uriel said. "Do whatever it takes."

16

Smack! Cera's head hit a patch of bare dirt in the grass.

She sat up as blue water droplets in the air shrank into mist then faded and disappeared. Nimue was gone. Merlin's slain soldiers lay in the alley with Cera. Two townspeople at the end of the street pointed at her and where the soldiers had come from and spoke quietly to each other. A full day's ride away, on Mont Tombe, Arden withered in his bed, set to die halfway between midnight and sunrise, based on the hour Nimue's letter had arrived in Tours. Cera had time, but just.

She stood. Nimue had been correct—Cera felt a lot better after the rest. Sharper, more focused. Nimue had revealed Arden to be King Arthur's heir—true heir to the British throne. Son of Perceval's beloved liege. A young dragon, Gethen had called him. Cera might have known.

She headed back to the house she'd been baited to, for her horse. She hoped the lying woman had been safely reunited with her daughter but couldn't spare the time to check. For all Cera knew, Merlin was hastily organizing reinforcements for a second attack, and based on what

Nimue had said, she doubted Nimue could soon leave her waters to come again to Cera's aid.

Cera was not alone, Nimue had claimed, and in the alley with her, for a fleeting time, Cera had not been. But Nimue had spoken of a fantasy. She had left. Cera was alone. Alone, she would ride while Nimue passed the time however she did in a lake or river somewhere. *Or does time not pass for Nimue as it does for humans?* Cera had no idea.

Her horse remained tied where Cera had left him. Cera's time with Nimue had also given him a rest. After food and water at the livery, Cera would ride half the day then trade him, with some gold, for one last fresh mount. She untied him, got up on the saddle, and looked herself over.

Cera smiled at the sliced gown stained with blood, grass, and dirt, which had once been pure white. Red splattered the inside and outside of her cloak. Eventually, she'd change and not into another gown. Along with something sturdier than sandals, if she was to be constantly hunted or under attack, she needed something easier to fight in.

It would be even better, Cera noted, to find a way not to be under constant attack. *But first, to Mont Tombe to save King Arthur's son.*

––––––––––––––

Two hours outside Laval, Cera rode northwest on the path through plains of rolling grass and patches of trees. Warming May morning air filled her lungs and billowed her cloak. Occasional puffy clouds blocked the bright sun's rays from hitting her face.

Arthur had been as bright. Perceval had called his king a beacon in the darkness, matching all accounts Cera had heard of the Briton, including Nimue's. Perceval spoke of the joy of Camelot and Arthur's hope for a world full of that joy—his intent, in fact, to see the world that way, before Merlin cruelly betrayed him, abruptly ending his reign at fourteen years. It should have stretched on for glorious decades.

King Hengist ruled Britain now, a hard and absolute monarch, having subdued the Angles and Saxons in every battle as his terrible machine of war swept across the island. The last report to reach the order had given a concerning account of the situation for his growing number of subjects. He killed men who refused to fight for him, so few resisted. Hengist ripped them from their families, along with anything of value—including most of the food—to feed the war machine. Women left at home lived at the mercy of foreign governors and their sinister cronies. Children suffered through it all.

With his army swelled with men, horses, weapons, and ambition, Hengist's attention had finally fixed fully on King Constantine, the last holdout, defending Camelot and the lands beyond in the southwest. Good-intentioned, good-hearted Constantine could not last long, and darkness would cover all of Britain.

Cera stared into a dense patch of trees on the left, wondering if Arden could rally his people. *Can he save Camelot—or recover it if it has fallen already? Will the Britons remain united and follow him, despite his mother's origin, so he can be the bright light Merlin tried to snuff out?*

Or perhaps Merlin tracked Cera at that very moment, following beyond her sight, bent on stealing the Holy Grail and poised to also finish the job of ending Arthur's line when she led the wizard to him.

Cera focused on moving forward. She had no choice. Arden would die if Cera did not reach him. If Merlin followed, they'd just have to deal with him after Arden drank from the grail. *Dammit, Perceval, why couldn't you have found another way? You should be here with me. You should be part of this fight.*

Dirt, far ahead off to the right, rose from the grass. Cera squinted to see—maybe it was someone on horseback. She felt for the dagger on her right leg. It was there as it should have been, so she trusted the other to be sheathed on her left.

Dirt farther ahead to the left formed a low cloud off the plain. To Cera's right, it did indeed look like a rider. Cera's shoulders sank. Dirt was being kicked up from dry land because her route had taken her away from any river or lake, away from Nimue. Cera wished Nimue had spoken true and that she would be there to help her. It sure had sounded like Nimue wished it, too, but in that moment, when it mattered, Cera was all alone.

But she'd manage. She'd find a way.

She saw red on the chest of the rider coming from the right. And then Cera made out the same cross shape on the rider from the left, in the center of a white tunic. The Order of Nolvan had found her.

Cera glanced backward. A pair of mounted knights rode

in the distance. She couldn't have turned back, anyway, because Arden lay to the north, not the south.

Cera focused on the knights ahead. She picked up into a gallop, her horse breathing hard and the grail stowed in the satchel strapped across her body. She wondered which of the knights were charging at her—which of the knights who'd vowed to God to protect His grail and who had belittled Cera and underestimated her for decades.

Sir Hunald, Cera thought, was closest, off to the right. The wide-shouldered, chiseled-chinned second knight to drink from the Holy Grail, all those hundreds of years ago, charged hard.

She couldn't make out either of the pair behind her. Ahead, on the left, it appeared to be Sir Alan, who'd accompanied her on many journeys across Europe. Cera gritted her teeth. He'd always insisted she hide in the damn carriage.

The hooves of Sir Hunald's horse hit the ground hard and loud on his route to intercept Cera. Four knights of the order would not be easy, but she had no choice but to get it done. And she had to get it done fast.

Hunald raised his sword. Cera considered firing a dagger at him, but he had the speed to knock it away, and she'd have only her other dagger against so many. Her eyes met his. He must have been timing his attack, counting down the last strides before he swung. He snarled.

"Ya!" Cera pushed her horse faster.

Hunald shifted course and—arm outstretched, leaning from his saddle—swung at her head. Cera bent backward, low and away, beyond the blade's sharp edge.

"Halt!" He turned to follow. "It is not yours!"

"You've hoarded it long enough!" Cera yelled to him, checking left. Sir Alan was nearing.

Her horse jerked to a stop, and she held on tight. Behind her, an arrow stuck in her mount's backside, and Sir Hunald held the bow. He nocked another arrow. Cera's horse kicked its hind legs out, and she slid from the saddle to the grass.

Cera drew a dagger and turned to Sir Alan… and ducked—*swoosh*—under his sword. Hunald's arrow flew inches above Cera's head.

Sir Alan spun to attack again, and she flung her dagger at his horse's chest. She drew her other knife and sprinted at him. Alan dropped off the angry, rearing animal, and Cera leapt feetfirst at the knight, sending him violently into the horse and his sword out of his hand. She jumped up, swinging her knife at his neck, but he raised his arm to block. The back of his other gloved hand slapped across her face. He punched to follow, but she ducked and drove her knee into his stomach. Alan gasped for air and punched her chest, and it hurt, but she thrust her knife into his gut and dragged the blade until the gash opened to the air his lungs had sought.

Sir Alan shoved her away. Cera pulled her knife out and slashed it through his neck. He slumped onto her, his blood covering them both as he fell.

Cera turned to Sir Hunald. *Thunk!* "Agh!" An arrow lodged in her left shoulder. "Stand and fight me." She grimaced. "Or are you scared?"

"Huh!" Hunald threw his bow to the ground, rode closer, and dismounted. "It won't matter. You and your little daggers cannot defeat me."

Cera snapped the arrow off near her shoulder and winced but found she could still use the arm.

Hunald pointed at Sir Alan. "You'll pay for what you've done." He drew his sword. "You'll pay in this life and forever after."

Cera sheathed her knife and picked up the fallen knight's sword. "*He* attacked *me*. My conscience is clear."

"You stole God's Holy Grail. You're killing its guardians."

In the air before her, Cera swung the sword twice to test its weight and balance. "I will save the suffering and the sick. I act *for* the grail so it can fulfill its true purpose, which is not to travel around Europe as an idle object, a mere witness to the pain surrounding it."

"The grail is an ideal for knights to—"

"It's a cup!" Cera screamed. "A real thing! You all wasted centuries of people suffering and dying. But now *I* have the grail, and I will use it."

Sir Hunald shook his head. He and Cera glanced at the approaching riders, Sirs Felix and Berthold. Cera needed to deal with Hunald before they arrived.

She started toward him and he toward her. With a quick step, she swung her sword.

Hunald met it. "As hard as your mother!"

Cera cut low.

He met it firm. "You do believe you're in the right."

With all her strength, Cera swung high.

Hunald parried. "You're wrong, but you believe."

He cut high and fast. Cera barely blocked it. He went low—she blocked it—and high, across her left arm. "Agh!"

"There are worse ways to die," Sir Hunald said. "The Lord may pity you."

"I pity you all," Cera spat. "Brave knights become babysitters."

Hunald frowned.

Through her arm and shoulder's throbbing pain, Cera cut high and fast. Hunald blocked and moved quickly to parry her low strike, and her next. She faked high, and he went that way—she sliced across his hip.

"Gah!" He shifted backward, favoring that side.

Felix and Berthold reached them.

"Give us the grail!" Sir Berthold shouted from his horse.

Cera pointed her sword at him. "Come down and take it!"

"No!" Hunald pointed at Berthold. "Stay there. She's mine."

"No." Berthold dismounted and drew his sword. "The grail is all that matters. Once we have it, fight her—prove yourself in combat against the princess, if you must. But first, we get the grail."

Cera backed away from Hunald and Berthold. Sir Felix dismounted and drew his sword. The trio of knights spaced themselves around her. *Better on foot than on horseback*, Cera thought, grasping at the silver lining.

Despite sharp pangs in that arm and shoulder, with her left hand, she drew her dagger to go along with the sword in her right. Cera needed to cut them down one at a time but

"*The* Lord. God. Uriel sent me to take it from you."

"The archangel?"

"The archangel."

"From heaven?"

"Him, yes." Roan shook his head. "Me, no."

Cera squinted. "Then why kill Sir Hunald?"

Roan stopped, separated from her by only the length of his big sword. "The Lord doesn't want them to have it either. I am to destroy the grail."

"What? No…"

"Yes. Give it here." He put out his hand. "I don't need to kill you. But I do need the grail."

"I don't believe you."

"You saw me dead." Roan spat to the grass. "Wasn't the first time."

"Perceval—"

"Didn't kill me. Lady Tadman did. I was drunk and exhausted from fighting that wretched knight."

Cera raised an eyebrow. "*Lady* Tadman?"

"I was a mess!" Roan growled. "God took everything from me!"

"Yet you'll do this errand for Him?"

"Look—"

"Do you know what I mean to do with the grail?" Cera asked. "Did Uriel tell you? About those I mean to help?"

"I don't care." Roan leaned forward. "I've been to hell, princess. I won't go back."

Cera stood firm. "You think destroying the Holy Grail will keep you out of hell?"

"It's your God's will."

"I do *not* believe you."

Roan's eyes widened. "So be it."

He raised his sword and wrapped both hands around the handle. Cera tucked her hair behind her ear on the right and raised her blade, sliding her hand down over the pommel to fit her second hand on the grip.

Roan cut hard, and Cera slid aside, shocked at the big man's speed. He swung, and she blocked, holding as firm as she could to keep his blade from inching nearer.

"It doesn't have to be like this," Roan said.

"Then go away!" Cera gritted her teeth. "I ride to the aid of a young man. He's dying. Let me save him!"

"And then you'll give me the grail?"

"No." Cera pushed his sword away and stepped back. "Never."

Roan nodded. "Perceval didn't deserve one with such spirit."

"Perceval believed as I did."

"And he's dead for it, and I missed the chance to kill him myself. I won't miss out on you." Roan thrust, and Cera dodged. He cut, and she blocked, stepping back at the powerful blow. On he came, stronger with each swing. Her weak leg made it hard to get set, and her wounded shoulder hurt with each parry and move.

Roan swung high, and she blocked, then low, and she deflected it. Then, leading with her good shoulder, Cera sprang at him. He absorbed the blow and threw her staggering away.

Roan swung at Cera's neck, and she ducked as the blade swept over her hair. He kicked Cera to the ground, and when she started up, his blade's tip was there. She rolled aside and flung her leg across his ankles. Roan fell to his knees.

He lunged forward and plunged his sword down into Cera's gut.

"Mmh!" She pushed up against his chest, like pushing against an iron wall.

Cera dropped her sword to use both hands, but Roan didn't budge. He twisted his sword's blade. She screamed as the steel in her stomach spun all the way around.

"I'm sorry it came to this." Roan withdrew the bloody blade and used it to cut her satchel's strap. "You're a worthier adversary than most I've fought." He pulled the bag from her. "And I've fought many."

Cera lunged for the bag. Roan's fist hit her face, which smacked into the ground. He towered above her.

She spat blood, chest heaving, holding her ripped-open stomach tight. "You don't understand what you're doing!"

"No!" Roan put out his hand. "I don't understand God. I hate God. But He offered me a way out of hell, so I took it."

Cera's gut oozed blood. Her breaths became agonizing. Her eyes slid closed as Roan walked away with the Holy Grail. Clutching herself, she gulped. No sacred drink to heal her, Arden's time ticking away. Maybe she couldn't save him any longer, but—

Cera cracked open her eyes, got a foot under her, and

rose. "Think about what you're doing!"

Roan glanced back, then he turned to Sir Berthold and crouched to the wounded knight. Cera's hurt leg wouldn't take her weight, and she crumpled to the ground.

She stared into the sky, and tears welled up. She pictured Arden dying in his bed. She thought of all she would never get to do, those she would never get to help. All that she'd dreamed of but failed to make real played out in her mind.

She screamed, "Think about what you *could* do with the grail!"

Her eyes shut, her head turned so that her cheek felt soft grass, and she thought of Perceval.

17

Riding through the grass, with Cera's satchel holding the Holy Grail in the large pack on his horse's side, Roan wiped wisps of hair from his face. He headed south to where the dying knight of the order said he'd find the nearest bridge where he could turn northwest to the nearest town where there'd be a blacksmith. Roan had already forgotten the town's Frankish name, but there, he would get the smith to melt the grail down.

Roan recalled Cera's last words. He *had* thought about what he was doing. Uriel had told him why God wanted the grail destroyed. It was too powerful for anyone to possess. *Fine. God willed it.*

What did Cera want me to do? So she'd sought to save some young dying man. Roan glanced back at his pack. *Who cares?* Aedre had died. Madeline and his son had died. *People died!*

How brazen of Cera—how presumptuous to think she could change that. Change death, that young man's fate. *Maybe God demanded the grail be taken from her and destroyed because she shouldn't have been meddling with His plans—*

Roan gripped the reins tight—*however cruel His plans were to their victims and those who loved them.*

Uriel hadn't told Roan why God doomed Aedre and Madeline to their early ends. Uriel hadn't assured Roan they'd gone to heaven. Madeline must have—his kind, gentle Madeline, who was always faithful to her Lord. But Aedre had slain so many on all the battlefields after the days' outcomes had been decided and she might have let them live as prisoners, so Roan didn't know her ultimate fate. And he hated not knowing. Uriel had presented Roan with a god who needed a task done that He didn't care to do Himself. Uriel hadn't changed Roan's mind about God. Nothing the angel had said dulled the venom that coursed through Roan's veins at the name or notion of Him.

God had shown Roan hell. He hadn't held that back. Roan spat, remembering for so long not having the saliva to manage such a thing, parched in Satan's infernal pit. Yes, Roan was doing an errand for that heinous Lord, and he didn't like that. But he didn't have much choice.

You fought well, Cera, Roan thought. *You died well. I understand why Perceval died for you, if he saw the same passion in you that I did. And Perceval did not actually send me to hell. I understand that. God and I are to blame, I know.*

So, Cera, I have thought about it. I've thought about plenty, but it doesn't change a thing. I'll stay out of hell, and destroying a holy relic in the process sounds damn satisfying.

After that, I'll be done with God. I'll know He's up there and the Devil down below, but I'll have done my task. I'll have earned the rest of my years on earth. And I've fulfilled my vow to kill you in Perceval's stead, so I'll live better than the mess I was—for me, not for God.

Clang—clang—clang! In the small town, early that afternoon, a grizzle-bearded blacksmith beat his hammer against an orange-hot sword's edge on a stone table outside his shop. Heavy heat hit Roan hard as he walked over, carrying the satchel with the grail. The blacksmith flipped the blade. *Clang—clang—clang!*

"Hey!" Roan called.

The man ceased his banging. Along with his soot-covered tunic, trousers, and apron, he wore a rope necklace with a wooden cross at the end.

"I need something done," Roan said. "Immediately."

"What do you need? As you can see, I'm busy."

"Melt an old cup for me. It's silver and gold."

"Why?"

"Bad memories," Roan said. "And bad luck. I need it gone."

He lifted the sword he had been hammering and inspected both sides.

"I'll pay extra for interrupting you," Roan said.

The blacksmith leaned close to look down the sword's edge. "Must be really bad luck."

"The worst."

The smith motioned behind him to the source of the heat, a bed of red-hot charcoals surrounded by black stone. "It'll melt silver and gold."

Roan stared into the familiar red and black. Beads of sweat formed on his brow.

The smith set the sword on his table. "Do you have the cup?"

Roan tore his eyes from the fire and produced, from the satchel, the Holy Grail.

"Wow." The blacksmith rubbed his chin and took the grail. "Where'd you get this?"

"It's been in my family."

He examined it closely. "If you don't want it, may I keep it?"

"No." Roan pulled a gold coin from his purse. "It's bad luck. It's cursed. Melt it."

"Are you—"

"Do it right now." Roan produced a second coin. "Over those coals."

The smith took the coins and put them in his pocket.

Roan looked around for any members of the order but spotted no knights at all, let alone ones with red crosses on white tunics.

The smith put on thick gloves. "A sad end for such a fine thing."

Roan stepped to him. "Melt it down."

"Sure." He backed away. "Sure. No problem."

Roan followed him to the bed of charcoals. With long tongs, the blacksmith grasped the grail. Roan stared at the waves of heat above the coals and saw the towering walls of flame that had surrounded him. Crackling filled his ears. For years, the ceaseless breaking of those massive wooden trunks had fueled hell's blaze. The stench of sulfur oozed into Roan's nostrils. Roan closed his eyes and saw Aedre tortured by the demonic army, so he opened them again to the smith's earthly coals.

At the end of the long tongs, the grail moved above the black-and-red bed. The roar of hellfire rose in Roan's mind. The infernal pit's insufferable heat blew across his face, pebbles mixed in, grating his bone-dry—

Schvt! Steel slit Roan's neck.

"Stop!" Cera called, bloody dagger in hand. "Get it away from there!"

The smith moved the grail away from the coals. With both hands, Roan clutched his bleeding neck as he turned to her, the broken arrow still in her shoulder, a wide strip of bloodstained white tunic wrapped tight around her stomach where he'd plunged his sword through her.

Roan gagged, choking on blood. Cera wrapped her arm around him and, straining at the effort, drove her dagger into his gut. "You underestimated me again, Roan."

He dropped to his knees, and she moved low with him, speaking into his ear. "God gave me the strength to endure, as He gave Sir Berthold long enough before he died to lie to you. Due west would've gotten you here long before me, but Berthold's last words led me here in time to save God's Holy Grail from the fire." Her eyes flared. "God doesn't want it destroyed. He wants me to *use it.*" She pulled the dagger out and leaned away. "What did he do to you that you hate Him so?"

"My…" Roan coughed more blood into his mouth. "Wives and son… died…"

"Did they rot down in hell with you?"

Roan shook his head.

"Then what were they doing with the likes of you in the first place?" She stabbed her knife into his heart. "Go back to hell and stay there. Long for them while you burn forever."

Roan's eyes rolled up, then they shut.

18

"Give it to me," Cera said.

The blacksmith guided the long tongs over, and Cera took the grail by the bowl—warm but not melted. She'd made it just in time.

"Do you have water?" Cera asked, rotating her shoulder where the broken arrow remained lodged.

The blacksmith looked at Roan's lifeless body on the ground. "He didn't seem well."

"He stole this from me." She raised the grail and grimaced, holding her stomach as adrenaline gave way to sharp pain and wooziness. "Did this too. I need water." Arden flashed to mind. "Please hurry."

The smith rushed inside. Cera leaned against his stone table and wondered if Roan had hesitated for even a second, after they fought, before deciding to go through with destroying the grail. She considered binding his hands and feet and taking him with her. *If Roan's wounds heal, his pierced heart restarts, and life springs forth in him, would those bonds keep him at bay? Or would he return freed of whatever ropes I used and—already so near to me—be able to succeed, finally, in his designs?*

The blacksmith brought a small cup of water. Cera poured its contents into the Holy Grail and drank it fast. Breathing easier, she stood straight, her hamstrings no longer cut. Under the torn tunic she'd tied around her, she felt whole, inside and out.

Cera handed the blacksmith his water cup. "Please fill it again."

He hurried away.

Cera couldn't take Roan with her, she decided. If he revived again, she wanted to witness it, but after the diversion westward, she couldn't afford to be slowed by traveling with him. She couldn't even spare the time to tie him up.

The blacksmith returned with his cup filled.

She handed him the grail. "Pour it in."

He poured, and Cera set her right hand against her shoulder, grabbed the broken end of the arrow, and pulled hard. "Mhm!" It came out, and blood flowed after it. She dropped the arrow and reached for the grail. The smith handed it to her, and she drank.

He watched in wonder as the hole in her shoulder mended. She rotated her arm—good as new. She shifted her eyes to the heavens. *Thank you.*

The blacksmith's hand covered his heart. "My God."

"It is His gift, yes."

"The Holy Grail!" His face lit up, then he hurried inside with his cup.

Cera took her satchel from Roan. She put the grail in it, slung the bag across her body, and tied the strap in a tight knot where he had cut it.

The blacksmith returned with his filled cup.

She produced a coin from her satchel. "Would you burn this body, immediately? It's… dangerous."

The smith bowed his head. "Of course." He closed her hand around the coin. "May I drink from the grail first?"

She pulled the grail out and handed it to him. He poured his water in and gazed adoringly at it.

"It's now or never," Cera said. "I have to go."

He drank, crossed himself, and held the grail before him. A tear slid down his cheek. "Who are you? Are you an angel?"

"I'm a woman." Cera put the grail away. "A righteous woman who isn't afraid to wield God's Holy Grail."

The blacksmith fell to his knees and wept. Cera ran to her horse, but Roan's looked fresher and more eager, so she mounted his.

———————

Hours later, before sunset and dangerously farther south than she should have been because of Roan's diversion from her route, Cera rode her stolen gray horse northward. She rode as fast as she dared, with eight or ten long hours between them and Mont Tombe, depending on what the animal could manage. Far ahead, no cloud of dirt rose from the ground, and no riders approached. Cera checked behind as she'd been doing constantly. No knights of the order in white. No Merlin or his soldiers in gray. No Roan in black.

She might not make it if Nimue's predicted timing was accurate. *How does she know it will be that hour, in the middle of the night? How can she know in advance how much time Arden has before he dies?*

"Nimue!" Cera called out, though there was no water in sight. "Lady of the Lake!"

Her horse's hard-hitting hooves and steady, effective breaths continued, interrupted by no words of response on the air. *Can he get me there in time?*

Cera checked behind her. No knights, no Merlin, no Roan. If only they'd stolen the grail sooner…

But they couldn't have. They'd barely succeeded when they had acted.

Yet at the terrible cost of Perceval's life, in what mattered most, they had indeed succeeded. And now mere hours separated the grail from doing something so important.

Hold on, Arden. Give me the time Nimue foretold. Merlin didn't stop me. Roan failed twice. Give me the promised hours, and maybe an extra one or two if you've got it in you, and I will be there. You will be healed. You'll have your chance to lead your people against King Hengist, if you want it.

Cera hoped then that Arden proved to be the kind of man—the kind of leader—she imagined. She'd only seen him sickly in bed. She wanted to see the young dragon take his father's mantle.

The tide. Cera pictured water surrounding Mont Tombe. *Will it be out when I arrive? If it isn't, could a boat ferry me across fast enough?*

"Keep it up, Gray." Cera patted her horse. "You're doing great."

Cera looked to the heavens, wishing for the tide to be out

when they arrived, then stared straight ahead and asked God to give speed to her horse.

Hold on, Arden. I'm coming with the Holy Grail to save you. Just hold on.

19

Roan's eyes opened, and he stared through the cutout in the stone floor that revealed the inferno of hell. A wave of heat lashed his face. He jerked backward.

Uriel stood beside the bench in the middle of the square gray room, arms crossed, wings folded in behind him. "You want to return to those pits as Cera commanded? To be once more and forever tormented by Satan's fire?"

"No!" Roan marched to the towering archangel. "I thought I killed Cera. I left her for dead."

"Decades of drinking from the grail have made her strong," Uriel said. "As her conviction makes her strong. I assumed your conviction would do the same for you, but maybe someone else would be more up to this task."

"I'll kill her!" Roan roared.

Uriel pointed his pale finger. "You'd better."

"I'll cut off her head. She won't survive that."

"No." Uriel smirked. "Not even the Holy Grail would save her from that."

"She rides to save some young man."

Uriel nodded. "In the north of Francia, King Arthur's

son, Arden. Merlin poisoned him, and he's dying, slowly but surely."

Roan raised an eyebrow. "I didn't know Arthur had a son."

"Few do. She is not Guenevere's. Before Arthur became king and married her, he fell in love, and the child was conceived."

"And you… God doesn't think Cera should save him?"

Uriel leaned close. "God's will is that the grail be destroyed. He will give you one last chance to complete the task, but no more than the one."

"I'll get it done." Roan gritted his teeth. "Send me back."

20

Merlin sat sunk in a creaky wooden chair in his big tent, with his eyes closed, head bowed, and long wooden staff leaning against him. The rolling ball of fire at its end provided the only light on his wrinkly skin at the late hour. His knees hurt, and his back ached, but Merlin had grown used to ignoring those things until he could drive them away completely.

In his mind ran scenes from towns and villages in the aftermath of King Hengist's many conquests. Defiant men's lives snuffed out, women taken against their will. A younger Merlin—one who trusted in many different gods than the single Lord he cursed now—would have hated seeing it or remembering it, but that had been a long time ago. The scenes just played out now.

Merlin's tent flap parted slowly, and Captain Ulrich peeked in. "Sir?"

Merlin opened his eyes to the big, gray-haired, neatly bearded leader of his soldiers. "Have the scouts returned?"

Ulrich stepped inside. "They have, sir, with no sign of Arden. I'm afraid the trail has gone cold."

Merlin scowled.

"Maybe…" Ulrich scratched his beard. "Maybe he's dead. The poison really should have—"

"No." Merlin shook his head. "I would know if he was dead, I assure you. And you would know too! It would be obvious for you to see."

Ulrich made a confused face then started to leave, but he turned back.

"Yes?" Merlin asked.

"The men," Ulrich said. "They wonder, why Arden? I told them it's because he is King Arthur's son. And that makes sense, but none ever heard King Hengist give the order. And in fact…"

Merlin leaned forward. "Go on."

"Well, some claim they heard Hengist say he was *not* worried about a lost supposed son of Arthur at all."

Merlin nodded. "It's simple, really. Like you, Captain, I don't always get to choose my target."

Ulrich appeared confused again.

"I chose Arthur," Merlin said. "That murder was of my own design and long in the making. But not Arden. Maybe we hunt Arden to rob a loving mother of her son—a mother whose ancestry cast her and her son apart from everyone around them and who never got to live her life with the man she loved, who loved her with all his heart. I knew them back then, you know. Arthur, before he was king, and his Ayodele."

Ulrich clasped his hands before him.

"They could have had such a life together," Merlin

continued, "had he not become king and been convinced that his people would never accept a king married to an African. Which seems, despite all her merits, a fair assessment, though the decision caused such pain. So maybe we target Arden to bring even sadder days to that good, once joyful woman." Merlin paused. "Or maybe it's because Arden could become an even greater king than his father." He shrugged. "Whatever it is, I do not know. But when it is done, there will not be an old man sitting before you. My sharp mind will not be trapped in this failing body. I will be a young man once more."

Ulrich's eyes widened.

"Yes," Merlin said. "The stories you have heard are true."

"But…" Ulrich shook his head. "But how?"

Merlin smiled. Then he sighed and sank into his chair. "It matters not. With Arden alive and hidden, my long life is finally at its end."

Another soldier burst into the tent. "Sir." He looked from Merlin to his captain. "Sir." Then back to Merlin. "We've spotted the princess riding north, headed for Mont Tombe."

"How near the island is she?" Ulrich asked.

"An hour. Maybe more. Her horse is slow and spent."

Merlin stood. "The Holy Grail is no substitute for Arden, but it would stop time's assault upon me and give me however long I need to find the boy and end him."

The soldier gave the captain a confused look.

"I'll tell you later," Ulrich said.

"Let's go." Merlin's face glowed in a flare of his staff's

fire. "I can already picture the abbey atop Mont Tombe in flames. After we have the grail, what a horror for all to witness from near and far—that holy place ablaze against the black of the night sky."

21

Gray's hooves hit the path hard. Ahead, a scattering of dim lights shone on the hill of Mont Tombe rising from the water. Cera's horse labored, sucking in the bright night's warm, humid air, but she couldn't let him slow any further. Midnight had come and gone hours before, by her best estimation. Arden couldn't have much time, but he had to still be alive. He *had* to be.

The Couesnon River, flowing to the bay, ran on Cera's left. Her hair blew across her face when she scanned the grassy plain to the right—no Order of Nolvan, no Merlin, no Roan.

Roan… a wholly different kind of obstacle than she'd expected. *Sent from hell? Sent from somewhere.* Cera had killed him twice. Perceval had seen him dead.

Roan seemed hardened by it all and by whatever had come before for him. The knights of the order, though physically strong and talented, had been softened by years of comfort, content to be guarding the grail. There was no softness in Roan. No eternal youthfulness. *Troubled,* Perceval had called the rock-solid Saxon. Cera wondered about his life's struggle. *What happened to his family?*

She checked the trees in the distance behind her… a blur. Cera squinted. Movement was visible in the full moon's light but not clearly.

She veered left off the path toward the river, to be nearer Nimue if she happened to be watching for Cera from the water. If that was how it worked with her at all.

Mont Tombe grew closer, wide-based, lording over the flatlands, with rings of dark forest wrapping around it in between the rings of smooth-sided buildings where a scattering of lights shone. A bright light burned at the abbey at the top.

Behind Cera a ways, horses and riders emerged from the woods, ten or a dozen in drab colors, not the white of the order. She didn't think Roan, once more risen from hell, was among them, because he'd come alone both times before. That meant Merlin's men followed, gaining on Cera and her weary mount.

Facing front, she stood in her saddle. "Shit."

Water—its calm expanse reflecting the moon's light without interruption—separated her from the hill fortress, not a plain of sand she could ride quickly across. She sat. The tide was, most unfortunately, in.

But there'd be a boat at the water's edge, and when Cera woke whoever rented it and told them of her quest—and, if needed, that King Arthur's heir lay at the end of it—she had no doubt they'd let her take it immediately, and maybe they'd even help row across the bay.

Cera coaxed more speed from Gray, who mustered the

energy, perhaps seeing the shore and understanding it meant his desperate ride's completion. Ahead, a figure stood at the edge of the water as those behind grew larger in pursuit—Cera counted fifteen of them. There was no ball of fire burning atop a staff in any of their hands, but surely, Merlin himself couldn't be far.

"Hurry!" called the woman ahead of her, a familiar sweetness in her voice, her dark hair blowing in the breeze, her light skin and soft features practically glowing. She beckoned Cera toward her. "Let's go!" Nimue's face was warm, her attire dark, pristine, and again fit for fighting, a sword sheathed on her hip. Past her, a small boat bobbed in the water.

As she reached Nimue, Cera slowed Gray and slid off his saddle and into a hug. "Nimue, thank God."

Nimue tightened the embrace, then she moved Cera away and pointed at the boat. "Get in. I'll get you across."

"How's Arden?" Cera asked.

"Dying. Any minute."

Cera stepped off the land's edge, stumbling into the boat, then turned back to Nimue and the approaching riders. "Merlin's men?"

"Yes."

"And you're sent here to stop them?" Cera needed to understand her.

"Not sent." Nimue crossed her arms. "I came. I can't let Arden die. He can't follow his father to the grave."

"He *won't* die."

The boat glided away from the shore.

"Merlin and his men will bring boats," Nimue said. "I'll make the water impassable for as long as I can." Her face fell, and she spoke louder, growing smaller and farther away. "Then my energy will fade, and the waters will calm. They will reach you!"

"Fight with us!" Cera yelled.

"I will!" Nimue stepped into the water. "For as long as I am able. Save Arden!" She faded to droplets, then mist, and then as the boat sped faster, to nothing, leaving Gray, who'd worked so hard to get Cera there as quickly as he could, standing all alone, breathing heavily. Cera gave him a nod then turned to Mont Tombe and gripped the boat's sides.

Faster, she cut through low waves, salty wind buffeting her face and blowing her hair. It felt good to be off the horse, her tired self enjoying moments of rest while Nimue guided her.

While Nimue could guide her, at least. Cera had her daggers. Once he was healed, presumably, Arden could fight. Sir Gethen, his protector, would as well. That made three. Nimue made four but only for as long as she could stay in human form on land. Cera glanced back at the shore. There were more riders than before, maybe twenty.

As she glided across the bay, the hill grew increasingly imposing. Cera recalled—vividly, for it had been so recent—walking there hand in hand with Perceval.

And she cried. Cera whimpered, and her nose ran. With Perceval in the impending fight, she knew they would win. Perceval was supposed to be with her. They both wanted a better world. For so long, it had been her alone, but Perceval had come, and he *had* understood. Cera sniffled and wiped her nose with her sleeve.

She gazed skyward at the stars the moonlight did not drown out and wondered again if perhaps Perceval had been right. *Has everything since he first showed up in the order's ledger of prospects been wrong?* Cera worried for Perceval's soul. If doom awaited, she could handle it, but he didn't deserve such a fate.

The boat rose against a wave and gently lowered.

No. Cera wiped her eyes dry. She'd made it this far. It would not be doom for herself, and Perceval had earned a better fate than that.

Four fighters were not many, but they would find a way to save Arden, survive, and keep the grail safe and out of Merlin's hands. She was ready to fight for God, to share the power of the grail with His people. Somehow, she would pass this test so she could.

At the dock on Mont Tombe, a lone figure waited, a broad-chested man in a red tunic—Sir Gethen, it became clear. He motioned her to him, though Cera could do nothing to increase her speed. Her boat slowed, in fact, as it got closer.

"Hurry, Cera!" the short-bearded Briton called.

"You knew I would arrive now?" she called back.

"The Lady of the Lake foretold it."

The boat hit the sandy shore. Cera took his hand and stepped out.

Gethen pulled her into a jog up the hill's coiling path. "Looks like you've seen a little action."

"You have no idea. How's Arden?"

"I pray he's alive when we get there. His breaths come so shallow. He no longer eats or drinks. His mother is with him."

Cera ran faster, and Gethen, sword on his hip, mail armor rattling, matched her pace past the mostly unlit houses and shops.

"Merlin is coming," she said.

Gethen gripped his sword handle. "I know."

"Once healed, will Arden be helpful against him and his soldiers?"

For the first time that Cera had ever seen, Gethen smiled. "Oh, yes. The boy can fight."

Past stretches of woods and low buildings, up the winding dirt path they ran, legs pumping, Cera's satchel pushed around toward her back. Halfway to the top, Gethen pointed ahead at the house on the right. "There."

Perceval had been with her in that house the last time. She couldn't help thinking about it, even though it would do her no good. He should have been with her still.

The door to the next house up the hill opened inward. Out stepped Roan in his black-and-coal-gray clothing. Gethen and Cera skidded to a halt.

The Saxon positioned himself between them and Arden's house and drew his mighty sword. Cera's heart sank.

"Give me the grail!" Roan roared.

Sir Gethen drew his sword.

"Stand aside!" Cera yelled. "Arden is dying. We don't have time!"

"I don't care." Roan shook his head. "Give me the grail, and go say your goodbyes before he does."

"Emh!" Cera drew a dagger and pointed it at Roan. "Why are you doing this?"

"God wants the grail destroyed," Roan said.

"I *don't* believe you."

"I told you, Uriel said—"

"Uriel?" Cera squinted. "*Was* it Uriel? You were in hell first, yes?"

"Yes."

"What did you do that sent you there? You said your wives and son died, so either those women were insane, or you weren't always such a wretch."

"I had a wife, and God took her." Roan's tense body relaxed. "A lifetime later, I had another. God took her, too, in childbirth, along with my son."

"And you went to hell?"

"I deserved it!" Roan screamed. "They died. Aedre first, and when Madeline died, my guts were torn out a second time, and a fresh, vicious gash ripped across my brain. I came back from it once, but… you have no idea." He lowered his sword. "In my misery, I stole, I murdered. I broke apart families. I didn't understand how He could take them all. I still don't understand!"

Cera lowered her knife. "I don't either. And I want to stop as much of that kind of suffering as I can." She shifted her satchel toward him. "With this."

"God doesn't want that," Roan said. "He doesn't want you to have the grail. I explained it before."

"An angel told you? You're sure?"

Roan raised an eyebrow. Perhaps he realized what Cera was driving at.

Gethen stepped forward. "Arden doesn't have time for this!"

Roan raised his sword, both hands on the handle. Cera put out a hand to stop Gethen.

"What if you're wrong?" she asked Roan. "What if it was not Uriel who pulled you from that pit, but it was Satan or one of his devils in disguise? What if *Satan* is bent on destroying the Holy Grail, and when you've done his bidding, you're sent straight back to hell?"

"What if it *was* God's angel?" Roan asked. "And *you* are the one who's wrong?"

"I may be." Cera nodded. "But I don't think so. My heart says I'm right, and my soul. And you know what? If I'm wrong, so be it. I will live my one life how I believe God wants me to."

"God told me to destroy the grail," Roan said.

"Maybe."

Roan lowered his sword, his eyes pleading. "How can I know for sure?"

"Trust me! Or the grail. Trust your heart."

Roan shook his head. "I need to *know* what's right."

"We're out of time." Cera drew her second dagger. "Fight me, and I'll give you the chance to ask Uriel, or whoever you've been talking to. I've killed you twice. I'll do it again."

"I underestimated you." Roan wagged his finger. "I won't this time."

"They're coming!" Nimue ran up the hill, huffing for air, and stopped, bent over, hands on her knees. "Merlin is with them. I held their boats to a crawl, but he figured out why. He whispered my name and scorched the bay. I felt it everywhere, burning me, until I could not command the water and hold them any longer, no matter how hard I tried."

"How many?" Gethen asked. "How long do we have?"

"Sixty men." She stood straight. "Fifteen, twenty minutes. As for me, I have less time than that on land. It was all I had left to come warn you."

Cera went to Nimue and grasped her arm. "Thank you."

Her eyes looked so sad. "I long to do more."

The door to Arden's house cracked open. Roan and everyone watched it open wider as Arden leaned his gaunt body against the frame for support. He held a gleaming sword low and lazily.

Cera stepped to him. Roan got in her way, glancing back at Arden.

"Leave…" Arden failed trying to raise his blade. "Leave her be."

"Let me help him," Cera said to Roan.

Arden collapsed to the ground. His eyes closed, and his sword rolled from his grip.

"Please!" Cera said. "He's dying!"

Arden's mother rushed to him in the doorway.

Cera asked Roan, "How many did you murder after tragedy befell you?"

"So many." He watched motionless Arden.

"Then *save* one. Let me. You're here—now—not in heaven and not in hell but living on earth in this moment. When it's time for God to judge you again, who will stand before Him? The man who destroyed His Holy Grail, or the man who let me save King Arthur's son?"

Roan turned to Cera. "I can't be wrong and be sent back down to burn. How do you *know* God wants you to save him?"

"I don't." Cera walked past Roan, knelt to Arden, and said to his mother, "Bring water, quickly."

Arden's mother sprang to her feet while Cera sheathed her daggers, unlatched the satchel, and pulled out the grail. Sir Gethen gasped behind her. He and Nimue came over, then Roan joined them. Nimue held her weary self against the house's side.

"Here!" Arden's mother set a pail half-full of sloshing water on the ground and dropped to her knees.

Cera dunked the grail in and brought it out to Arden while lifting his head. "Drink, Arden."

His brown eyes cracked open.

"Drink, and be healed by God's Holy Grail."

His lips parted, and Cera brought the grail to them and tilted it slightly. With great effort, he swallowed, then his caramel skin warmed and his face filled out, punctuated by its strong jaw. Cera tilted the grail farther, and Arden drank faster.

His mother grabbed his hand. "My son!"

Cera finished tilting the grail, and Arden drank the last of it.

He breathed in, and his broad chest filled with air. "Thank you."

"Thank God," Cera said.

Arden took the grail and refilled it from the pail. "Thank God." He drank the grail's water, and his muscular form filled out. His mother held him and kissed his recently shaved head.

Arden's relieved, welcoming countenance changed to a focused one, fixed on Roan. "You would have seen me die instead of drink from this life-giving cup."

"It wasn't about you," Roan said. "Just the grail."

Arden picked up his sword and stood, matching Roan's height and rivaling his physique. The young Briton glared at him with a fresh energy that dominated the Saxon's tired attempt at a response.

"You may die yet," Nimue said. "Merlin draws near." At her fingertips, droplets formed in the air. "I'm so sorry I can't do more for you—with you—tonight."

"What if you could?" Cera dunked the grail into the pail and rose with it full to Nimue. "What happens if you drink this?"

"I…" Her eyes widened. "I don't know."

"Would you try?"

Nimue reached for the grail, but her dissolving hand passed through it. "Help me!"

Cera brought the grail to Nimue's still-solid mouth and tilted it. Nimue drank, and the mist about her hand collected into drops, which rolled off her fingertips like rain to the ground.

She swallowed the last of the water then took the grail from Cera, able to hold it in her fingers, which were once again solid. She bit her lip. "I cannot hear the water calling me back to it. I cannot hear it talking to me, nor can I talk to it."

Cera grasped her shoulder. "But you're here."

"Yes!" She grasped Cera's shoulder. "Because I want to be."

Cera took the grail from Nimue and returned it to her satchel. "Ten minutes until Merlin and his men arrive?"

Nimue closed her eyes. "I cannot see the water as I could."

"It's all right. You're here with us." Cera pointed at Roan. "And you? Will you stab me in the back while we fight Merlin?"

Arden raised his sword. "I'd kill you if you did."

"Or will you join us?" Cera asked. "There's sixty of them, five of us. Help us rally the people on the island and fight them."

Roan stepped back. "I vowed to kill you."

Cera stepped to him. "I vowed to marry Perceval, and that didn't happen either. So I know a little of your life's pain, and it stings, and later, when I get a chance to really think about it, it's going to hurt a lot more. But I'm moving forward in a way he'd be proud of. What about you? After all you've lost, what kind of man do you want to be? You saw to it that Arden was saved from the wizard's cruel poison. Now help Arden see through his next attack."

Roan nodded slowly then faster. "I'm a better man than… I've been lately."

Gethen pointed his sword at him. "Try anything, and I'll have your head."

"You couldn't," Roan said. "But I won't—you have my word. I've been many things I'm not proud of, but I've never been a liar." He turned to Cera. "I don't understand… much at all. I don't know who pulled me out of hell. I don't know what I'm supposed to do. But your words ring true, and I can't be still. I want to fight, and with you is the fight that feels right."

Cera nodded, ready to keep a close eye on him for anything suspicious.

Roan turned to Arden. "How old are you?"

"Seventeen," he said.

"You're King Arthur's son?" Roan asked.

"I am."

"Then I guess I'll be fighting alongside teenage British royalty. Ever been in battle?"

"Small skirmishes—not like this. But I'm ready, I assure you."

"He can fight," Gethen said.

Roan asked Arden, "You got any armor?"

"Yeah."

"Saving it for something?"

Arden hurried inside with his mother following.

"We should hide the grail," Gethen said. "In the abbey."

"No." Cera clutched it in her satchel, to her side. "It stays with me."

"The people. The others…" Gethen looked at the handful of islanders who'd gathered to see the commotion, then he turned to Nimue. "What will Merlin do to them?"

She shrugged while pulling her hair tightly behind her. "Dunno. Probably nothing good."

"Any fighters among them?" Roan asked.

"A few," Gethen said. He called loudly into the air, "We're under attack! Everyone, to the abbey!" He went to the house across the path and banged on the door.

"We'll warn down the hill," Cera called to Gethen then ran to the path and down it, with Roan and Nimue following. Cera yelled, for all to hear, "Get to the abbey!"

While islanders evacuated their houses, weary eyed at that hour, Cera snuck glances at Roan, who seemed focused on the task at hand.

A sturdy man came out his front door. "What's going on?"

"Merlin attacks!" Cera answered. "Get your sword. See your family to the abbey, then meet us. Sixty men row for the island!"

He turned inside. "It's an attack! Children, let's go."

"To the abbey!" Cera yelled as house doors opened, and they ran on. "We're under attack!"

Near the bottom of the path, between trees, Cera spotted a flickering glow out in the water, which must have been the sorcerer's. Past the next house that a family exited, Cera saw flames in the boat leading a pack of other boats. Trees blocked a better view until the woods ended and they reached the bottom, where the low wall encircling the island began.

Halfway across the bay, Merlin sat at the head of the lead

boat, his staff leaning against him, his wrinkly old face staring straight ahead, while two of the other five men aboard rowed. A flotilla of a dozen ships scattered behind him. The roaring ball of fire atop his staff blazed, lighting their way.

"Sixty," Roan announced. "Plus Merlin."

"Told you," Nimue said.

"What do we do?" Cera asked. "We couldn't outrow them at sea, and I wouldn't risk leaving the islanders to Merlin, anyway."

"We could use the wall defensively." Roan scanned the stone barrier one direction and then the other. "Except I don't think we have the numbers to man it."

"No," Nimue agreed.

Arden came running down, wearing mail armor and a white tunic with a red dragon—the emblem of Arthur's line—at its center, his sword sheathed on his hip. Merlin stood in his boat. In the firelight, his lips turned up at the edges.

"Well…" Cera looked at Arden. "He knows you're here now."

"Good," Arden said. "I'm not a snake like him, dealing in poisons and assassins sprung upon me out of nowhere. My enemy should know full well it is I who oppose them."

"Bold. Brave." Roan cocked his head. "Also foolish. Surprise is a powerful weapon."

Arden crossed his arms. "I—"

"Horses." Roan pointed at him. "Got any on the island? You've given me an idea."

"We do," Arden said.

"This path at the base…" Roan pointed. "It goes all the way around the island?"

"It does."

"Row!" Merlin's man cried from out in the bay. "Harder! Row!"

"Come on." Roan motioned for everyone to follow him and began jogging up the hill.

As they ran after Roan, Cera glanced at Merlin, who smiled smugly until the tree line blocked him from view.

"Is it a *good* idea?" Nimue asked.

Roan turned back. "Worked last time."

They passed families walking up the hill. "Hurry!" Cera urged them. "They're close!" The people hustled faster.

"What's the plan?" Arden asked Roan.

He looked back again. "We surprise them. We spring upon them out of nowhere."

"On horseback?" Cera asked.

"No," Roan said.

Cera caught sight of Gethen running down the hill with the sturdy man she'd seen earlier and two others with swords. They all stopped in front of Arden's home.

"That's all?" Nimue asked.

"It'll be enough," Roan said.

"What's the plan?" Gethen asked.

"Can I see it?" the islander beside him asked. "The Holy Grail."

"We don't have time," Roan said.

Cera glared at Roan and pulled it out. "He may see what he's fighting for."

The islander's hand went to his heart. He crossed himself, as did the other two. "Thank you, m'lady." He nodded at Arden. "We fight for the King of the Britons as well."

"Aye," each of the other two said.

"I told them," Gethen explained. "Figured it was time."

Arden nodded, and Cera put the grail away.

Roan opened his arms. "What a touching moment for you all. If you're through, and it is now an acceptable time to discuss the imminent danger..." He nodded. "Good. We're on a pretty flat stretch of the path right here." He pointed at Gethen and the other islanders. "You four, go past the houses"—he gestured toward the area beyond Arden's house—"into the woods, and down the hillside, and wait on the path that goes around the base of the island, on horseback. Find a white robe for one of you to wear if you can."

Gethen squinched his face. "A white robe?"

Roan motioned to Cera. "So they think it's her. And as close to blue as you can get, to match her cloak." He gestured to Nimue, Arden, Cera, and himself. "We four are going up the hillside"—he pointed past the houses on the opposite side of the path—"into those woods to hide. Merlin's men arrive any minute. No one's in their homes, so Merlin and his soldiers will march up the path and think everyone's holed up, ready to make a stand in the abbey. When they're nearly past us, we rush down from the trees, down to this section of the path right here, and take out as many as we can. But we don't stop to fight for long. We keep going past the houses on the other side of the path, into the woods, and down to the bottom of the hill, where you all are. And Merlin's men will chase us."

Roan pointed at Gethen and the others. "When they reach you, ride hard, and since it's the same number, and one of you is also in white, it's dark enough out that they'll think it's we four fleeing. But actually, we four will stay behind, hidden again. Merlin and his men don't know there are *two* groups of four. Why would half of us not attack in the first place? They'll see you riding away, assume it's us, and expect the next attack to come at the head of their line, on horseback. And you will do that. But unknown to them, we'll remain behind them in hiding, creeping closer, waiting to attack at the same time from the rear."

Gethen rubbed his chin. "Not bad."

"There's sixty of them," the sturdy islander said. "Eight of us. Is 'not bad' good enough?"

"It worked last time," Cera said. "Didn't it?"

"Aye," Roan confirmed.

"And there's no time for anything else," Cera said. "Or to argue. Go, now."

The islander nodded.

Sir Gethen looked at Arden. "Good luck."

"You too," Arden said.

"Go!" Roan urged.

Gethen and the three islanders hurried toward Arden's house.

"We can get Rocatos's horses," Gethen said to the others, "and Grunu's." They passed the house and disappeared into the woods down the hill.

Cera started the other way off the path, past a house on that side, with the others following. She asked Roan, "When did you do this before?"

"In Britain, in Essex with my first wife, Aedre. It was her idea."

"Were you outnumbered then too?"

"Not this badly."

Up the hillside and into the woods they went. Roan veered right and motioned for Arden to follow. Cera veered left behind a big tree trunk. "Nimue," she said. "You look worried."

"I was thinking, what happens if my body falls in battle?" Nimue shrugged. "Before, I would have returned to the water. Now, who knows?"

Cera grasped her shoulder. "Don't die. I have the grail. If we get separated, find me."

Nimue pulled Cera close and hugged her tight. "Thank you. I cherish the worry—the risk. The fear of loss unlike any I've ever known." She backed away. "I won't die. I can't bear to lose this gift you've given me."

"Shh!" Roan had a finger to his lips, hiding, crouched behind his own large tree.

Arden had gone to the next big one over. He peered down the hillside at the path. Cera nodded to Nimue, who went to the tree to her left. Cera crouched low and pulled her cloak close around her.

The gift given to Nimue came from God, of course, but Cera's heart beat proudly. She'd delivered the gift, as she had to Arden and when healing Herbertus's back in Tours. Already, the grail was doing real, meaningful good, no longer in the clutches of the Order of Nolvan.

She turned to watch the path down the hill… and heard the soldiers first, the soft sliding and rattling of armor to the right, farther down the hill through the trees and houses in the darkness where the path wound. Nimue watched from behind her tree, Arden and Roan from behind theirs. The rattling grew louder.

The ball of fire came into view, small but blazing, illuminating Merlin and his soldiers in a column behind him. Two men wide, they marched onto the flat section of the path near Arden's house, most swords sheathed. Some soldiers held spears, and many carried round shields, turning their heads right—toward the trees where Gethen and the others had gone to lower ground—and left, into the trees where Cera's group hid at higher ground.

Cera kept perfectly still. As Merlin continued in front of them on the path, one of his men with a torch broke away from the column, moving toward a home where light glowed through the windows. He kicked the door. The wooden frame broke loudly, and the soldier looked inside then back out.

"No one." He moved to Arden's house and its already open door and checked inside. "Empty," he called to Merlin.

The wizard stopped. "They must be in the abbey, counting on God to save them. We'll burn it, and we'll catch any who flee and burn them as well."

"Ya!" The soldiers cheered and raised weapons in

approval as Merlin led them on.

Worry had fled Nimue's focus-filled face. She looked like a tiger about to pounce. Roan appeared firm, solid, ready to strike but not in a hurry. Arden breathed fast with his sword already drawn, held down—low enough, Cera hoped, to keep from reflecting light and giving him away.

Another soldier held a torch in the middle of Merlin's column moving down the path. Merlin himself had passed out of sight. Cera turned her back to them and rested it against the tree trunk then slowly, quietly drew her daggers. They could not fail. No longer did Arden alone depend on it, but his mother and the whole island awaited Merlin's wrath in the abbey. Speed would be paramount. They needed to deal lethal blows to as many as possible, as fast as possible, before the soldiers organized their response.

Cera glanced at her satchel. She couldn't bear thinking of the end for Nimue or Arden, so *she* had to survive, in case they needed a drink from the grail to recover from injury. *Arden, stick to the plan*, she urged in her mind. *Don't run immediately after Merlin to avenge your father. Think of the cost, to yourself and everyone, of the reckless act if it fails.*

She wished she'd admonished him against that course, but there hadn't been time. Just as there hadn't been time to consider the risk of putting everyone under one roof in the abbey. Cera blocked out the thought. Certainly, she had no time to waste second-guessing herself.

Except... can Roan be trusted? Cera leaned toward yes. While he seemed a mental mess, aside from their initial conversation about a horse he had for sale, he also seemed sincere. But she'd been wrong before, so the safest course would be for him to lead their charge, where he would be in her sights instead of with a drawn sword behind her.

Nimue had a hand on the tree, a hand on the ground, and both heels off the ground. She was ready to go. Cera peered at their passing enemies. The rear of the line of marching men appeared on the path down the hillside.

Roan and Arden turned to Cera. On her other side, so did Nimue. Slowly, Cera rose. Roan did the same. She made eye contact with him and nodded down to the soldiers. He shook his head no and nodded to her.

The end of the column was before them on the path. Most soldiers' swords remained sheathed. *Why won't Roan go first?* Cera nodded to him again.

Again, he shook his head no and nodded to her.

Fine. She spun away from the tree and ran hard down the slope, followed by the sounds of at least some of the others. Before her, Merlin's men marched forward, oblivious.

Cera glanced back—Nimue and Arden charged but not Roan. *Shit.*

She passed through the trees to the row of houses in front of the path. The last soldier in Merlin's line turned, angling his torch toward Cera. His eyes widened.

"Hey!" He went for his sword's handle.

But he didn't draw fast enough, and Cera's dagger slashed his throat. With her other one, she stabbed at the soldier beside him, but he blocked her arm with his shield. He drew his sword.

Nimue thrust her sword into his stomach. Two of

Merlin's soldiers down—fifty-eight to go.

The nearest one stepped toward Nimue. Cera threw her shoulder into him, driving him back. Nimue focused on a soldier behind Cera, while Cera ducked under another soldier's sword swing and stabbed up into his gut. He lurched forward, and she slit his neck.

A few men up the line, Arden chopped down a soldier. He parried an attack. A second engaged him, and he fought defensively.

Cera started that way but shifted to avoid a sword. Another soldier stepped toward her, and she had a pair to contend with. She held a knife out at each of them, waiting for their next moves—to see what came too slowly or what was wrong with them so she could take advantage and take each of them out.

Merlin's whole line had their attention on the group. Arden was surrounded. A third and fourth soldier rushed Cera, Nimue thrust her sword into one of them, then three more neared.

Black streaked down the hill near Arden—a long sword held aloft. Roan burst into the line, hacking at Merlin's disordered men, hewing off limbs and heads. Arden resumed his offensive, and Merlin's soldiers crumbled before the pair.

Dagger first, Cera lunged at the nearest soldier distracted by Roan. His shield blocked her late, and she rolled off it, her cloak flying in the face of his attacking companion, whose gut Cera thrust her dagger into. His raised sword fell.

"Let's go!" Roan shouted. He slashed one last soldier in gray then motioned down the hillside. "Come on!"

Arden kept fighting. Roan went over, and together, they overwhelmed the soldier. Arden turned to the next, but Roan shoved the boy away, off the path. Arden came back. Roan got to him, wrapped his arm around him, and kept him moving down the slope. Nimue kicked away her foe and ran after them. Cera followed her.

"Get them!" Merlin cried as they raced past the row of houses, into the trees, down the hillside. "Get Arden!"

Trailing Roan and Arden, Cera watched Nimue's back and followed her route. Cera stepped over fallen branches, keeping her knife-holding hands out for balance. A dozen soldiers chased, the one leading with a torch, but they moved more slowly with their cumbersome shields.

Cera's foot slipped when the hill dropped fast, and her backside hit the ground. Nimue glanced back. Cera sprang up and kept going. Nimue smiled. Behind them, the distance to Merlin's men was growing.

Halfway to the bay, between trees, Cera spotted moonlight hitting the water then noticed a scattering of small buildings beside the path at the base of the island. Down they ran. Roan and Arden veered toward a tiny square building. *Where are Gethen and the others?*

Roan and Arden reached the building and rounded it. Nimue got there and waited. Cera rushed to her. *There!* Four horses stood before them, with one of the riders in white. They had indeed found a robe in the color and a dark cloak to go with it. Roan and Arden went into the building. Cera nodded at Gethen. He nodded back, and in a quick clattering of hooves, the four islanders rode off.

Nimue guided Cera into the building and pulled the door softly closed, and the four of them stood packed tightly inside, breathing hard, except Roan, who had his finger to his lips for them all to be quiet. They slowed their breathing. Outside, Merlin's soldiers clamored down the hill.

"They're getting away!" one called.

"Gotten away," another said. "We'd never catch up to them."

"What's the plan, Captain?" one asked.

"They've nowhere to go," a confident voice answered. "We have men waiting by the boats and on the other side of the bay. It's so bright out that if they flee, we'd see them in the open water, but I think if they meant to flee, they'd have done it already. We'll push on to the abbey, and they'll try to stop us. Except we'll be ready next time."

"Aye," came from a handful of voices.

"Come on," the captain said. "Back up the hill."

The clamoring of mail armor and feet in the woods rose, more slowly than it had during the chase, then steadily faded. In their hiding place, Nimue gave a wide smile. Cera couldn't help but return it. Nimue appeared unharmed, as did Roan and Arden. Cera sheathed a dagger on each leg. She heard only crickets outside.

Nimue said quietly, "So far, so good."

"So far," Roan answered as quietly.

Cera asked Roan, "Why didn't you tell me you'd delay your charge?"

"Afraid I wouldn't come?"

"You tried to kill me twice," Cera said more loudly. "I

wondered if this was all a plan for attempt number three. Maybe it still is. Since you couldn't do it yourself, have them do it for you."

"I gave you my word," Roan growled.

Cera cocked her head. "Didn't you give it to Uriel first?"

"You convinced me—or at least made me question." He motioned up the hill. "You'd rather you hadn't? Do you wish we'd fought it out while Arden died?"

"I've killed you twice. I'm really good at it!"

"Not again. I'd have your head!"

"Children!" Nimue put her arms out between them. "Children, please."

Roan knocked her arm away. "I'm no child."

"I'm sixty," Cera said.

Arden studied her.

Cera patted her satchel. "The grail."

"I'm significantly older than either of you," Nimue said. "And Arden, rightful king though he may be, is a wee one. So to me, you are all but children of this earth that is suddenly wondrously new and maybe extremely dangerous to me."

"How old are you?" Arden asked. "And I'm not wee."

"Old," Nimue said. "But none of this matters now. We need to get in position for when Sir Gethen attacks the front of Merlin's column."

"Which means Merlin himself," Arden said.

"Which means Merlin himself," Nimue echoed.

Arden said to Roan, "I'm sorry I didn't heed your call to stop fighting and leave the path."

301

Roan shrugged. "I would have done the same at your age."

Arden shook his head. "I know better."

"You fought well up there," Roan said.

"That's better!" Nimue said. "But we still have to go. I'll take the lead. I've walked the woods on this enchanting island often—on both moonlit nights and dark, star-filled ones—over the centuries."

Nimue cracked open the door and peered out. Slowly, she exited, pushing the door wider, and Cera followed. The night was quiet, the bay's water calm.

They followed Nimue up the hillside and into the woods, in the direction Merlin's line had been marching. They moved carefully to keep from making too much noise.

"How many did we kill?" Arden asked softly. "I got three."

"Three for me," Cera said.

Nimue glanced back. "Four."

"I lost count," Roan said. "It was so many."

"More than a handful," Arden said. "Summing to fifteen or twenty in all."

They jogged slowly up the hill. Cera, without daggers in her hands, found it easier than the rush down. *Even twenty dead means a lot remain*, she thought, though if Merlin had kept some by the boats, that meant fewer were marching on the abbey. And her side would have Gethen and the three with him in the next encounter. Their odds had indeed improved.

Nimue halted and shot her hand out beside her. The rest

of them stopped, and they all crouched low. Ahead, up on the path, the rear of Merlin's line of soldiers passed in the space between houses. Nimue crept forward, and they followed behind the soldiers.

"Be ready," Roan whispered. "Gethen and the others could attack any time."

"But wait for the soldiers to rush forward to meet them," Cera added.

"We'd better get there fast," Arden said, "or they won't last long."

They continued behind the column, with Merlin's soldiers looking side to side repeatedly, especially into the trees where the group had come from the last time. The soldiers checked houses they passed, calling out upon finding them empty. When those in the rear glanced back, Cera and the others froze until the soldiers faced forward again, then the group continued their stealthy pursuit.

Nimue's hand went out. "Slow."

Arden began drawing his sword.

"No," Roan whispered. "They might see light reflect off it."

The young king eased the blade back into its sheath.

Clang-crack-clang!

Nimue sprinted up the path toward the noise. They all rushed after her. Cera drew her daggers, and Nimue, Arden, and Roan drew their swords.

They neared the row of houses. Merlin's soldiers surged forward toward Gethen and the three other islanders without paying any attention to what was behind them.

Roan made eye contact with Cera for a long second, then he raced faster between the houses toward the path so at the moment Nimue thrust her sword into the nearest of Merlin's men, Roan thrust his into the next one over. Arden and Cera headed farther up the line. From the corner of her eye, Cera saw Roan and Nimue take out another one each before Arden reached the path and slashed a soldier's back. Cera stabbed into one's heart and got one more before others turned around, newly aware that they had attackers behind as well as in front.

Her daggers dancing, Cera stabbed into soldiers' guts and spun to parry, dodge, or slash through an exposed neck at any opportunity. Arden stood tall, his sword chopping down foes or meeting their attacks firmly. But so many soldiers surrounded them.

Arden and Cera gravitated toward each other until they were back to back. Swords came from everywhere. A flaming torch whipped past Cera's face. A spear's tip—*schvt*—slid across Arden's arm, and another sliced Cera's leg. She dropped to a knee but only to launch herself low at a soldier's knees, driving him to the ground. She sank her dagger into his chest and called to Arden.

"We need to get Merlin!" Avoiding a stabbing sword, she rolled off her dying foe. "We won't last here!"

Arden kicked into the midsection of his adversary, who rushed again to Arden, who thrust his blade into his stomach. Arden withdrew his sword in time to parry a blow from the attacker behind him. Cera hurried up the side of the path, ducking under a sword swing, sidestepping a second. The soldiers nearby crowded toward Gethen's group, who had lost a man and were down to three.

Behind Cera, Arden followed more slowly, dispatching foes as he went… but he didn't see the soldier behind him. Enraged, the soldier gripped his sword with both hands and raised it high.

"Arden!" Cera cried.

Schvt! The attacker's hands separated from his arms, Roan's heavy blade slicing both wrists. Roan emerged from the crowd, eyes wide and wild. He hewed his sword clean through the torso of the mutilated soldier. Arden nodded to Roan, who slashed an oncoming soldier as the crowd enveloped the Saxon.

Nimue, a smirk on her face and dirt and blood covering her clothes, grabbed Arden's wrist and pulled him, lurching forward, toward Cera. Quick air blew Cera's hair. She leaned away from a blade then stabbed backward into the soldier's side. She spun and jabbed her other knife straight into his neck. Choking, he slumped to the ground.

"Nice move." Nimue appeared behind her with Arden.

"Thanks." Cera looked ahead, where Gethen and another of the islanders on horseback fought Merlin and a dozen soldiers. "If we kill Merlin, maybe the rest will quit."

"Let's do it," Nimue said.

From that direction, three soldiers broke from the group, coming their way.

Arden glanced back at the chaos around Roan. "Think he's all right?"

"They call him Relentless." Cera readied her daggers. "We'll see."

Nimue and Arden raised their blades, and each engaged an oncoming foe. Cera's opponent, with his spear, faked right then jabbed left, but she sidestepped it. *Swoosh!* Nimue's sword swept across his chest.

He fell, and Nimue turned to Cera. "Too slow."

Arden dispatched his enemy with a thrust to the gut.

"I was getting there," Cera said to Nimue.

A shrill cry rose ahead, a burst of fire died, and a burnt islander fell from his horse like a sack, leaving Gethen alone atop his mount, swinging his sword at those below. Cera headed that way with Nimue and Arden. A soldier thrust his spear into Gethen's horse's chest, and the British knight fell, as the animal did, to the ground. Another soldier raised his axe above him.

Cera hurled a dagger up the path between Merlin's men, into the shoulder of Gethen's attacker, who cried out in pain. Gethen got to his feet. A column of flame swept over him from atop the staff held in Merlin's outstretched arm. The fire dissipated, revealing Gethen's unrecognizably blackened face and body, which slumped to the ground.

Merlin turned to Cera, Nimue, and Arden. Eight soldiers preceded his advance. Nimue drew a knife from inside her boot and threw it into one's forehead. *Seven soldiers.*

One swung his blade at Arden, who smashed it aside and sliced the soldier's neck. *Six.*

Cera charged at one and ducked under his swing. She stabbed, but he blocked her arm. She grabbed his sword arm, got her shoulder and body under him, and lifted him over and with her to the ground. He punched her nose, and her head rocked back. It rocked forward, and Cera drove her dagger into his side and twisted it.

Heat! Cera lifted her cloak and retreated until the heat beyond died out. Merlin, well out of reach, turned to Arden, who fought two soldiers. Arden took a slash across his arm and barely blocked the next attack. Merlin raised his staff toward Arden, the ball of fire churning atop it.

"No!" Cera readied to throw her dagger, but soldiers surrounded Merlin like a shield.

She ran for Arthur's son. Flames streamed from the wizard's staff, enveloping a soldier and Arden all at once.

"*I* have the grail!" Cera cried, falling as a wounded soldier grabbed her ankle and held it.

"And I'll take it!" Merlin roared, fire pouring out. "After he dies, to fulfill my half of the bargain."

Arden and the burning soldier screamed. Cera drove her knife into the chest of the soldier holding her.

Schvt! A thrown spear lodged itself straight into the neck of the soldier in front of Merlin, whose fire died as he searched for its source. Nimue raced past Arden.

"You!" Merlin yelled, spewing his fire at her.

Nimue twisted her body mostly out of the way. "Get him out of here!"

Soldiers attacked her. Cera rushed to the burning young king, down on a knee, leaning on his sword for support. She threw her cloak over him, and the fires died, leaving his body, face, and clothes charred black. She crouched to him. "Can you move?"

He pushed himself up and groaned. She *couldn't* let Arden

die, not after everything she'd done to get to him—not after Perceval had died so she could reach Arden in time. She slipped her arm under his and took his weight as they rose.

Heat! Cera got her cloak up fast, before the fire did any more damage.

Merlin stopped the ineffective flames. "Kill him!"

"Let's go!" Cera helped Arden, hobbling off the path toward the nearest house.

From lower on the path, soldiers headed for Arden and Cera. *Four—no, five.* And one fell, chopped down by Roan from behind. Roan huffed for air, blood splattered across his face and dripping off it and his slashed clothes. He limped into a run after the rest of the soldiers.

With Cera and Arden at her back, Nimue positioned herself between that pack of soldiers and the others near Merlin, brandishing her sword. Cera watched what was going on behind her and Arden, where Roan and Nimue did their best to avoid Merlin's blasts of flame, furiously swinging their swords at the last groups of his men—wildly lashing out, trying to keep the greater numbers at bay. Arden wheezed and grimaced.

"Hold on," Cera said. "Some water's all you need."

He tried to speak but only rasped. His sword's tip dragged in the dirt.

"You're not dying today!" Cera marched them on. "You didn't survive Merlin's poison to die in a burst of flame."

Arden closed his eyes.

"I thought dragons liked fire." She lifted him a little, and his eyes reopened.

The pair struggled toward the house. Behind them, near Merlin, Roan took a slash to the back and fell.

But up he rose, slicing an aggressive attacker's chest.

Nimue, her clothes scorched and blood soaked, backed toward Cera and Arden, parrying attacks from oncoming soldiers. Past her, flames enveloped Roan.

Arden raised his hand to the door of the home, but his weak push did nothing. Cera kicked it open. In the center of the room, a bucket sat in a ray of moonlight beside a smoldering fire pit. She dragged Arden that way.

"Hurry!" Nimue yelled. "Need ya out here!"

At the fire pit, Cera peered into the bucket. "Dammit!" It was empty. She helped Arden to the ground and spun to the small table with a cup on it. Cera raced to it. "Thank God."

She grabbed the cup, rushed to closed-eyed Arden, and slid on her knees to his side, holding the cup high and balanced so only a bit sloshed out. Cera unlatched her satchel, took out the Holy Grail, and poured the water in.

She brought the grail to Arden's lips and lifted his head. He sipped... and his face mended. Its blackened skin grew smooth and returned to its natural brown hue. He paused to breathe, took the grail, and finished it on his own.

Nimue reeled into the home back first and crashed to the ground before them, her clothes and fair skin cut and badly burned. A long slash ran from her forehead across her bloody left eye and her nose to the opposite cheek. "Got any more to drink?" A huge gash in her leg bled, but she still held her sword.

A gray-bearded soldier entered at the doorway, then Merlin and two young soldiers followed him. The wizard's fire brightened the room. He stepped forward. "Your friend fought like a man possessed."

Arden put down the grail and stood. Cera stayed kneeling with one arm over exhausted Nimue.

"Like a man afraid of where he was going if he died," Merlin said. "Fought much harder than Constantine's pathetic band at Camelot before their end."

Arden pointed his sword at the sorcerer. "You'll pay for that, and for what you did to my father."

A fireball shot at Arden, exploding and scorching his side as he turned.

Merlin pointed his staff at him. "When I end you now and am young once more, I will live my newfound years saddened that God didn't save you from me, just as He did nothing to save Arthur or his dream of a better society." He turned up his palm. "I push God by my actions. I *pray* that God will show up and stop me. Or send an angel to do it— that He'll take an interest in our world He's abandoned." Merlin shook his head. "I thought He would be interested in saving my friend Arthur, but God was nowhere to be found."

Arden stepped forward. Flames streamed from Merlin's staff, burning Arden's side and back until Cera got in the way with her cloak before her.

Boom! The exploding fire launched both Arden and Cera flying into the wall.

"Die now, dragon whelp." Merlin extended his staff, and

a cone of flame blazed at Arden.

"Agh!" Merlin cried as the flames shifted downward and the wizard fell into them, charred-black Roan atop his back.

Merlin's staff clattered to the ground, and its fire died. The older soldier rolled Roan off and lifted Merlin, patting out persistent flames on his robe. Another soldier stabbed into Roan's stomach.

Nimue sprang forward on the ground and grabbed the fireless staff. Cera got in front of her with her dagger out. Arden, grimacing but not as burned as before, raised his sword. Merlin, his wrinkly skin untouched by the flames, curled his lips and raised his palm, his ball of fire burning just above its surface.

Cera hurled her dagger—Merlin turned. "Ah!" he cried as it lodged in the side of his chest.

With her eyes fixed on him, Cera reached back and low. "Sword."

Nimue placed her sword's handle in Cera's palm, and Cera marched toward the pained wizard. The gray-bearded soldier stuck to him as one of the two younger soldiers blocked Cera's way.

She met his sword strikes high and low, and worry covered the soldier's face. Cera swung, and he parried. Then she sidestepped his attack and slashed his throat.

Grimacing, Merlin—her knife still in him—raised his fiery hand, and a blast torched his falling soldier as Cera shielded herself with her cloak.

"Gah!" Merlin backed out the front door, his last two men following.

Cera stepped over the burned, lifeless soldier in pursuit. Arden followed. She halted and turned to him and the flickering flames around the house, which Merlin's fire had left.

"No, protect Nimue." Cera glanced at the gashed, stabbed, shallow-breathing cinder of a Saxon warrior on the ground. "Find water. Use the grail. Save Roan."

Arden lowered his sword. "All right."

Cera took a deep breath, then she ran out the door after the pair of soldiers hurrying downhill as fast as their wounded old leader could manage.

"Merlin!" she cried.

From down the dirt path, he scowled back. The older soldier flung Cera's dagger. Cera shifted her hips, leaning away as it flew past.

Then she charged. The younger of the two soldiers stood his ground while Merlin and the other continued down the hill. The young soldier raised his sword. Cera neared and raised hers.

He swung his blade. Cera met it, and passing him, she slashed his side.

Spinning toward her, he clutched the wound. Cera swung hard. He parried weakly. She chopped his thigh. The soldier fell to a knee. She sliced her sword clean through his neck. His head rolled, and his body crumpled.

The faint light of Merlin's fire seeped around the bend lower on the island's coiling path. Cera wondered how many soldiers had been left guarding the boats.

"Merlin!" she screamed.

She sprinted past empty houses, down the hill. If Merlin left the island, Cera had no doubt he would chase Arden, wherever Arthur's son went.

The glow she chased intensified. Merlin coveted the grail also, and Cera knew he'd hunt it and her as well. She rounded the corner to find Merlin and the soldier protecting him ahead and, down past them, their boats at the end of the path.

"Stand and fight!" Cera yelled.

The older soldier turned to her while Merlin kept going. The soldier was bigger than her previous foe, and with his age, surely, came more experience. He raised his sword, and—his eyes angry—rushed up the hill at Cera.

She charged straight at him, gritted her teeth, and raised her sword.

The soldier didn't veer.

Cera didn't veer.

He swung, she met it, and they collided and tumbled to the ground.

Cera sprang to her feet while the soldier collected himself on his back. She slashed down at him. He parried then flailed his sword. She leaned out of the way, angled her sword downward, wrapped both hands around its handle, and, dropping to her knees, plunged the blade into the big man's heart. He lurched, then he turned his head aside and ceased moving.

She stood, the soldier's blood dripping off her sword, and spied a rowboat in the bay with two soldiers fleeing the island. Cera raced after unprotected Merlin, who neared the other—empty—boats, clutching his wounded chest.

"Merlin!" she cried.

He spun and sent a ball of fire at Cera, who ducked in plenty of time.

"You're all alone!" She resumed her pursuit, drawing close enough to see fear on his face. He shot a pair of fireballs. Without breaking stride, Cera raised her cloak, and the fire dissipated with soft taps against its blue fabric. "That won't work. Not against me."

At the base of the path, Merlin stopped and turned to Cera, huffing for air, hunched. With his off hand, he held the spot where her dagger had sliced into his chest. She skidded to a halt a few paces before him.

"Now you pay for what you did to my mother!" She pointed her sword at him. "You pay for killing King Arthur."

Merlin glanced skyward. "I think not." He stood tall, angling his palm down as its fire grew. The sphere expanded into the space between them, growing faster, bulging against its curved surface.

Cera stepped to him. With all her might, she swung her blade.

BOOM!—the fire burst.

Off her feet, into the air, Cera flew, blinding flame everywhere. She pulled her cloak over her stinging face. She dropped her sword and, midair, used both hands to get the soft fabric around her and keep it there. Air rushed everywhere. At her feet past the end of her cloak, she saw treetops and house roofs sliding by fast on her way up the island.

Then the trees grew larger and the roofs nearer as she descended. Cera curled into a ball, closing her eyes and wrapping her arms around her head.

Crack! Crsh—crack! Cera fell through tree limbs and leaves.

Thud. She hit the forest floor, and her head smacked the mud ground.

Cera took a breath, then another. Her face hurt. She opened her eyes and brought both hands before her. Ten fingers. She checked, and sure enough, she still had two legs and a foot at the end of each of them. Cera felt a bump on the back of her head then noticed its throbbing.

She touched her burned face. "Ow."

Her hip aching, she got to her feet. There was a glow beyond the trees, out in the bay.

Cera crouched but couldn't see the light better. She headed up the hillside, and between tall trunks and leaves, the orange-yellow out in the water grew and shrank.

It brightened, and she crouched again, seeing a lone figure in a boat, headed toward the mainland. Merlin's fire flared at his boat's rear, seemingly propelling him through the low waves.

"Cera!" Arden called from up the hillside.

She spun to him. "How's Nimue? How's Roan?"

"Nimue's fine," Arden said. "Pretty pleased with how she fought, happy to have gotten to fight. She's... just generally excited."

Cera smiled.

"But Roan! He won't drink from the grail. He's dying.

What happened to Merlin?"

"He got away." She hurried to Arden, and they got back to the path and ran for his house.

Arden glanced at her. "Are you all right?"

"Yeah." Cera pointed at her face. "How bad is it?"

"Not that bad. Relatively speaking."

She burst into his house, and he followed.

Beside a burning candle, Nimue sat on the table, twirling Merlin's staff in her hand. "He's very stubborn."

Roan coughed blood, adding to what already covered his ashen face. Gashes, long and short, and stab wounds littered his body and limbs. The grail lay knocked over beside him, next to a bucket half-full of water.

Cera dropped to her knees, took the grail, and dunked it into the bucket. "Roan."

His eyes cracked open.

She held the grail out to him. "The grail will save you."

"It's God's grail."

"Yes! God's Holy Grail."

"How many grails do you think she has?" Nimue asked.

Roan closed his eyes. "Damn him."

Cera slapped Roan's charred cheek, and his eyes shot open. "He took from you, but think of what He gave you! You must have been in love. Think of *those* times. And Arden. He lives, even after Merlin's poison. Think of that miracle."

"Let me die," Roan said.

"To go back to hell?"

His eyes shifted to Cera.

"You've been to hell," she said. "You know the pain there."

"I know the pain here!" Roan roared, a sudden strength in his voice. "On earth."

"There's more than that here," Cera said. "More than just pain."

"Haven't I done enough to deserve a better fate?" Roan asked. "Today, in this battle?"

"Maybe," Nimue said. "Maybe not."

Arden knelt beside Cera.

"Fight with us, Roan," Cera said. "Fight against Merlin. He got away, but he *will* return for Arden, if not for the grail. Fight mad at the world if you have to. I do. Be furious at God if you must, but stay, and keep fighting. If you die, maybe you've done enough. God is forgiving, but—"

"No!" Roan yelled. "I won't beg such a god for mercy. For anything!"

"Then maybe you haven't done enough," Cera went on. "And you'd return to hell. But here, in between heaven and hell, you *know* there's good for you. You've lived it before."

"And then agony," Roan said.

"Sometimes," Cera said. "Yes."

He looked at Arden then closed his eyes.

Cera grasped his shoulder. "Roan!"

He lifted his arm. "Give me the cup."

Cera placed it in his hand.

"They used to call it that," Nimue said. "The Holy Cup."

"Really?" Arden asked.

"Of course not." Nimue shook her head. "That would be ridiculous."

"Not for God," Roan rasped, bringing the grail to his mouth. "You all would have burned without me. You need me." He drank, and his cuts and stab wounds filled, and most closed. Roan breathed deeply and gulped the rest of the water. His eyes opened wide. "Damn good drink, though. I'll give Him that."

He handed Cera the grail. She sat back, and her shoulders and whole body relaxed. Listening to the stillness nearby, her eyes grew suddenly heavy. But it was not quite the time for real rest.

Cera refilled the grail from the bucket and gave it back to Roan. "This'll finish the job."

He pushed the grail to her. "You first."

She nodded then drank. Her face soothed, her head stopped throbbing, and coolness swept through her. She refilled the grail and handed it to Roan.

"What now?" he asked.

Nimue held out Merlin's staff. "This seems dead."

Roan paused his drink. "I recognized that fire. The way it flared, flames rolling over each other, the way it smelled when it burned me. That was hellfire."

Cera crossed her arms. "He said he needed you dead, Arden, and that once you were, he'd be young again."

"He tried to kill me before the poison," Arden said. "Since he murdered my father, he and his men have been searching for me and sending assassins wherever Gethen and my mother and I fled. I don't know how he learned of my existence, but since then, he's been after me. We have at least discovered why."

Roan set the empty grail down and labored to get himself up.

"Why the show?" Nimue dropped off the table with a springy bounce. "You feel fine—I know it. You drank from the grail twice."

Roan scowled. "Force of habit."

Cera got up and smiled.

Arden stood and asked Nimue, "Do you know how my death would give Merlin new life?"

"I don't," she said. "But he's looking pretty old at the moment."

"He is," Arden said. "So he won't stop. Even if he flees back to Britain, he'll return. His life apparently depends on it."

"Unless we take the fight to him," Roan said.

"The Britons need you," Nimue said to Arden. "With Camelot and Constantine fallen, they suffer under King Hengist. They need their true king."

Arden nodded. "They need their land free from foreign rule. Then they need the world my father dreamed of."

"The Order of Nolvan won't stop coming for the grail," Cera said. "To Josephus and those knights, the grail is everything. They've sworn to God to protect it."

"Now *we* protect it," Nimue said.

"If you're wrong…" Roan crossed his arms. "If God really does want the grail destroyed, He'll be after it too."

"He would be." Cera nodded. "But I'm not wrong." She looked from Roan to Arden to Nimue. "This is not what I expected. For so long, I sought to steal the Holy Grail from the order, to rescue it from an idle existence, but only to help people. The idea of having the grail and seeking revenge for anything never once crossed my mind… until Merlin killed my mother and King Arthur—Perceval's king." Cera clenched her fist. "Merlin has caused too much pain for too long. His fire burned Gethen to ash. His council fuels Hengist's domination of the people of Britain. He is a force of evil."

"For ages," Nimue said, "Merlin has been at the center of things like King Hengist's tyrannical rise to power. I could tell you such stories."

"You heard him tonight," Cera said. "However he's lived so long on this earth, he lives to perpetrate those atrocities."

"We responded today," Arden said. "Gave the old man what he wanted."

"Yes," Cera said. "We most certainly did. And while I don't think he'll soon forget, I doubt we satisfied his demand for a response from God."

"If something bigger is his aim," Roan said, "something worse to get God's attention, then he won't stop with Britain."

"No." Cera shook her head. "And through King Hengist, Merlin's evil will be a plague spreading across Europe, oppressing its people. I can't let that happen. I can't let so many suffer."

"Then we do as Roan suggests," Arden said. "We stop them now, in Britain, before things get worse."

Nimue's eyes widened. "Yes!"

Roan nodded. "Now you *really* need me."

"We do," Cera said. "And that settles it. We protect the Holy Grail, and we use it to stop Merlin and King Hengist in Britain."

THE END OF BOOK I

Connect Online

Thanks for reading. If you enjoyed the story, please leave a review at your favorite online retailer.

Get the latest updates about S.M. Perlow's works by signing up for his newsletter:

smperlow.com/newsletter

Find him online at:

smperlow.com

twitter.com/smperlow

facebook.com/smperlow

WORKS BY S.M. PERLOW

Vampires and the Life of Erin Rose

Novels
Choosing a Master
Alone
Lion
Hope
War

Short Stories
Alice Stood Up

—

The Grand Crucible

Novels
Golden Dragons, Gilded Age

—

Other Works

Novels
Stealing the Holy Grail

Short Stories
The Girl Who Was Always Single

CPSIA information can be obtained
at www.ICGtesting.com
Printed in the USA
BVHW080039290321
603598BV00004B/336

9 780999 285855